MW01485741

ALSO BY RYAN COLLETT

The Disassembly of Doreen Durand

George falls Through Time

George falls Through Time

A NOVEL

RYAN COLLETT

WM

WILLIAM MORROW

An Imprint of HarperCollinsPublishers

Without limiting the exclusive rights of any author, contributor or the publisher of this publication, any unauthorized use of this publication to train generative artificial intelligence (AI) technologies is expressly prohibited. HarperCollins also exercise their rights under Article 4(3) of the Digital Single Market Directive 2019/790 and expressly reserve this publication from the text and data mining exception.

This is a work of fiction. Names, characters, places, and incidents are products of the author's imagination or are used fictitiously and are not to be construed as real. Any resemblance to actual events, locales, organizations, or persons, living or dead, is entirely coincidental.

GEORGE FALLS THROUGH TIME. Copyright © 2026 by Ryan Collett. All rights reserved. Printed in the United States of America. No part of this book may be used or reproduced in any manner whatsoever without written permission except in the case of brief quotations embodied in critical articles and reviews. For information, address HarperCollins Publishers, 195 Broadway, New York, NY 10007. In Europe, HarperCollins Publishers, Macken House, 39/40 Mayor Street Upper, Dublin 1, D01 C9W8, Ireland.

hc.com

HarperCollins books may be purchased for educational, business, or sales promotional use. For information, please email the Special Markets Department at SPsales@harpercollins.com.

FIRST EDITION

Designed by Kyle O'Brien

Art by © Jasper.K/Shutterstock

Library of Congress Cataloging-in-Publication Data has been applied for.

ISBN 978-0-06-346350-9

25 26 27 28 29 LBC 5 4 3 2 1

For Blake

George falls Through Time

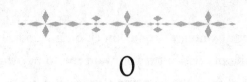

0

My ex-boyfriend's name was listed on my internet bill and I could not remove it. One year ago we had moved into a new flat together—renting, renting, renting, oh how the wool gets pulled over your eyes with faux crossing-the-threshold assurances, live-work-play, rooftop solar panels, utopian architectural mock-ups of the sunniest day in London you'll never see. We set up our bills together like giddy kids, newlyweds but not wedded, and not new, pushing mid-thirties. Water, heat, electric, internet, TV, rent, rent, rent—these things all happen in a smear so of course details get bungled, lines get blurred, names get put where they don't belong and the names have to match, the postcode has to match, block capitals and the space, Google autofill always wrong—whose card is that anyway? What are the last four digits? I hate talking on the phone, I hate dealing with people, I hate waiting, I hate telling strangers in intricate detail exactly how they can take my money and having to repeat that conversation up the call tree, around the maypole of managers. By all means, come and get my money. Come knock on my door, I said to the woman on the phone. But if you want me to pay this bill, then you've got to change the name on the account because my name is George. No, listen to me. My name is George, there's no one else using the internet, there's no one else here and I won't pay the bill until it's in my name.

That was what I was doing when two of my dogs ran away. I had six of them (too many, pushing my luck) but while I was spelling out my email address, confirming my postcode, my mother's maiden name, with the woman on the phone saying, "I've just sent you a text can you read me the code?" I looked down to check and noticed a fluffy white cloud missing from my periphery. No fluff, just grass and shadow, dark green turning blue. It was getting darker earlier. Summer was winding down.

"Hold on," I said into the phone but my cheek pushed the hang-up button on accident and ended the call. Shit. Ryley, the fluffy white bichon frise, was missing. Vanished.

He was one of my regulars. For six months I had been walking Ryley four days a week and his presence was the moral foundation for the five other dogs I walked at the same time. I could let Ryley off the lead without issue. He was levelheaded, calm, less blatantly doglike than the others, he never barked, he never ran away. So shocking was his absence that it took me an extra minute to notice that Matilda, an enormous Afghan hound, was also missing. Her owner was a Russian billionaire in exile who was already upset with me over how much energy she still had after our walks. You don't run her enough, he said. All your dogs are too small, Matilda's not like the others, she needs to be pushed.

She was gone too.

"Shit, shit, shit." I looked around. I was in the middle of Greenwich Park, in an open field with shallow woods all around me, shrubs and summer brambles. The walk was done and I was about to leave and return the dogs to their homes, but these stupid internet people, these stupid fucking bug people had finally returned my call to fix my bill and I had to answer or risk another delayed payment, another late fee, another dent of debt, tanking credit score, multiplying fees, did anybody read the letters they sent me? Was anybody on the other end of the threats? They sounded so oblivious over the phone, the whole hive of them nattering away in the background of every call.

"Matilda!" I hated calling the dogs by their twee little names. I spun in a circle. The four remaining dogs shuffled around me, their leashes wrapping around my legs. I didn't call for Ryley only because he was the sensible one—I wouldn't be surprised if he had gone and walked himself home—but not Matilda, no, she would be going berserk on her own, modelesque and dramatic, tied up in sticks and nipped at by foxes.

I roamed the perimeter of the field, peering into bushes, scraggly trees. Rain and heat had done a number on the woodland and it was lush, impenetrable, a nightmare of hay fever. The sky was overcast, darker than usual and moonless as dusk fell, with Canary Wharf looming in the distance, the windows of empty office buildings twinkling piss yellow. The four other dogs (a Yorkie, a Boston terrier, a mixed collie thing, and a princely Shiba Inu) had caught wind of something wrong. Their faces were pointed and jittery, their trust in me waning. Ryley was the best friend of the best friends—his absence alarmed them. And as far as the pecking order went, Matilda was the prized racehorse and for them this was the desertion of God, it put their very existences askew, their dog world governed by genetic chaos and codependency.

No, I wasn't supposed to be walking six dogs at once. The dog walking app has a limit of four but you can trick the system with some timetable foolery and stack your pickups and lie about your drop-offs. I could do six at most. Once I had tried eight and that proved to be too much—I had lost track of things and a kid got bit. Not badly! But dramatically. Catastrophically for a London mum and a lawsuit was threatened and stalled mostly because I was nonresponsive—but more than threatened because I got a letter, I got an email. Did you know you actually have to create a login if you get sued? You have to set up a username and password of your own volition, as if to say yes, I'm happy to be sued, thank you very much, I'll scan all these documents, I'll upload them to your *portal* because by the way I don't have any money for you to take in the first place so what else have I got to lose. God, my internet bill. Why had Matilda bolted? She was worth thousands. I was embarrassed to call her name. I was embarrassed when the kid had gotten bit. I was embarrassed to be seen with six dogs. Four dogs. To be a shepherd of the ugliest sheep imaginable.

But this was what London did to a person. This was a city that made you put up with such ordeals because otherwise you'd sit and stew too long on hypotheticals, imagining how much money you could earn by just selling all eight dogs instead of returning them. OK maybe killing one (the Yorkie), but ransoming the rest, and not even on the black market because this was a city where you could get away with selling a stolen dog on Gumtree, where you could buy drugs on Deliveroo. This was a city where you wondered if maybe your ex-boyfriend was legally responsible for paying your internet bill because his name was listed as the primary account holder, so technically the bill was his and maybe you had a case there and he should be getting all these letters and you should even go ahead and ask some not-free legal advice about all this from the same people who were suing you because of the dog that wasn't yours who bit a kid you didn't know. This was a city where you acted out imaginary scenarios like this—near-cartoonish courtroom arguments—where you'd justify the actions you took for cruel commercial gain, the desperate measures your pride forced you to take. That kid was asking for it! The bill wasn't in my name! You roamed the city like this, imagining blowout, end-all arguments with strangers, with tourists on the tube, with your boyfriend who wasn't your boyfriend anymore and your boss who wasn't your boss anymore. This was a city where your boyfriend became your ex-boyfriend because you quit (you weren't fired, no way) your data entry office job because you were beginning to imagine arguments in your head like this, actually mutter under your breath as you walked aimlessly in circles on your lunch break and ran into people, smacked shoulders, and your boyfriend was worried about you—but only worried enough to leave you, not worried enough to stay.

And not *you*, obviously I mean me. I mean *I* did all these things. *I* prowled the giant underground shopping mall in Canary Wharf on my lunch break cursing humanity, long before the dogs, long before everything. *I* became one of those people you see muttering to themselves in public—it's never the homeless, never the poor, it's always the rich, those banker types, those Canary Wharf lads with their fat asses shoved inside their tight pants, muttering to themselves like sociopaths because they are sociopaths, and me in the background, their data entry fiend, staring

5

at their huge asses without shame, at their steroid nipples jutting through their thin white shirts, cursing them to hell, cursing myself for lusting after them, for not having enough money to justify quitting my job (*not getting fired!*) but trusting that my boyfriend was making enough for both of us but apparently that not being the case, or at least he said it wasn't and I had to start dog walking and then we just sort of broke up. Less than broke up. He said he was worried about me, he said it wasn't about the dogs, and then he was gone. This was a city where you just sort of broke up. Case closed. This was rental economics. This was actual living breathing mushy human beings dysmorphing their body clocks to fit six-month break clauses and three-month renewal periods and one percent annual salary increases and timing breakups to match paydays and due dates and all for the sake of a tiny one-bedroom shit flat because they're all shit flats, they're all mildewy and smell like your cooking and fucked—even the ones you take your mum to when she comes to visit because she's worried about you and you need to get your mind off things. Have you seen the peeling paint in Buckingham Palace? Have you seen the shit carpet? Even the new builds in Vauxhall, in Southwark, in everywhere a Shanghai developer has snatched and built a modular little circuit board tower, entombed in flammable plastic—or maybe it's brick—let's argue that it's real brick, sure, it looks real convincing but it's just plastic composite, just aerated fiberglass, blowing off in the wind, buckling in the heat, up in flames in seconds, all sense of permanence, of nesting and community nothing but big fat adverts on scaffolding because look, it's a new month and your Singaporean landlord would like another two thousand pounds and *you* have to give it to them. God forbid they take it themselves.

(I don't think I'd be able to kill a Yorkie. That was a joke.)

Messages started appearing on my phone.

"Are you on your way?"

"Where's my Luna?"

"Did you forget to send your pic of Daphne today?"

These sick freaks actually demanded photos of their dogs on their walks. No, I can't send a "pic" right now because me and Luna and Daphne and the other two bitches are climbing through bushes, sloshing through weeds. I pulled them along, forcing them to be the wild animals they didn't know they were until we reached the deer enclosure in the far corner of the park. I searched the bushes along the fence. The deer on the other side were fascinated by us, these desperate barbarians.

"Ryley! Matilda!" I called into darkness.

The dogs by now had abandoned all possibility of trust. Luna, the Boston terrier, was dragging on her lead, refusing to go any farther but luckily she weighed about the same as a squirrel. More messages appeared on my phone. The owners had to use the dog walking app to communicate with me, which was a battery-suck, and I had already spent so much time talking to the internet people. 17 percent now 10 percent. Someone called, I answered. It was the Russian.

"Sorry yeah we're just on our way, sorry." I said. "Got a little sidetracked."

"Sidetracked by what?"

"By, um . . ." I stopped. And there she was. Twenty yards away. Long-limbed, long-haired, with her hellhound sunken face. Matilda.

But she was behind the fence. Matilda was inside the deer

enclosure. She was standing among the deer as if she were one of them, just as limber and gallant, only furrier. They didn't seem to mind.

I hung up on the Russian and went to the fence. I walked along it, looking for a way around. I could climb it easily but what would I do on the other side? The dog was too big to climb back over with. I called her name and tried to lure her over, but she stayed put, watching me with her skeletal smile, taunting me.

I cursed aloud and decided to climb over. I could at least get ahold of her, then figure a way out of the enclosure. I tied the leads of the four other dogs to the chain-link fence—they were all in varying degrees of bafflement and peril but I shushed them, reassured them it was all fine. The Yorkie was trembling. The Shiba Inu was reverting into something more feral and wolflike, flinching at every sudden move. I made sure their leads were securely tied, then climbed over.

I landed on the other side and the deer scattered. "Stay!" I said to Matilda. She turned her head and contemplated running off with her new friends. I pretended I had a treat in my hand (I never had treats) and slowly approached. As soon as I was within reach I grabbed her by the collar and put her back on the lead. She shook herself and wagged her tail, letting her long hair wave and flutter like a 1970s glamor model. Her eyelashes were thick and coy. Her teeth were white and haunting against her black lips. I walked with her around the enclosure, looking for a way out. There was a large brick wall along the far side with no doors or easy exits, but farther down the meadow was a work shed and a garage where I could see a large wooden gate. The gate was locked up with chains, but there was a significant gap between it and the ground—this had to be how she had gotten in here in the first place and now we'd both have to squeeze back out. I headed toward it. The deer continued to scatter. More calls and messages chimed on my phone.

And then something happened.

Four things happened, actually, but all at the same time. These four separate events occurred at the exact same second and created what I can only describe as a rip or a kind of smear, like the world around me had boiled itself to an evaporated state and formed this millisecond injection of pure undiluted stress that I think would have killed my body if it hadn't done what it did instead. These were the four events:

First, Matilda growled at a passing deer and I was afraid she was going to try and attack one of them, so I reached and grabbed her collar instead of just her lead to keep her closer to me.

Second, it wasn't Matilda that had growled, it was the Shiba Inu, back at the fence, and he hadn't growled, he had barked. He was fighting with one of the other dogs. I turned and looked and all four of them were in a sudden, ferocious brawl.

Third, a security guard entered the enclosure and called out to me. Light from a torch flew across the meadow. The eyes of the deer flashed yellow and red and I couldn't stop and explain what I was doing there because I had to turn back, I had to run back to the fighting dogs.

And fourth, my phone wouldn't stop ringing and chiming with angry dog owners, internet providers, boyfriends, lawyers.

Every one of these things happened at once like the artful dropping of four synchronized divers from the sky, causing no splash, just undulating ripples. A chain reaction of paradoxes. I had to stop the dogs from fighting but they were on the other side of the fence but I couldn't let go of Matilda because she was spooked and lurching forward, trying to escape, turning and biting my hand gripping her collar, and I tripped and fell. The policeman yelled. My phone rang. And all this time I couldn't stop thinking about my misaddressed internet bill, the shit flat I couldn't afford, the job I had lost, and the gig work I had found myself lost in the middle of. I fell and kept falling through these things, the world becoming liquid, slipping out from under me.

I didn't land on the ground. But I felt pain—it was Matilda's teeth gnawing at my wrist but then it wasn't. Sensation—pain, sounds, the night air—it all flushed out of me. The policeman's voice was farther away. The snarling dogs were somehow above me, as if I had fallen down a well and for a second I thought that I had, that I had fallen down a hole in the ground, but that couldn't be true because everything was white, flashing, iridescent, and somehow below me, not above, looping and inverted. Matilda's fur swirled out like grass as we careened into each other. The policeman was below me. The dogs were above me. The park was spherical. The sky was inside me. I felt sick and vomited but the only thing that came out was myself, flipping over myself, regurgitating my own body like the flipping panels of an old alarm clock. Bells ringing. My hearing blurred. My vision split. My nervous system, my fingernails, my hair, my skeleton, all displayed themselves like jars of separated herbs, sealed off, naked, preserved, then shattering back together again, too fast, too hard and somehow, in a way, disgustingly sour.

When everything finally settled, when the tingling across my body stopped, when my mind unclenched its pulsing and my lungs gasped for life, it was as if whole days had gone by. But in reality, they were yet to come.

1

Your body knows where you are, it's your mind that needs convincing. In hindsight, I knew exactly what happened to me right when it happened, I just didn't have the words, I only had the sensations.

I was lying flat on my back and the first thing I noticed was the silence, or maybe I should say the noise. The world was so noisily silent. Quiet enough that I could hear my blood moving through my body like a big sloshing bag of water. My heart a propeller. Tubes, valves, and holes opening and closing, contracting, sliding around. My eyelids opened and shut too loudly, like two heavy wooden shutters, so I kept them shut. My body recalibrated. I could hear actual sunlight filtering down around me like pebbles scattering across my body. It was daylight. That was a change. It had been night and now it was day. (Again, your mind wants to jump to easy conclusions like this, make connections, despite the body knowing inherently where in time and space it exists, knowing where it's not meant to be.) I must have passed out, I thought, and sure, that had happened for a moment, technically—my body granted my mind this bit of recognition.

There was birdsong above me. The loudest thing I have ever heard. Screaming into me. A chorus of birds sang as populous as the leaves in the trees. My eyes opened again, wide like jaws agape. There was so much greenery. I squinted and blinked furiously. Flip, flip. Slamming shutters. The light was like water to look through. I sat up and my surroundings tightened their grip on me. Greener than green.

I was in a thicker, denser part of the park. (But we have not moved an inch, my body said. It's the woods that have grown denser, and how might that be?) Above me: canopies, leaves, the sky like a vaulted ceiling, held up by wood beams, trees all adorned. Beneath me: moss, grass, bugs, dirt, thick ropes of weeds and brambles, truly the softest bed I have ever laid in; grass like jade feathers, like the earth itself was still miles beneath it all.

Hey the deer were still there, a short distance away, watching me. Again the noise! I could hear their breathing, like one organic, festering dough, munching their grassy meals, jaws moving in silly circles, their blinking as loud as my own, my barn doors flipping open and shut. But the deer were larger in number than before, and they were grander-looking, more sturdy and golden. Matilda was nowhere to be seen. The brick wall and chain-link fence surrounding the deer enclosure were also gone and my mind continued its charade of wondering where I was, if I had perhaps stumbled into a deeper reach of the enclosure, my body clock tsk-tsking me all the while.

I stood up. I walked. The deer moved away from me. Their hooves clattered in heavy parade across the grass. I walked in the direction of the fence where I had tied up the dogs, but I walked too far, I had to have walked too far because I never reached the fence.

I stopped.

"OK," I said. That was my first word. My voice rang loudly in my head.

I never met the fence. I turned and walked in the opposite direction but never met the brick wall, nor the main road beyond, always choked with car traffic on the Blackheath side of the park. I heard no cars. I turned again and walked back, walked south, past the place where I had woken up, past a dense thicket where I knew for sure the deer enclosure ended and the rest of the park continued, but still no fence, no dogs, no park. There were no gardens, no pathways. The bandstand gone, the café gone, the parking lot gone. I walked into another open meadow, but it wasn't easily navigable, the grass wasn't shallow and thin, it was thick and riddled with shifting earth. There were rocks, holes, sticks, branches. Field mice appeared and disappeared. There were gnats everywhere and birds everywhere eating the gnats. I reunited with the herd of deer and they skedaddled again, still wary of me. Those aren't the same deer, I thought to myself. Something about this isn't the same.

I followed the natural slope of the meadow to where I knew would be the crest of the hill, where there was an overlook by the Royal Observatory, with a statue of a general, some benches, always filled with tourists taking in the view of the river and Canary Wharf, and what a fine day for it. But my body continued to mock me, laughing and shaking me with a sudden nausea because there was an overlook, yes, but no Royal Observatory. No statue. No bench. Not even a road or a hint of pavement or a sign.

I knew I was in the right place because there was the river, there was the view—I had been to this overlook a hundred times and I knew I was in the right place, but I was trembling, I was sick, because—there was no—yes no—there was no Canary Wharf. It was missing. What wher- whe—I looked around. I looked again. The buildings were gone. The Isle of Dogs was completely bare. Greenwich was gone. Everything was only trees as thick as marshland, right up to the edge of the water, checkered in places with lime-green and yellow fields, but no buildings, no roads, no streetlamps. No university, museum, or market. My whole body shook.

"What," I said. My second word.

Only the bright blue dome of the sky was still the same, sculpted and heavy like lead around me, and I wheezed. My legs buckled. I fell to my knees. I stared at this view for a long time, unbelieving, hunched over on all fours as if in a trance, watching alien things in the distance pass by like banners that hinted at my whereabouts, my whenabouts. There was a boat down in the river, moving slowly along. It was a large canoe-like thing, with a covering over it, like a barge. Wooden. People rowed it forward. There were more boats farther up the river, where it bended and turned, closer into central London—a London that wasn't there, or wasn't the London that should be there. The Shard, the City, all the faint landmarks you could spot from the top of Greenwich Park were gone and in their place was what could only be called a shantytown, dusty and yellow-green, smoke rising everywhere and fading into a pastel horizon. It was a beautiful summer day, but it wasn't my day, it wasn't my season. It was a joke.

My stomach walloped and moaned, my vision went teary and flushed. The delirium of green all around me and the noise, the non-noise, were like sudden, irreversible maladies, and I heaved with sickness. Everything I knew was gone. Everything had been replaced with woods and smells and noise. I wondered for a moment (my mind's first crude attempt at understanding what my body already knew) if some horrible apocalypse had occurred. A nuclear bomb or an earthquake had simply washed away the city. Then I thought of drugs—maybe I had accidentally inhaled something or brushed up against a toxic plant or mushroom and this was some wild confusion, but every explanation only served to dull and cheaply nullify what was ringing its blaring truth in front of my eyes, deep inside my ears: this was a world that was clearly existing and I was contained within it now, physically, as real as ever. I could concede that moments ago (hours ago?) I had not been here and now I was—but actually that wasn't true either because I had been here before just not in the here that was now and so what was here had to have transformed, but not transformed because the river was still its shape, the land was still its form, the air was air, the sun was sun, so what had to have occurred was a sense of age. Of changed time.

Hours ago? Years ago? That was what my body felt innately. It felt like years ago I had been walking the dogs, chasing after Matilda and Ryley, years ago in the sense that years were measures of distance, in any direction, years ago in the sense that I had moved away from the time with the dogs and the fence and the wall and the phone calls into another time without them. I had stepped across these units of measurement. I had traveled time. That was what I could call it.

I felt painfully, piercingly alone. I was the only person in the entire world this had happened to—that was the prevailing, insane feeling.

Along the banks of the river there was actually a version of Greenwich still—a small settlement of stony buildings and dusty lanes, thatched roofs, some tiled, rising smoke. In the center of the town there was a church but not the one I was used to seeing, and there were more trees surrounding it, more trees than ever before, peppered throughout the town. This is psychosis, I thought. I have lost my mind and this is what I am seeing; I am doing something worse than dreaming, oh my God.

My instinct was to pray so I prayed. I wasn't a very religious person, but the entire world had shifted—or I had shifted through the entire world, like a sieve, and from what I could tell, I was the only one this had happened to, everything was continuing at pace with or without me, and I felt the pressure of cosmic attention. I had *time traveled*—I held the thought for the first time, consciously, seriously—and surely that was indicative of some kind of irreparable breaking. If there was a Creator then surely he or she was watching me this very moment, watching this creation of his or hers that had dripped through a hole in what was supposed to have been an impenetrable net, was already trying to fix this, was saying a holy "oops" at the least and would make amends, would answer me and put things right. I didn't say anything in my prayer, just sort of wallowed and cried, said "God" both as an address and a curse in vain, felt dizzy and stopped, felt embarrassed, like I was getting ahead of myself, being too dramatic, and I laughed. I closed my eyes. I waited for the world to change back, for myself to wake up. I can wait on top of this hill for a long time, I told no one. Surely the disrepair will repair itself if all I do is wait.

Here are the things I was wearing and had on my person: a pair of white Reebok trainers, white socks, black running shorts and underwear, a white T-shirt with a navy blue line drawing of a cartoon octopus printed across it, my wallet which contained no cash, just two credit cards, a debit card, and various rewards cards; the keys to my flat; the entry fob to my building; my phone; and a tangled pair of headphones. I no longer had Matilda's lead in my hand, nor Matilda obviously, but there were long strands of her hair stuck to my shorts, which I brushed off.

I checked my phone. It still had 10 percent battery, but no cellular or Wi-Fi signal. Like a freak, I took a photo of the view from the hilltop and the photo on the screen looked modern and normal, like I was out on a hike at a nature reserve somewhere— and you would believe it if the Thames wasn't right there, bending the same way it always bent, like a familiar guide smiling at my lostness, saying hello, you're not supposed to be here right now, please kindly could you leave.

I started to panic again. I walked downhill, I had to move. Everything was so loud! My feet roared with every step and kicked up dust. I pushed through bulky shrubs and stubborn, slanted trees, and soon there came signs of development, but nothing I could understand. I passed small enclosures built from rocks, wooden posts, a faint trail carved across a clearing, ivy that had been cut back, and crude hedgerows. These were signs of life but not my life, not anything close to it. I was trespassing. Surely I was out in the country or something. I had had a psychotic break and wandered all night.

A woman and two children appeared on the path in front of me—I saw them and they saw me and we all froze. I gasped. It was like I was seeing humans for the first time in my life. Their clothes were brown and goldenrod. The woman wore a sort of tunic with deep pockets, sleeves, and a cap on her head. The two children wore similar tunics, which were essentially rectangular tubes of fabric fitted to them. But it was their faces—their bodies—that shocked and made me stop. Their faces were normal. I don't know what I mean by normal, but that's the best I can describe it. Their expressions, their eyes, how they darted, the way they breathed as any other human would breathe, how they blinked—they were like me, like anyone else. I struggled to speak.

They stared at me but kept walking down this simple dirt trail that cut through the thicket. The children looked over their shoulders and stared longer, until the woman said something to them I couldn't understand, ushering them along.

"Hey," I called after them, but the woman pretended not to hear. They walked faster and disappeared. I listened to their footsteps trampling down the dirt path until they were far away, and yet I could still hear them and their voices, echoing through the trees as if we were sharing a small, private room. "Hey," I said again, but quieter this time. I exhaled.

I followed the same path down to the end of the park—of course I couldn't be sure where the park actually ended as there were no roads or walls and there was no "park" to speak of, but the trees thinned out and the trail became wider and more solid, more like a road. There were wooden fences in places now, stones that had been stacked together for purposes I couldn't assume, swaths of meadowland that appeared to have been divided up and tamed. There were crops. There was a collection of small buildings in the distance.

"Shit," I said out loud. Again my voice sounded so strange. It rattled my brain when it left my mouth, unmuffled, too crisp. I was acutely aware of the movement of my tongue, how sharp the

T-sound sounded. I said *shit* because this was ridiculous. "What the hell. I can't—this isn't—what the." I stuttered and shook, talking to myself, afraid to walk any closer to the settlement—to Greenwich! To my flat! I lived over there! My flat, which I couldn't afford to live in anymore, with the view of the river, the Waitrose downstairs, the coffee shops, the pedestrian bridge, the pub along the water. It was right in front of me but it wasn't there! It wasn't there!

A man's voice sounded from behind me. His intonation was like that of a greeting, like saying "hey" but it sounded more like "hail," like a guttural tic. I jumped and turned around.

An older man, weathered and red, was sitting on the ground against a fence on the side of the road. He wore almost the same type of clothes as the woman, only more tattered and wrinkled. His fingernails were long and mangled. He was barefoot. He sat in a crouched manner, it didn't look comfortable, but he was smiling at me, teeth all broken. He repeated his strange-sounding greeting and nodded his head, inquisitive.

"Hi," I said.

Eh?

I walked tentatively toward him. I looked down the road, then back at him. He was still smiling, pointing at me now. He spoke a full sentence and truly for the life of me I couldn't understand him.

Hah-eel been fareh yeh?

"Sorry," I said. "I've just come from the park and I don't know what—"

Koonst ow spekest thow ayngleesh?

"I don't know what's going on." My voice mumbled off. I stood next to the man and gripped the fence. I had to hold on to something to steady myself. Everywhere I looked, everything I heard, dismantled my senses, and I was afraid I would pass out. Time travel? How could my mind so easily make such an assumption when just saying hello to a stranger was overwhelming.

The old man kept speaking to me, asking something, repeating himself. He noticed my trainers and pointed at them and said something loudly. I said sorry again, shook my head, that was all I could do. I closed my eyes and leaned against the wooden rail. The sun bore down on us. The man's voice sounded as if we were inside a soundproof recording studio. Everything that made up the essence of him—his rugged breath, the wetness in his speech, the movement of his clothing—strummed illegible rhythms right inside my ear and I winced at the sharpness.

"Where am I?" I demanded. My voice was too loud, I couldn't get a grip.

Eye ben marvey-loos yeh shoes thow kanst understant?

"No. Where am I? Where are we?"

Been boath stuk hey-er outen ah wey. Ha ha.

"Greenwich?" I said and pointed down the road. "Greenwich?"

Grenwych?

"Greenwich."

Gren ich?

"Greenwich."

No—Grenwych.

"OK, Grenwych," I said, trying to imitate him. The man laughed. And surprisingly, despite my panic and the world that was spinning too loudly, too lush, too green, something in my heart floated up. We had communicated, just barely, but we had communicated. Contact. Greenwich. I had said it wrong, or wrong to him, and he had corrected me. Oh my God. I smiled. I laughed. Oh God, oh God.

The old man kept talking, now even faster. His language was thick and coated in heavy-sounding syllables that dug deep into the dirt. He pointed at my shoes again, he patted his cheeks and laughed. He pointed at the octopus print on my shirt. His gnarled yellow fingernail. All I could do was smile and apologize while I tried to think what to do next.

Al hayle! the old man suddenly yelled. *Al hayle!* He waved his arm at someone behind me and called again. I turned.

Two men were coming down the road. They were younger—they looked about my age, both were dressed in the same sort of tunic and rags as the old man but cleaner. Again the normalcy of their faces was the only thing I could focus on. Their faces were the sorts of faces I would see on the tube. Just two young men, with whole lives, features, and quirks behind their eyes. They saw me and looked puzzled, almost wary.

The old man called them over and they approached slowly. It was my clothes that set me apart from everyone. I started to worry. I had no means of explaining myself. Even if I knew what I needed, I wouldn't know how to say it. I could say "Greenwich" again in that strange way the old man had said it. I could point. I heard the old man say it again when he spoke to the men. All three of them talked back and forth. Their language was strange and barbed, slurred into each word, sounding almost German, but with an Italian inflection, each voice with its own life, tics, timbre. One of them gestured to me. The old man kept laughing about something. One of the young men coughed—that was weird because coughs sound the same in any language, to any ear.

He cleared his throat and spit. He wiped sweat off his face with his tunic. It seemed unreal. Their faces, their gestures, and how they moved felt so natural and recognizable, but I couldn't understand a word they said and I had nothing to say for myself. They were unplaceable and so was I. I had no home, no reason, no sense of time. No life. I felt it all slipping out from under me again. One of the men addressed me directly but his words, this language, was like an offering of slop I could only shake my head at, step back from. I was more passive with the two young men. Something about being closer to them in age, I felt a self-consciousness I hadn't felt with just the old man, a more desperate admission of purposelessness. I wanted to fall in line, but I didn't know where the line was.

The man asked me a question. I said sorry what and he asked again. He stepped forward. There was a seriousness in his tone, a hint of aggression. I hesitated.

"I live here," I said slowly. "I live here in *Grenwych*. Actually, I think—" I stuttered and laughed at myself. "I think I traveled through time." I figured I might as well just say it, not that anyone could understand me.

But the man didn't like what I was saying. He shook his head and stepped closer to me—too close—and said another long string of words. He pointed to the old man and to the other guy with him. He asked me something, then repeated himself.

"Sorry," was all I could say again and again. I held up my hands to show passivity. "I truly don't understand what you're saying. I'm out of my mind right now I don't—" Then the man touched me. He reached and grabbed my shirt. I flinched out of fear, but also out of awe—at the physical sensation, at reality proving itself. This was a human touching me, as real as any other. I saw the faint wrinkles in his face, the coarseness of his hair, and a sense of custom, a sense that there were principles of tailoring and hygiene and self-determination built up inside him. He grabbed my shirt because he wanted to inspect it. He seemed almost aghast at it, running his hand over the fabric. I gently pulled away but he grabbed me again. He pulled harder on the shirt.

"Where are you from?" he asked. Or at least his intonation sounded as if he had asked something to that effect. He repeated himself. Whatever he was saying was aimed at me and demanded an answer. He was impatient.

"My name is George and I live here," I said, carefully. "I'm a dog walker and last night—or an hour ago, or something I don't know—something happened to me when I was at the park. Two of my dogs ran away and something happened. I passed out, I think, or something else. I fell. And I woke up here. Or well, I woke up at the park, in the same place, but here. Here in London but at a different time. Because this is like, what? Medieval times?" I laughed. "Time traveling isn't a thing but this is what's happened to me and I'm here and I'm just as freaked out as you are."

Recognition flashed across the faces of the men when I said key words. London. Dog. Time. They kept looking at my trainers and shorts. By now, another man had walked up from the settlement and joined us. He wore a thing—a leather sort of armor over his chest. He also held a long knife. You could call it a sword. There was an older woman farther away leaning against the same fence, observing. I was becoming an attraction. I was disrupting the flow.

The man who was keeping hold of my shirt this whole time

said something to the man in the armor. While they spoke to each other, the second man pulled at my running shorts. His hand groped at the waistband and I tried to step away from him.

"Stop," said the man holding my shirt, or something like it. He jerked the fabric to get me to hold still. The armored man said something, a sort of command, or a permission, addressing everyone in the group. Tension ran through everyone's voices now. There was a hierarchy.

"Please," I said, trying to lean back. The neck of my T-shirt was stretching out. "I just need help, I'm not going to cause any trouble, I'm a nobody." But I struggled too hard and the man yanked me back with equal force. Panicking, I ducked my head down and tried to back up, but he kept his hold on me and I lost my footing. As I stumbled, he grabbed more of my shirt, pulling it up my back and over my head. He laughed. With the shirt slipped off, I was free for a moment, but the armored man grabbed the back of my head by my hair. My scalp exploded with pain.

"Stop!" I yelled.

The armored man yelled instructions to the two men, who proceeded to strip off the rest of my clothes. I yelled and thrashed about, but they had me firmly detained. There was a sense of methodology at play here, as if the men were sentries and had done this before, but there was also marvel in their voices. They pulled my shorts off and awed at the fabric. They tried to grab my underwear but I twisted away and fell onto my back, hard against the ground. They pulled me back up and one of them grabbed my arms, twisted them up. I tried to kick the other but he grabbed both legs, laughing, and had my feet, amazed at my shoes. His voice reached a delirious pitch as he pulled them off my feet, then my socks, then finally reached and pulled off my underwear. I flailed around and tried to elbow the other man, but he put his hand across my entire face and put me in a twisted headlock. I bit him and he forced his whole fist inside my mouth, gripping my tongue. My jaw sprang open. I screamed and gagged, spitting, realizing all this was happening while we were walking, we were on the move. They were forcing me along. I was gagging, hunched over, moving forward, struggling to breathe, my bare feet on rough, packed earth.

They walked me into Greenwich, but of course it wasn't the Greenwich I knew it to be. The church was like a lone farmhouse, fenced in and rough-hewn. Gone was the market, the *Cutty Sark* museum, the housing estates, the McDonald's, and Starbucks. There was only a greenery encroached upon by wood and stone structures (buildings? houses? It was incomprehensible.). There was an order to the land, but not one I could make sense of nor see through my tears, the dust, the pain and exposure.

They walked me naked through the settlement. Men, women, and swarming flies of children gathered and watched us pass. They spoke among themselves in that chewed-up language of theirs. Someone yelled something, the armored man replied. Someone threw something. More instructions, hurried voices, laughter. The man tugged at the rope I was tied to—they had tied me up; when had that happened? It rubbed dry and rough around my wrists. More men joined us, they carried my clothes and shoes, ecstatic at their new treasure. With a sting of ultimate shame I suddenly worried about my phone—I was being dragged through the street and that was what my mind went to—worrying if it had fallen out of my pocket during the assault, worrying about the screen cracking, the battery life. I realize now this was my brain scrambling its autopilot, clinging to the last vestiges of modernity it knew, just a mental by-product of time traveling, but of course how could anyone know that when I was the only person this had happened to. I was alone. I felt the painful awareness that I was the only human being on the entire planet worrying about his phone at this moment. The worry echoed out across the land, into space, noticed by no one. Loneliness was too trite a word. This was banishment. Exile. I began to weep and howl.

They took me to a large stone and brick building. They threw me in a dirt cell.

They kept me there for days. Then weeks.

Darkness and solitude compounded on itself.

Time.

Itself.

Zero. Then One. Starting over.

At first, there was only brutality. My memories of those early days blur into a single dram. I remember the sunny awakening at the park, the assault, but then there was a period of darkness and silence during which I underwent a sort of prolonged mutation, with no clear moment when I knew I was out the other side.

Men visited my cell and questioned me. They pushed me around, hit me, demanded answers in a language I couldn't understand, each visit ending with me bloodied and barely able to move. I vomited and shook. I was given no food or water for days, and darkness, pain, and cold was all I received, abandoned and never checked on, never spoken to. After a week, they finally poured a grayish slop on the floor for me to eat, which tasted of nothing. I kept bleeding. They poured my cold meals directly over my body as if I were a plant taking water, twitching. I lost the ability to sleep. I lost the ability to stay awake. My toilet was the floor. Fever rattled through me. Physiologically, almost electrically, I'm sure my body remembers exactly how long I stayed like that and exactly what was done to me, but my mind struggles to recall with any exactness, only dark blurs of pain, a steep downswing into agony, and perhaps, most horrifying, an adjustment of expectation. Acclimatization.

What I came to feel was a pure grayness I had never felt before. The idea of joy had not ceased so much as it no longer felt applicable to my existence and so it was moved elsewhere. Everything was pain and so nothing was pain, there was no sense of contrast. I felt immutable. I simply dripped.

Then suddenly, momentum shifted. One day I was naked and one day I was finally given clothes—just a square tunic, but at that point I was a roach, deadheaded and almost *thankful* in a desecrated sense of the word. The fabric was coarse like burlap and frayed all over, but I treasured it. I thought about my old clothes—of course they had spooked these people. Surely they had never seen cotton fabric so tightly refined, machine-woven, mass-produced. I remembered the drawing of the cartoon octopus on the T-shirt, the rubber insoles of the trainers. Alien technology. I couldn't imagine what they were doing with them now. I ran my fingers over the new tunic with recalibrated awe. I cried, in fact, at these people's generosity. Something was happening inside me and I allowed it.

Captured and held in a cell, stripped, starved, beat—I didn't feel the sort of terror I knew I was supposed to feel. I felt the freezing bite of night and the musty heat of day—both sunlight and moonlight cutting between wood slats, striping my sores— but this wasn't suffering. This was abject pain, I could note, but a greater shock cushioned the blows, a new validity that was coming to my senses, a new benchmark, a new degree of aliveness that I can only describe as being able to hear things I had never heard before. Seagulls called from what felt like miles away. People swept, negotiated, hammered, dug, simply walked—whole lives were happening outside my cell and their sounds were of such a pure, undiluted crackle.

What would have been (or would be?) my old flat was just down the road from here. And if I closed my eyes and listened to the seagulls, it truly felt as though I could leave this cell, walk down the street, and be back at home with the same seagulls singing the same songs as if nothing had ever happened. Maybe my ex would be back there too, complaining about something— the rubbish needing taken out, the weather, the birds. A family of seagulls lived on our roof back then. They had made nests on the roofs of the buildings in our development. They would caw all day and my boyfriend hated the noise but I thought they were fun to watch, silly when their screams bubbled up any odd hour of the day, their little wars. They were drawn to the "green" roofs on all the buildings in the development—a tax write-off that mostly grew pollen-rich weeds in spring, burnt and dead by summer, and it was that barren greenery that made an attractive nest for the birds. They shit everywhere and swarmed the sky in the mornings. Sometimes I'd hear the gentle swoop of one passing the window in the middle of the night.

Workmen would come out on the roofs and try their best to make a hostile environment for the birds. From our top-floor flat, I'd watch them out on the lower buildings trying everything just shy of outright extermination. I'm sure the birds were a pestilence to people of consequence tied up in property values, hygiene concerns, but not me, barely able to make my half of the shared rent. The men erected tall poles onto which they fastened kitelike fake birds that fluttered dark and menacing in the wind to scare them away. This caused a week or so of chaos and screeching, but it only took one calm summer day, when the plastic crows hung flaccid and motionless, for the gulls to realize they were nothing to be afraid of. Other days the wind would blow so strong that the decoys would get wrapped up in their own tethers, knotted and stuck to the poles, and the gulls would cackle, victorious. Eventually the workmen stopped coming out to reset them.

I'd watch the seagulls from my balcony on days I wasn't working (i.e., couldn't find work, gave up on finding work, content to walk dogs forever) and smile at their tribal infighting, their comic dawdles, their fluffy new chicks flapping limber wings learning to fly. I'd hold my breath if one of them came too close to the roof edge. I applauded when I saw them soaring high above me one morning, little gray feet splayed out with joy, then gone only a few days later, flown away.

Our balcony developed a spider problem that summer. The seagulls would eat flies and other bugs, but when they were too busy fighting the workmen and the plastic crows, the flies proliferated and attracted spiders who wove enormous webs all over our balcony in order to catch them. My boyfriend refused to step outside, refused to open the windows despite the heat, would scream with great charade when one of the spiders crept inside the flat. One day I killed them all, sprayed bug spray all over the balcony, swept away their webs and mummified meals, totally ignorant to their purpose—and the next day we had a fly problem. The day after that, I had a boyfriend problem. We had a blowout fight over cleaning and the recycling, over the spiders and the flies, and everything became barbed in the way these things tend to, seagulls screaming all the while, refusing to be our metaphor for domestic neglect and elemental incompatibility. When our breakup finally happened it happened immediately and without fanfare. When I received a vague text from him the day after the night he had walked out and not come back, my first thought was oh, this is going to be a thing, but it should have been oh, this *was* a thing and now it wasn't because it was already over. He never came back. My boyfriend had also had a boyfriend problem, and he had taken care of it.

It was very London how we broke apart via admin, like defaulting on a loan, deleting a spelling error, sweeping away a cobweb. It didn't feel real when I half read the long, wordy email from him—he had never sent me an email before, why start now? He sounded so contrived and not himself that I googled the whole thing to see if he had used a foolproof breakup template or AI, but he hadn't, he really was that wordy and contrived. I tried replying with my own screed but only regurgitated the same shallow phrases, sounding like the back of a cereal box. I deleted the draft. I deleted the email and blocked his.

A few months after that, I traveled through time. Now there were centuries (I assumed—I didn't know what year it was) between me and the breakup. Actually, technically the breakup hadn't even happened yet. If someone were to ask me why I was feeling gloom (aside from the imprisonment, the beating, the gruel) I wouldn't be able to say "I'm getting over a breakup," because that wouldn't be true. "I'm *going* to be getting over a breakup" would be more accurate and that sounded like non-sense, that sounded like nothing. "I'm going to go through a breakup many years from now"—of course I would, that was no surprise. Everything broke eventually.

But the truth was I didn't feel gloom at all now. I could say these days imprisoned passed like nightmares, but like the nightmares of a newborn, who wakes each day with tremors and shrieks not from any logical pain or need, but from his body simply being just-born, unfolding like a leaf and trembling, knowing not which way to move. I held spiders in my hands now. I watched them weave and sew all night in the corners of my cell, understanding the patterns of their days more than anything else in this world. I wanted to know what their secret to the universe was, how they had managed, as a species, to stay the same for so long, content to weave the same patterns unchanged. I whispered to them my fears and asked if they had ever met a time traveler before. If they had, they certainly didn't make it known, just as God had left my desperate prayers at the park unanswered. I had slipped through time itself and not a peep. But this was no longer loneliness, I realized. This was no longer abandonment. The spiders carried on and so did I, and in the darkness, their leggy movements felt like instruction, the calls of gulls sounded like guides.

2

Another week and my captors let me outside. Prescribed sunlight. They took me to a small, walled yard and let me walk around on my own like a grazing animal. The world opened up in batches. The sky was gray but stately. I smelled the river nearby. I was no longer bound with ropes, and the men, who were numerous and varied, only watched from afar as I blinked in the sunshine, smiled at the fresh air. They looked at me and I looked at them and there was no animosity between us. I felt no pain or rage. That dark, withering solitude had been a baptism, releasing me into this walled garden with a new dryness of mind where the air tasted brighter and more saturated with oxygen than my body knew what to do with. My brain felt holey and overinvigorated, as if I could scream, and on that first day outside I did. I let out an enormous, full-throated scream that woke up the morning, that ripped open the already open air and lasted until the men ran over and beat me again, bound me up and threw me back in my cell for another week, then we did it all over again.

Each week, my new life gained complexity and thus was more enjoyable—and the fact that I was already calling it my new life was enough indication alone that something had been cracked open and drained inside me, beyond easy categorization. I would count the days with tallies scratched into my cell's stone and wood walls, filing a fingernail down to a pulpy nub to mark one day, then moving to the next finger the next day. After ten days, I'd have a fresh fingernail ready. With this structure came sophistication. I was kept in my cell, but the beatings ceased. My screaming stopped. They gave me a blanket and eventually started to leave the door to my cell unlocked, trusting me.

I went to the walled garden daily. At least one man always accompanied me, sometimes more, and as the days and fingernails passed, I began to communicate with them. They all seemed to be workmen at this house, this compound. We volleyed simple words back and forth at first: *Greenwich, London, food, bird, fish, warm, cold, sleep, wash*. I discovered that the words they used weren't foreign words at all, in fact, we shared nearly the same vocabulary, just spoken differently. They had that crunchy dialect—syllables budging against each other like sliding rocks, with a rhythm and sentence structure that was slower, using words sparingly but imbuing them with more meaning, relying less on accuracy via sheer quantity (how I would sputter and over-qualify each noun, stack interjection on top of interjection) and more on finding that one single word, almost like a kanji, that would encapsulate what needed to be said. After nearly a month of this, and with little warning, like a train hurtling through consciousness, we began to communicate more fully.

"Ready to go back?"

"Yes. Can I have a cup of water first?"

"Of course."

I drank from a clay cup, grainy against my lips. Water warm and earthy. I walked back to my cell. The guard followed casually. My shadow filled the cell as the door closed and I sat on the floor, leaned back against the wall, sunken and thankful for what counted as silence in this world but teemed with cooing owls, creaking branches, footsteps over floorboards, water thrown from basins, foxes, crickets, and mice; the overwhelm of this orchestra, the gulls, flies, dogs, a horse chortling somewhere. I thought about the future as the past and the past as the present. I soaked. Perhaps unwisely, I felt a form of love.

After two months of this—yes, two whole months—there was the sense that my status as a prisoner had been cast aside into a bureaucratic nothingspace, which isn't surprising in London. Where at first there had been only barbarism, I now saw organization and hierarchy, with myself simply part of the stock. The people who loomed over me were actually not much higher up the chain and had their own superiors to answer to. There was a warden, then a master, then another master, who reported to a lord, who was absent but hung like a cloud over every day—a man who would one day visit, who existed mostly as a rhetorical device for threats and panic, such as how would they explain this new prisoner kept under lock and key and fed their food, so they might as well put me to work, or shunt me away, or shunt me away and put me to work, or bring me out, put me away. A holding pattern was in play, no one could really make a decision.

They gave me chores to do—sweeping the courtyard, cleaning my cell. Trust was established, the tasks expanded and therefore the world. I was shown other rooms of the house: a kitchen, bedrooms, a dining hall. I met cooks, day laborers, children, more hierarchies unfurling faster than I could interpret or use as a gauge to determine, theoretically, where I might fit in.

The house I was in was a large manor house near where the old Royal Naval Hospital and University of Greenwich would be in the future. It was two floors and a basement, made of brick, stone, and timber, with a tiled roof, and beyond the walled courtyard was an expansive yard that led down to a boat dock on the river, which I caught a glimpse of one day through an opened gate.

"Watch out," said a man coming through. He pulled a wooden cart filled with heavy sacks, closed the gate behind him, and secured it with a lock. "Help me carry these to the storeroom. Do you understand?" He spoke slowly and I nodded. I had a stronger understanding of the language now—mashed up and underdeveloped but easier to grasp than a completely new tongue. I could carry on simple conversations if I had a willing participant, which I rarely had. Everyone regarded me with standoffish glances. The only words spoken to me were blunt commands.

"Take this one first. No, set that down, move it over there. Grab this one by the corners."

I spent the afternoon helping the man move sacks from the courtyard into the house, down a narrow hallway to a storage room at the far end. Though we said little to each other, he seemed more patient than other workmen I had encountered. He was older and seemed more at my level in terms of meekness than the others. I summoned confidence in my new wayward English and took a chance. When we were nearly finished, I said to the man, "I've seen you here a few times, but you don't live here, do you?" The words didn't come out right. I had wanted to make myself sound like myself but it was hard.

"Pardon?"

I had mixed up a verb tense. I repeated myself and rearranged the wording, stumbling into greater simplicity.

"Where do I live?" the man clarified.

"Yes."

"Over by the mill." He heaved the last sack into place and made to leave. My small talk was too small.

"What's today's date?" I blurted out.

He pretended not to understand, or maybe he really didn't, and kept walking, heading back to the courtyard. I followed him down the hall.

"Wait," I said. "What year is it?"

"I don't know what you mean." He chuckled. He walked faster, glancing into adjoining rooms and hallways as we passed them.

"What year are we in?" I repeated. "Like right now. Today. What is it—the year."

He relented and mumbled over his shoulder. "Twenty-eighth."

We stepped out into the courtyard.

"Twenty-eighth?" I said. "What do you mean twenty-eighth?" He kept walking away. "Come on, I just spent all day helping you, will you stop for a second?"

"Shhh." The man swept dross from his cart with his hand. He wiped his hand on his shirt. He went to open the gate, looked back at the house, then at me. "Just because you're picking up English all of a sudden doesn't mean you can talk to whoever you want."

"I've always spoken English, just not your English," I said, as fully in his accent as I could. "What do you mean by twenty-eighth? Like sixteen-twenty-eight? Fifteen-twenty-eight?"

"As in the twenty-eighth year of King Edward," he said. "But of course they wouldn't teach you that where you come from. Now get your hands off my cart."

"Twenty-eighth year . . ." My mouth hung open. "That does nothing for me."

"Does nothing for me either." He jerked the cart loose and pulled it through the open gate, slamming the doors behind him. I was left alone in the courtyard with no further knowledge of where I was.

King Edward?

I knew nothing about history—or well, I knew some things about history, but no more than the average person, not enough to know when the twenty-eighth year of King Edward's reign was. I had studied the kings and queens of Britain just like everyone else in school, done flimsy presentations about Henry VIII, getting the Roman numerals mixed up, bored out of my mind. There was Victoria, Elizabeth I, Henry VIII, too many Edwards, always getting the Charleses turned around. The mad King George? Boudica? Which Edward? Were we as far back as the Romans? When was any of that? I was terrible at dates.

What I knew was there was no electricity. There were horses, there was money, but no plumbing aside from what gravity could provide. The people spoke a smeary kind of English that I could grapple with, so it wasn't like we were completely prehistoric. I recognized snippets of French here and there, and stranger languages I couldn't pinpoint. "When was English invented," I heard myself googling, with the entirety of British history clouding my brain. It wasn't like knowing the date would make things any easier, but it would at least anchor me to a timeline, a sense of perspective I could tie to this new batch of humans I had been spat into.

Twenty-eighth year of King Edward. Handcarts and horses. Thinking about it only served to rattle me all over again and remind me of my bodyshock: stripped, beat, starved, held in a cell. Held in a cell until I enjoyed it—not like that was any measure because I had enjoyed dog walking until I had hated it. I had been walking six dogs. I had lost two of them. I had lost my job. I had lost my boyfriend. I had traveled through time. I had to get out of here.

I had to get out! The thought slithered its way through my mind full of panic and rush. That was the simple fact: I had to get out. I focused my intention on that because what was I doing here anyway? Being some kind of nobly austere stableboy? Basking in these monkish routines? I couldn't not be moving, I couldn't be complacent. I had to at least escape the manor house, then I could worry about the loftier, metaphysical time-crisis I was trapped inside or whatever this was.

But did I? I felt the knee-jerk itch to flee, but I had always felt that, all the time, not just now. I had felt that on the tube, on holiday, online, at work. I always wanted to leave. The only thing different now was the assuaging simplicity of being human in the sense that being human meant waking at dawn, defecating into a pit, performing labor, eating, resting, retiring with the sun, feeling the earth, feeling my skin tightening, burning, callusing, becoming uncontemplative. There was a coldness, sure, but there was a warmness—my awakening from shock and maybe the shock wasn't coming from where I thought it was. I wanted to flee, I wanted to stay. I also wasn't sure what either of those things entailed.

Over the next few days, I made a point to bond more with the people I interacted with—the guards and workmen, and all the daily visitors who passed through the house. Everyone had a purpose beyond my understanding and so I tried to understand. I carried more heavy sacks. I opened the heavy sacks and scooped out bowlfuls of barley and learned how to soak them, how to sift and strain them, how to cook them. I carried firewood, emptied latrines, washed floors, swept the courtyard, washed linens, repaired linens, and slowly reeled myself into greater circles of trust and was rewarded for it. They gave me new clothes—just another worn tunic, but slightly more substantial, and a belt, shoes. They gave me a bundle of straw to improve my bed. I smiled more often. There was hard labor to perform at all moments of the day, but I made sure I was smiling. I laughed. I smiled.

"Your teeth are very straight," said another servant.

"I had braces when I was a teenager," I said.

"Simon! Don't talk to him—leave, shoo shoo. Get out!" A woman whipped the man with a wet rag, and with serious force, not comically, batting him out of the work shed. I was helping her grind wheat grains, being as merry and charitable as I could be, ignoring the buzzing layer of mistrust that constantly surrounded me.

Through a window I watched this Simon wander off, look back at me and stare, then look at the ground. His hair was dark and slightly curly. His clothes were shades of tattered brown, but cared for, tucked in; there was intentionality. It was still unreal how real these people were.

"Where do you think I'm from?" I asked the woman later. The unreality of their realness made it easier to elbow my way into conversation with them like this, like I was surveying ants.

She said nothing. A fly hovered and bounced against the window. We continued grinding the wheat. Later, we ate it in a porridge. And that was the kind of day I had. Small inroads met with bewildering walls. Pools of otherworldly silences.

Simon was one of the men who had stripped me naked and tied me up. Wulfric was the name of the other one. Together they had beat me up and pulled off my clothes. One of them had shoved his whole fist inside my mouth, nearly broken my jaw, egged on by their superior. They both lived in the manor, in quarters close to my cell, but spent their days outside hunting and running errands. It took two months before I no longer felt a tightness of fear in my chest whenever I saw them—two months of learning, through observation, that their lot in life was as similarly dire as mine. They were indentured servants and a fist in the mouth was only what the task at hand had required. Their days hinged on unquantifiable blessings bestowed by an absent lord. They squabbled with each other like brothers for the last inch of status one could hold over the other—Wulfric's ancestral promises, Simon's northern roots, the sad buoyancy of religious superstition. I felt sorry for them. It didn't take long for both of them to earn— only abstractly, never stated out loud—my forgiveness. I couldn't blame them for what they did.

Simon always mentioned land an uncle had promised his father up north, which was subsequently his, now that the uncle had died and his father was already long-dead (trampled by three horses when Simon was a child; Simon's mother had died giving birth to him). The land there was lush, awash with arable soil, bordered by woods and a brook. His eyes misted when he spoke of it, even though he had never been there before. He had never left London.

"Why don't you go there?" I asked one night. We were huddled around a fire in the yard, too filthy to be let inside the main house. We drank root water, ate boiled roots, the cold at our backs. Summer was glancing in another direction—it felt like early September, maybe later—still no one would clearly tell me the date.

"Because I need an apprenticeship in London first," Simon said. "An apprenticeship in anything—maybe carpentry or engineering, I want to build things—with someone who'll give me room and board for a few months, which will buy me out of service here. Then I can buy back my earnings and pay my way north."

I struggled to see the math in the nightmare he described—and winced at how it all relied on handshakes and verbal confirmations more than anything else; maybe there was a scrap of paper somewhere in a registrar far away, but nothing warranted being an unpaid servant. There was a modern part of me that only saw the potential for anarchy in the way this old world functioned. Most of the fences these people swore by were all invisible.

"Why not just run away? If you have the land, just go there."

Simon balked. Wulfric glared at me and said, "Nobody *has* land. That's not how people do things in this part of the world." His tone was pointed and sharp.

"Everything has momentum," said Simon, trying not to dismiss me, but recognizing a clear division between my logic and his—if it could be called logic at all. There was genuine surprise in his eyes, like a part of him hadn't considered escaping outright. The way he spoke with his hands was measured and smooth. "But anyway, I'll need to save enough to hire protection for the journey, once I decide to go. I'll need a knight, or a mercenary from London. It's dragon territory."

I blinked. "Dragon?" I said.

"They don't have dragons in the future?" Simon said this with an impressive mix of cloying jest and seriousness. I had tried and failed to get anyone to believe my story. My being the time traveler was a running joke now and I guess I was happy to be one, happy to be anything. I was *happy*—I noted. A scary feeling.

"They don't have dragons in the past, present, or future," I said and tried to clarify what he meant. A dragon like a big lizard? A Komodo dragon? I dared wonder if we were as far back as dinosaur times.

Simon performed the swooshing wings, the fire breath. Wulfric nodded his head. They debated the size—bigger than a cow, bigger than the manor, a wingspan that can block out the sun.

"And these dragons have a territory?" I asked, incredulous. "They can't just fly wherever they want?"

"They eat sheep, so they stay in Yorkshire, they're afraid of humans. They won't come near a village but they will torch a single house out in a forest or a moor. The king has a special envoy devoted to tracking them."

"My cousin saw one," said Wulfric.

"They say it's what killed my uncle actually."

I tried to suppress my laughter. Their earnestness was too sweet to deny and from the looks in their eyes, too deeply believed to suggest an alternative explanation.

"Keep smiling," said Simon, looking at me with blue eyes. I stopped. But he hadn't meant it in a threatening way. "No really, keep smiling," he said again. It was my teeth he wanted to see.

He gazed with wonder. He compared them to dragon teeth. I laughed even louder, smiled wider. Wulfric went and pissed in the yard. A dog barked and was shushed. Smoke stained our clothes and I felt the warmth of the world's reasonability melting away, leaving me delightfully full and still.

The first time I was taken out of the house was with Simon and Wulfric to hunt deer in the woods—no, in Greenwich Park, not "the woods." My mind was constantly forgetting, then sprinting back with panic to old terms, old maps. But the park *was* the woods. It couldn't be anything else because there were no cars, planes, radio waves, construction, and in this absence was a purity of sound and air I can only describe as pure sensation flooding my bloodstream, the trees my teeming lungs and wind not an external phenomenon confined to objectivity but everywhere, in and out of me. Even the smell of dust and pollen, warmed and blown away—it was so simple but such a manifold betrayal of everything I had ever expected a scent to be. What I mean is that it was better. This world—everything about it—was just better than anything I had experienced in my life before. Sorry.

Simon and Wulfric took me into this open wilderness to serve as their smiling pack mule, happily tasked with foraging and carrying anything they managed to shoot with their bows.

"We'll make do with a few rabbits, but we need the stag. There's an eight-pointer I saw the other day past the road to Dover."

They spoke as if we were at a grocery store, trampling through forest like shoppers trawling supermarket aisles. Grab those berries, pick these leaves, find the stag.

"What for?" I asked. The only meals I had seen or eaten myself so far were bowls of barley porridge and root vegetables. Eating was less a pleasurable activity and more a purposeful fueling, flavor taking a backseat to the simple stacking of calories. Some days I swear I could feel my blood and muscles sucking up basic building block nutrients, shrinking and expanding like eager sponges. I hadn't had any form of meat in three months save for the hairlike bones of a fish left in a briny broth once. Three whole months of this, my god.

"The lord is coming tonight," said Wulfric. "We need to get him the eight-pointer."

"Where's he been all this time?" I asked.

Wulfric told me—in their manner of speech—to shut up. I was too loud and would scare the animals, he said. I sighed and trudged behind them, scanning everything we passed. And along these shores of silence we stalked, my complacency—this kind of happy idiot I felt myself becoming, this jolly camper—began to give way to other thoughts, to reality, to something serious.

Simon shot a rabbit. I collected the rabbit. I felt it slip away into death in my hands as I fastened it to my belt, and I felt this slippage of mortality like a knock on the door, confirming that my current reality here was *the reality*, the only one—that if I were to die here, I would be dead here, I would not wake up from whatever time-travel reverie I might have tricked myself into thinking I was in. This was real life. This was blood from what had been a living organism and this would somehow, someday, be me, still here.

Panic began to flutter inside me. If I was going to get out of here, this was a chance. Maybe not my one and only chance, but a chance nonetheless, and there was no telling how long it would take for another to come along. I watched Simon and Wulfric, how they walked so lightly over the ground, barely making any noise, their bodies lean and trim, but with rounded, well-worn muscles that could overpower me in a snap. They both carried bows and plenty of arrows. And Simon . . . Simon watched me closely. His blue eyes looked over his shoulder every so often. He'd find an herb or a mushroom and hand it to me to place in the foraging bag I carried, while making clear, decisive eye contact. It was the eye contact I feared the most, how it communicated that he wasn't some caricature of history or background foot soldier, but a man of my own, living and breathing exactly like me at the same intervals, a mind working just the same, if not better.

"Look!" said Wulfric.

We arrived at a clearing. On the map in my head of future-London we had walked up the slope of Greenwich Park and beyond Blackheath, past where there would one day be a large stone cathedral, a high street strangled with cars, a train station, then Kidbrooke and all the new builds. There, in the center of the clearing, a family of deer was grazing. Among them was the stag, with his sturdy antlers, all eight points, just as Wulfric had said.

Wulfric drew an arrow from his quiver and readied his bow. Simon also drew an arrow but instead of placing it in his bow, he took both and pushed them into my chest, giving them to me.

"What's this?" I asked. I looked at Simon—he was unreadable. I looked at Wulfric—his bow was pulled and pointed but not at the deer. It was pointed at me. He was smiling. "Show us your shot, soldier."

"What the hell?" I said. "I don't have a shot."

"Don't lie," said Simon, serious and steady. "We know what you are."

I was rattled. "What do you think I am? I've told you what I am—and I can't shoot a bow and arrow, I've never touched one in my life."

"You're a soldier."

"I'm not a soldier." I couldn't help but laugh. I sputtered and winced at Wulfric's raised bow. "That's what you've thought this whole time? That I'm a soldier—for who? From where? I've told you what I am and what happened to me—a soldier wouldn't have any reason to make that up."

"A Dane would."

"A Dane! You think I'm Danish?" I couldn't believe it. I laughed again and tried to back away but they accosted me, Wulfric's arrow was pointed right at my chest. The two of them were agitated and hyped up on each other the way they had been the day they attacked me. It was strange to imagine how their voices had sounded to me back then, so alien and abrasive. Now they were just two jumpy lads, eager to see me shoot a deer.

"I'm not going to shoot a deer," I said. "I'm not a soldier, I'm not Danish, and I wouldn't know the first thing about how to use this thing."

"You shoot the deer or I shoot you," said Wulfric. His arm was tensed, and I knew, based off this world's ease of quickening I had already witnessed, that he was deadly serious. "Look at your arms, your shoulders—those are the arms of an archer."

I shook my head. "These are the arms of someone who went to the gym a few times a week. This is why you took me along? Because you think I'm a soldier and can help you hunt? Look I

47

don't even know—" I fumbled with the bow and arrow. It was a limber, slippery thing. "I don't even know which way to hold it!"

"You shoot it or I shoot you," Wulfric repeated.

"Stop—you're both scaring them away," said Simon, shushing us. Across the meadow the deer were clued in to our presence. The eight-point stag had tensed up. The fawns seated around him were now standing.

"It's now or never," said Simon. He looked at me with a curt, disappointed expression, and at Wulfric with the same chagrin, like he knew this had been a bad idea from the start.

"And we really do mean now or never," said Wulfric, running his thumb across the back end of the drawn arrow.

"Seriously, I swear I've never shot—"

"You'll shoot the stag," said Simon, finally dead serious. Between the two of them, Simon was the more reasonable, or at least the more stable and coherent, and his tone confirmed this wasn't a joke. Whatever lane of logic they were running on had brought them to this point and there was no going back—they had planned on taking me out here to do this exact thing. They truly believed I was capable of shooting a deer from a hundred yards away, that my arm muscles, which had faded and leaned out considerably over the months, were more than just inflated vanity projects.

I sighed and looked around the meadow. Wulfric tightened his grip. "OK then can we at least get a little closer?" I asked.

"Some soldier."

"Well that's correct because I'm not."

We crouched low and shuffled around the edge of the meadow. The grass was dry and snappy no matter how slowly I tried to move and I could sense the gathering skittishness of the deer, they were about to bolt. No, I didn't want to shoot a deer, but there was an emotional detachment in having to use a bow and arrow—it didn't feel real and I knew there was no way I'd actually be able to hit anything. I'd scare them off with my bad shot and we'd all go back empty-handed and hopefully Wulfric wouldn't shoot me.

When we were closer, I drew the bow—I had never done this before, save for maybe a Scouts camping trip when I was ten, shooting targets with blunt plastic sticks. The bow was wound tight and difficult to pull back. My arms strained, the arrow wobbled, the stag's muscles twitched, it knew what was about to happen, and in a split second, just as the whole herd was about to vanish, I let go.

The arrow thunked off a rock ten feet away and twirled into the bushes. I flushed with relief. The deer scattered and fled and—

"What in God's name is that?" Wulfric cried. He dropped his bow in shock. As the deer parted . . .

There was a dog.

"No way," I gasped.

It was Matilda.

I erupted into a fit of laughter, I couldn't hold it back. All tension gave way to delirium.

Matilda the Afghan hound was sitting prim and proper in the shade of an oak tree, too unbothered to run for cover with her newfound family of deer. I couldn't believe it. She watched me from across the meadow with her panting smile. If she remembered me at all, she couldn't care less.

"What kind of bastard deer . . ." said Simon.

"It's a wolf!" Wulfric readied his bow and pulled back hard with the arrow.

"No, wait!" I lunged and grabbed Wulfric's arm as he let go. The arrow whipped through the air and disappeared into the trees. Before he could pull another, I jumped in front of him, putting myself between him and the dog.

"Stop! Look. Just stop for a second and let me talk. I am what I told you—I was a dog walker. I swear to God. I traveled through time and right before that happened, I was with that dog." I pointed at Matilda. "That's my dog. I was holding on to her. I must have pulled her through whatever wormhole I got sucked into." My English stumbled over itself. Even if I had gotten every word exactly perfect in this new dialect there was no way I was making sense.

"That's no dog," said Simon.

"It's some kind of hellhound. A wolf at least," said Wulfric.

I tried to explain the concept of a Russian oligarch's pure-bred Afghan hound worth more money than any of us could imagine and insisted this was irrefutable proof that my story was true, that I really had come from the future, but Wulfric and Simon remained apathetic, more in awe of the dog. Even if my rudimentary description of time traveling was understood, it meant nothing to them. I could be an oracle, a god, it didn't matter, I had been their prisoner the past three months, wasting my time not on reading tea leaves or predicting the weather, but staring with traumatized awe at dirt, wood, insects, people's eyes. My personality was only just reawakening with my ability to communicate and engage and I had nothing to show for it, I had nothing to offer these people. I wasn't a soldier and had just proven it. Anything else I was didn't matter.

Wulfric raised his bow again and pointed it directly at my

head. Instinctive terror fired and snapped through my body. "Wait! Wait! Please—wait," I cried with my arms raised. "Just watch."

Slowly, I made a fist and lowered it. I held it out toward Matilda and jiggled it. I called her name and whistled. And despite these methods never really serving me well before, her tail wagged, she stood up. Wulfric and Simon gasped at her height. She trotted over to me, smiling her devilish smile. Her fur was matted and her eyes read a touch more feral than normal, but otherwise she looked healthy and happy. Three months in the untamed wild had to be a nice escape for a pampered dog like her. The only thing that gave away her modernity (besides her exotic breed) was the thick designer collar still firmly around her neck, with a little gold-plated, diamond-encrusted name tag dangling from it.

A silence of calculations ticked between me and the two men. Wulfric and Simon saw the collar, saw my familiar maneuvering with Matilda, how she licked me, they looked at each other, and I looked at them, their twitching bows, a frenzy of silent, split-second communication. Before anyone could move, I unclipped Matilda's collar and jumped away from everyone with my hands up. Wulfric pointed his bow. Simon violently twitched. Matilda kept wagging her tail and panting.

"Just wait," I said, arms raised. The collar glittered in the sunlight. "Let's come to an agreement that works for all of us."

"Put your bow down," Simon muttered to Wulfric, but Wulfric refused.

"Simon, that's gold!"

It was gold plating at best, I thought. The diamonds had to

be cheap if not completely fake, but in the twenty-eighth year of King Edward—whoever the hell that was—surely there was no way of knowing any better. Plastic hadn't been invented yet.

The boys argued with each other over their next move.

"We'd have more money than the whole parish combined."

"And a bounty on our heads if you kill him."

"We were already threatening to kill him—"

"Only to get him to help us with the stag, I wouldn't have let you actually do it. The lord wants him alive."

There was more hesitance and murmurs between them, then Wulfric hissed at me. "Give it to me."

"Help me escape," I said.

"Give it to me and we'll let you go."

"No we can't," said Simon. "We can't go back without him."

"Put the bow down and let's talk," I said.

"Give it to me!"

"Put the bow down!" both Simon and I yelled at the same time.

Wulfric flinched, growled, and with a jerk of his wrist, let the arrow fly once again into the treeline. He threw the bow on the ground and conceded the floor to Simon, who stepped forward, unsure how to proceed. The childishness of the men was more apparent than ever and I realized the reason I could communicate with them so easily was because their language and vocabulary was more stunted than any of the others at the manor. They were working hands, nothing more. Simon had his imaginary talisman of a promised landholding and that was it. Their eyes could not unwiden after seeing this collar, something that afforded them an opportunity larger than they would know what to do with.

"Let me go and I'll give you the collar," I said. "And the dog. Honestly she's probably worth more. Just let me go and you'll never hear from me again."

"We can't let you go." Simon shook his head and looked at the ground, thinking. After a moment, he looked up and spoke methodically. "The lord arrives today with a caravan. It'll drop him off, then continue to London this evening." He looked at Wulfric, then at me. "We'll be helping them unload their goods—we can smuggle you on board one of the wagons. But no one can know it was us that helped you. No one."

The idea of freedom was so sudden and intimidating with its momentum. Just last night I had been lost in the sounds of my cell, lulled, really, by my environs. Now I was fully jolted out of the trance. Seeing Matilda, holding her collar—it brought a semblance of reality—of *my* reality—to this one. I felt the metal clasp, the tightly wound polyester and leather, the fake diamond studs, all factory stamped and sealed. It felt like I was dipping my hand back into where I had come from, and a very sentient part of me wanted to get back there.

I rolled the ragged sleeve of my shirt up to my shoulder, then put my arm through the collar, pushing it all the way up to my armpit, fastened it tight, then covered it. "You'll get this once I'm on the wagon. No one will know you helped me, I promise."

"Give it to us now," said Wulfric.

"No. When I'm on the wagon."

"Then swear to God," said Simon. There was a break of silence after he said this. The way he said it, the way his voice teemed with expectation, it wasn't how I had ever heard someone say it before—*I swear to God*, so flippant and tossed like a coin, not like this. I didn't know how to react.

"Sure," I said.

"No, swear it," he said. Unmoored earnestness blazed behind his eyes.

"OK, I swear it. I swear to God I will give you this collar once I'm on the wagon."

Simon stared me down. Wulfric watched both of us, wary, but calmed. I was reminded of how much this was a world I simply wasn't a part of. Perhaps we shared the same value sets at our core, about honesty and word as bond, but in terms of whatever bedrock of life experience informed our decision-making, we couldn't be further divergent. I had the upper hand.

There were more people at the manor than usual, and a buzz was in the air when we returned. Our little hunting party split up. Wulfric went to chop wood, Simon went to the stables, Matilda had tagged along and was giddily examined by other servants. But instead of having me help cook or clean to aid with the preparations, I was taken and put back in my cell. For the first time in two months, the guards locked the door behind me. And I was shackled. That had never happened before.

"Why?"

They wouldn't answer me.

Something wasn't right. I stood there in iron shackles, chained to the wall while the house rumbled with activity around me. For the first time, I smelled the wretchedly sweet stink of my cell. There had been a sudden change, a decision made, and I was on the outside of it. I began to panic. I twisted my wrists but the shackles were heavy and tight. They hadn't used these back when I was first captured, why did they have me in them now? I tried to push against the door but I couldn't reach. I had been in these people's good graces, but now things were set further back than they had ever been. I fought the urge to yell for help. I had no one to call for.

Smells of cooking slipped through cracks in the wall, mixed unpleasantly with my cell. They grew stronger as the afternoon settled into an evening that lit long lines of orange across the walls. Smoke laced with flavors of meat and herbs slipped inside, almost tauntingly. I paced. I felt for the reassurance of the dog collar under my shirt with my chin.

"George," said a voice. It was Simon.

Through a slim gap in the doorframe he pressed his face and saw me in the darkening cell. I showed him my bound hands.

"What's going on?" I said. I tried to remain calm.

Simon pulled at the door. The lock jiggled. His face reappeared in the gap. "It's locked," he said.

"I know. What's going on? You have to get me out of here."

"I can't now if they've locked it."

"Is the caravan here yet?"

"Almost." The thin strip of Simon's face was close to mine. I could feel his breath and how it rippled with nerves. I felt the disquieting swell of empathy, rendering him so eerily modern. "I don't think we can get you out of here anymore. Not tonight."

"Simon please. You can't leave me." The growing darkness gripped me. Blankets of air were thick and stale. For how much I had been tenderly swaddled by this isolation, I couldn't return to it, no I couldn't. My modern brain had snapped feverishly back to reality—I needed to get out. I felt my cheeks flush with anger and fear.

Simon said nothing else and disappeared. I resisted every

urge to yell after him, but it wouldn't make a difference because a swarm of noise was approaching. The whole house rattled. Doors and windows opened and slammed. Footsteps ran across the ground outside. Excited voices. And far away, but growing louder like a sturdy, rolling wave of stones, were horses.

The noise traveled from a mile away, then less than a mile, then less. I could see nothing from my cell as it arrived. Gaps in the wood slats of my cell looked out on only trees and a storage shed and a cloud of dust that was suddenly kicked up. The caravan was here. A thunderous team of horses was out front—chains, leather, wheels, boots all clattering together in a swarm. I questioned, for a second, if I had been transported back to the present day and was hearing a busy high street. Again I was awed by the voices—men and women disembarking, warm greetings, laughter, dogs barking. I thought of Matilda out there skipping around. The languages spoken were new slurry mixtures of English and French. But the awe I felt was only in a minor key this time, giving rise to an anger that was too familiar, too modern: I felt excluded. I was wholly on the outside, connectionless and adrift. I had no one. I thought of my ex, I thought of our home and all its thick lacquer, glass everywhere, not going anywhere, not saying anything, two clouds built up and smooshed against the walls. I was fired. I had lost my job, all my savings, lost my partner—boyfriend—boyfriend who I was starting to call my partner like a business partner, a transaction, failed, declined, lost him, lost my self-respect, lost two dogs, lost my sanity or, more accurately, lost track of time.

The door to my cell unlocked with a thud and swung open. Men I had never seen before entered my squalid space and surrounded me. One of them asked me a question in a language I didn't understand. The question was repeated, in what I believe was French. Then it was repeated one last time in English:

"I said why are you crying?"

"Huh?" I hadn't even noticed. I tried to wipe my eyes but scraped my cheek against the thick shackles. I lowered my head in shame and the first thing I noticed were the man's shoes. They were leather and well-made. Stitched and studded with adornment, pointed at the toes. Clean. I looked up.

The man standing in front of me was a mass of contradictions. Old, sallow-faced, painfully skinny, but engulfed in layers of fine clothing that upholstered him not like a wizened turtle, but like an exoskeleton. A barrel of tunics, robes, shirts, vests of leather and metal and thickly woven fabrics gave him an automaton body on top of which rested his shrunken, aged head. He was wealthy, obviously, and maybe to be wealthy meant to be saddled with it, to wear your net worth on your person.

The lord waved off the guards on either side of me and stepped closer. From a pocket in his cloak, he withdrew a small square of fabric and handed it to me. It was a swatch of black fabric, soft and stretchy, finely woven. It was mine. There was half a Reebok logo on it. It was a square cut from my black running shorts.

"Where did you get this?" asked the lord. "What kind of material is this?"

"This is from my running shorts," I said. "It's . . . I don't know, polyester or something? A spandex blend? I'm from the—"

"Yes, I know, you're from the *future*," he said in a mocking tone. "I can't have you running around my estate saying things like that. You've made people very uncomfortable. Now tell me where you came from. Tell me if you want your life spared."

"I'm from the future. I don't know what else to say. I have nothing else—"

"OK then let's say you are. Where in the future are you from? Even a time traveler has to come from somewhere."

"I'm from here!" My voice was breaking. There was an audience of onlookers behind the lord. "I'm British. I'm from right down the street. I live here in Greenwich, I work in Canary Wharf—or at least I used to. I was a dog walker—that dog! The weird dog with the long hair—that's my dog."

"A long-haired hound, yes." The lord was unfazed. "I'm familiar with the breed, they're nothing special. I've seen plenty at court before, which is why I'm asking you again, one last time, where did you come from?"

My hope was fading. The iron chains dragged on the shackles, cutting into my wrists. I had genuinely nothing to say. If Matilda the dog was deemed nothing special yet she had been out running free all this time while I had been imprisoned, then surely that made me less than the least. And maybe it was the intimidation of the lord—the vibrant dyes in his fabrics, the gray locks of hair that hung coiffed under his cap—and the desensitization of all I had been through—the loss of identity, the physical taxation of living here, of being human in such a primal, impersonal thrashing—that I felt like it was true.

"I'm nothing," I said. I was crying again. Or maybe I had been crying the entire time. I noticed Simon and Wulfric among the hushed faces of guards and servants behind the lord. "I don't belong here. I'm not a soldier, I'm barely a passable servant. I was born here—in London, farther west, then moved even farther west, then came back to London for university, France sometimes for holidays, Spain, never Denmark, I've never been there,

I don't speak Danish, if that's what you think I am, I can't speak anything. I'm not anything. I'm nothing. I'm truly nothing."

When my arms slumped to their sides in final defeat, they slumped too far. The wide neck of my tunic pulled too much to the side. A glittering, fat diamond revealed itself.

Everyone gasped and my heart sunk. I tried to shrug my shoulder to hide it but it was too late. It was over. The lord narrowed his eyes and smiled. He stepped forward and came inches from my face and towered over me not because he was taller but because I was slumped over, shortening myself, shrinking away. I showed no resistance, only a flinch, when he reached into the neck of my tunic and grabbed the dog collar. The crowd murmured in hushed, excited tones, sharing theories and disbelief. I felt the disappointment of Simon and Wulfric, the cruel inevitability of their life paths. The lord remained calm and slick, almost meditative as he inspected the fake crystals, the cheap gold plating, the thick leather and nylon. His cold fingers rubbed like wet reeds against my bare shoulder. He stared into my eyes. He stared back at the collar. He exhaled slowly and withdrew a large, curved knife from his belt. He held it up to my neck.

"Don't worry, everyone," he said over his shoulder. I closed my eyes and winced, waiting—I couldn't even accept my end with valor, with open eyes. But the lord didn't hurt me. With one jagged yank of the knife, he cut the collar off me and turned around to face his subjects. "The man is correct. Believe everything he says. He's nothing."

3

I resigned myself to the fact that it was over. I had no other choice but resignation because dissecting what had just happened inside me was too overwhelming. The lord had pulled out a knife, held it up to me, and I had closed my eyes. Earlier I had done the same thing when Wulfric pulled his bow on me and all I could do was wince—that was the pinnacle of my instincts, not to pull away, not to fight, but to in fact stifle those reactions in favor of something more compliant. I might as well have presented my neck to him. Please kill me. Please kill me now. I thought about Ryley, the bichon frise I used to dog walk, and how he would lie on his back, legs in the air, wiggling his body back and forth, ribs and abdomen exposed, expecting nothing but belly rubs from the world. "*Please kill me now, please kill me now,*" I would sing, imagining a voice for his body language. "He's so trusting, look at him, he doesn't have a clue—you don't have a clue, do you? You just want your belly rubs. *Please kill me,* he says, *please kill me now!*"

My boyfriend would watch this and laugh from far across the room with one single, forlorn haaaaaaaaaaa like a circle drawn around a lonely, empty page. I should have detected something wrong in that sound—no, I *had* detected something wrong. What I should have done was *do* something about it, but again I was compliant, I was nothing. I would appease the unappeased. When HR pulled me into a side office at work and told me I was being let go—not fired, not made redundant, just "let go"—I smiled and nodded, I did what wasn't even asked. I let them let me go. It's always "the needs of the business," the current situation is always "untenable," and it always seems to make perfect sense to my pigeon brain. Yeah sure OK. Anything I am or have done is only ever alluded to as a circumstance, a situation. There is discipline but there is also: let's get this over with. Dowdy HR varmints I had never seen before suddenly clinging to my every word like exhausting little pets. Please kill me.

Ryley was my first dog. His owner was a guy in North Greenwich who worked from home during the day and needed the dog out of the house for midday calls. In those early, freshly unemployed days I was militant with the dog walking app—sharing my location at all times, sending photo updates, bringing along an extra battery to keep my phone charged. I stuck to a prescribed walk up and down the river with Ryley, along the eastern edge of the peninsula, then a rest and a game of fetch in the park, then back to Dad's. "Back to your dad's, c'mon let's go," I'd say, and I'd feel a pit open in my stomach, a depressive pang at the earnestness I too easily slipped into despite the job/gig paying next to nothing and the fact that not long ago I had been just like this dog's yuppie dad, working/staring from home at my dinky plastic laptop, wiggling the mouse every twenty minutes to keep my chat status present, commuting to the office a few times a week to feel air con, lust for bankers, and purpose in an otherwise directionless morass all while the consequences of earlier transgressions grew wings and began to fan.

You don't learn from your mistakes, you only learn to make them in easier, smaller ways.

It wasn't long before I was more daring and took on more dogs, taking them for longer walks farther from their homes. One day I walked Ryley and a gaggle of other small dogs all the way back to my flat and set them loose inside. I sat on the couch and ate McDonald's and fed them all one french fry each, two for Ryley. I wrestled and laughed with them on the floor. I rubbed Ryley's belly.

"*Please kill me*—is that what you're saying? *Please kill me, George, please kill me now!*"

"Does he have to do that on the rug?" my boyfriend asked.

"It's fine, bichons don't shed."

"It's not the shedding I'm worried about. Don't they only roll around on their backs when they've got shit on their fur and they're trying to rub it off on something?"

He never played with the dogs. He resolutely withdrew himself from any glee I was faking my way into feeling. No, I wasn't where I wanted to be in life, but I didn't think I had to broadcast unhappiness for that to be clear. I wasn't going to be miserable. But my mind was vulnerable then and his obvious displeasure imprinted itself to devastating effect, beginning a self-policing inside me, when for every twee doggo-world charade I tried on, I would counter it with an invisible, deep hatred and anger, which I kept unfocused and vague to avoid confrontation. The only problem was I misdirected the negative energy so far out into the universe that it could only circle back into my own orbit and darken my own light. Self-hatred.

"I can't believe I'm getting paid to do this," I said, militantly carefree for my own sanity.

"I can't believe it either," my boyfriend said with a tone that stung through time itself.

I realized I had reverted to that same earnestness with Simon and Wulfric. Defense mechanism or not, I had sworn to God in front of them, I had contemplated what that really meant—only to be rebutted with cruelty, sarcasm, and theft at the hand of, well, at the hand of the lord himself. I felt my mind slipping just like it had before. I was so wayward and naive. I had convinced myself I was going to escape and been swatted down so easily. Of course I had fallen in with Simon and Wulfric—we were of the same crude, rudimentary mind, gutter slaves with enough pipe dreams to trick ourselves into keeping going. The lord of the manor had spoken two different languages before he stopped on crude, glottal-clogged English when speaking to me. His words and sentence structures had been difficult to understand and he had had to dumb himself down for my sake. I was more than two steps below him; that was my place.

I was a prisoner. I was a servant. And maybe that's what I had always been: exploitable by my own stupid trust in the world's sheen, in the mere idea of authority no matter who wielded it. I was one who could be swatted, that was all it took and all that was needed, not worth the effort to convince or sway.

◇ ◇ ◇

I didn't know whether to gnash my teeth and beat on the wall or just sit there resigned to my own filth and eventual doom. The lord of the manor would give the order to dispose of me for good after the party and that would be it.

Once again I let the silences of the world carry me away— only this time they were smothered with a noise I had rarely heard thus far: merriment. This is all a joke, you see, this cell you're in, this tattered cloth, your dumbass mind. I listened to rushing waters flowing, of wine or beer or whatever they drank here. Cutlery clattered—I hadn't used cutlery in three months. And I heard—again a first here—the most cauterizing decibel of alien sounds: music. Someone was playing a guitar, or probably not a guitar but a lute or something, and it sounded beautiful, withering, vibrating through the air to my cell like pornography pouring into my ear canal. I hated it. I hated them, whoever they were. It was the loudest party I had ever heard, like the house itself was mashing its woody gums on me, suckling silliness, spilling out into the yard, drunks vomiting, shrieks and dances, and the horses shifting around, snorting, flasks clinking together, songs, and in the midst of all that, a sliding lock, a chain moving, barrier lifted, door opening. My heart lit one feeble last time.

Wulfric appeared in the darkened doorway, straddling the current of noise, barely able to keep himself upright. He held a pair of keys.

"Let's go party boy," he said, slurring his words.

"Wulfric. Thank you. You have no idea. Thank you, thank you," I repeated over and over as he unlocked and unbound my hands from the shackles and chains. I stood up, immediately grateful and ready to go, snapped out of it. "I won't forget this, I promise." Word was bond to these people, even though I had lost him the collar and he had nothing to gain. Maybe it helped that he was drunk. I smiled and laughed and rubbed my sore wrists. I had worked myself up into such a frenzy.

"No," he said, slapping his hand on my shoulder to steady himself. "We're staying right here, you and me. We're gonna dance. Come on. We're. Dancing." Drunk or not, his aim was squarely stable, and before I had a second to react, his fist smashed against my skull. Warmth rang out—the pain wasn't a quick sharpness, more like a woolen blanket thrown over me, and I fell to the ground, tangled up in myself, double-visioned. Wulfric was immediately on top of me, kicking me in the stomach, cursing me with words and phrases I could only assume translated in one way or another to motherfucker.

"Happy now, you Danish piece of shit?" He pummeled me. "Fucking scum."

I held up my hands like a drowning victim. My spine felt wobbly, like it was about to come undone as I tried to worm myself away and I hobbled onto my knees. Wulfric grabbed me by my tunic and threw me out of the cell. I crumbled against the wall in the narrow hallway. I crawled, he grabbed again. I yelled but gargled blood. I felt myself fading into the pillowy warmth. I felt nothing. I felt no more pummeling. It was as if I had left my body and was watching my beating from the side, but that couldn't be right, because the other man I saw was fighting back, the other man wasn't me.

Simon threw a drunken, bloodied Wulfric into the cell and slammed the door. He turned to me.

"Get up," he said.

"I can't."

"You can."

And he was right, I could. I stood slowly and before I thought I was fully upright, we were running. We were outside. His arm was around me. The wetness escaping me cooled in the night air, moon reflecting in it, inner warmth fading rapidly. We ran past drunks and revelers, the caravan was gone, there were no more horses. I mumbled something about it, slurring my speech. Slipping on this or that. I was fading. We were in darkness. Black trees folded over us and grew darker. Slippery slipping. I could no longer see, hear, or feel. Slipped away. I was gone.

I woke up to a fully blue morning, everything either pure white or pure blue, no gray to ease the contrast. Blue leaves were wet and shivering. White sky was brisk and all-seeing. My breath emitted a weak curl of fog that barely obscured the figure seated next to me.

"Simon," I said. The whisp blew away and revealed his face as it turned to me. He had been waiting. He smiled but it was an inverted smile, hesitant, more like a grimace. It was daybreak, but barely. Less time had passed than I thought. I tried sitting up and felt immense pain all over.

"Careful," he said.

I stayed on my back. I lifted my head and looked under the neck of my tunic. I was bruised everywhere. My limbs all seemed to move as they should, but there was a sharp pain in my chest. I felt my ribs, unsure what to be feeling for—they felt normal, incredibly painful in places, but not broken. I was shocked at how skinny I had become, my ribs just sitting there, wrapped in paperlike skin. One, two, three, four, five I counted them. The heaviest part of my body was my head, which I struggled to keep held up, scenery blurring. Blues and whites.

We were in the middle of a dense forest, huddled together under two twisting trees. There was no trail anywhere that I could see, just shrubs and wet, wet woodland so wet it seemed to only be raining under the trees, water cascading down stairways of branches. I asked where we were and Simon said Deptford, but he said it like *Deep*-ford, which made sense to me only much later when I realized we had *forded* the *deep* River Ravensbourne to get to where we were. That was why we were wet. We had swum across it, Simon pulling me along against his chest.

"Thank you," I said. I felt embarrassed for being unable to defend myself against Wulfric's blows and passing out. Simon was no bigger than me, formed of slender, utilitarian muscles fit for his daily grunt tasks, nothing more. I was slightly taller than him and even though I was malnourished from the past three months, my body still had pockets of vanity muscles strapped to it—those archer's shoulders—serving no real purpose than to look attractive to a demographic that was centuries away. Simon had forded a small river with all that in tow.

He shrugged off my gratitude and was awkward and coy in his own way. He gazed off into the trees. His dark curls dripped with water.

"Why are you doing this?" I asked. "The lord took the collar, I've got nothing to offer you now. And I'm not a soldier. If I had any sort of status, I'd have used it by now."

"I want freedom just as much as you," he said. "And I know you're not a soldier. I believe you." His voice was calm but pointed. His words qualified multiple things at once and he sounded as if he had thought this all over. He looked at me again. "I believe you," he repeated. "Everything you said. I believe it."

How? A chill ran through me. I barely believed what had happened myself, and as much as I wanted someone else to believe me, Simon doing so would only create an external witness to my situation, a separate consciousness operating outside of what I could otherwise, on my lowest of days, convince myself was all a nightmare or a hallucination by just another Londoner gone insane. Saying he believed me made it all the more real.

"You haven't been very convincing, I'll admit that." Simon smiled. "But lucky for you, I found a stronger argument." He reached into a pocket inside his tunic and pulled out a worn, damp bundle of knotted twine and burlap and handed it to me.

I stared at it. Sickly, I knew what it was right away just from its subtle weight, the feel, the smooth blackness that revealed itself as I unwrapped it.

It was my phone.

"It fell out of your pocket the day you were—or I guess—the day we found you. I picked it up and kept it. Wulfric noticed but he thought it was just a piece of charcoal. We thought you were an illegal collier at first, stealing wood for burning. But it's not charcoal, is it. It's glass and something else. How is it so flat and smooth?"

"No idea," I said, turning it over in my hands. The smoothness was overwhelming. "Factories in China. I'm sure charcoal's involved at some stage of the process, so you're half right." It was strange to see my reflection so clearly in the black screen. I felt my hollow cheeks, combed through my matted hair with my fingers.

"It glowed blue," said Simon.

"I bet that was terrifying."

"I thought it was on fire. Some kind of super-charcoal that never burned out, but of course it did."

"It ran out of battery."

"What is it?"

For ten boring minutes I explained a phone, a phone call, a smartphone, and touched lightly on the concept of the internet, and realized simultaneously that these were the most boring, fruitless voids of inventions, and where in my previous, contemporary world these had ruled all facets of my life—my employment, my lack of employment, my love life, friendships, economics, education—here they were of lesser value than dirt. Dirt could be dug up, compacted into bricks to form kilns, makeshift infernos for creating charcoal or pottery or metalwork. My phone, which couldn't even turn on because the battery was long dead, was only a mirror held up to my people, showing how much we didn't want to talk to each other and how much of this enormous world we would rather consume through a siphon. Nothing that had been inside that phone was in my head now. No practical skill had been passed down. In fact, I was certain it had degraded key aspects of my humanity.

Simon couldn't be less interested and I agreed, stopping myself midsentence.

"No way to charge it anyway," I said. I halfheartedly tossed it, let it drop to the ground.

"We can sell it for some coins," said Simon. "Which we're going to need sooner rather than later."

"Want to bust it open?"

And so we broke the phone open. We smashed it with a rock. The screen cracked and shattered, the metal casing popped apart, revealing thin sheets of circuitry and metals. Copper, zinc, lithium, aluminum, glass. Simon was more impressed with these and together we carefully gathered them into his burlap pocket. His plan was to walk to London, stopping at merchants along the way, hopefully generating enough money to find a place to stay for the night once we reached the city, then we could chart a course farther north. He reckoned we could afford one night in London—it was too early for alarm bells to start ringing back in Greenwich, and even then it would only be Wulfric who would raise them. If anybody came chasing after us, they wouldn't come until their hangovers had eased up.

But something about Simon still seemed hesitant, as if his decision to help me escape hadn't been such a point of no return, that he was still teetering on the precipice of it. And it didn't make sense after all. Even if he believed wholeheartedly that I had traveled through time, I had nothing of real value to offer him. I was physically weak, had no idea of where to go or what to do next, no wealth besides what we could barter with the phone parts. I sensed a marked shuddering come over him, a crescent-shaped opening that demanded silence and careful, cautious prying much later, so I said nothing. Years spent under the thumb of Canary Wharf finance lads had given me a heightened awareness of another man's charms, and Simon had many. He had an earnestness built into his face—blue eyes too round, too open, hugged by cheerful, heavy lids—the same kind of earnestness I had once been afflicted with. It was an innocence but a calculated one—there was always something to be gained, no matter how selfless you tried to seem. I had to stay away, but I had to let it draw me in.

◇ ◇ ◇

Before the time traveling, before the dog walking, before the breakup, when everything was more than swell, I had been a midlevel software engineer at the venture capital risk management department of a giant hedge fund. The job was techy and complicated-sounding but ultimately just glorified data entry and accounting with a fancy veneer. A job like that comes with its own void of nothingness, which I wholly expected when I got it, excited mostly about the salary and looking cool on LinkedIn— maybe I'd become the kind of person who posts, be clever and witty, not too climby, not too sarcastic.

Against my better judgment I became motivated and self-starting, and volunteered to take on development projects with our billing software, more so to impress the boys who worked in account management and sales, the wolves who were hired in droves, fresh out of uni. They were incubated and there was a trajectory for them at the firm. Eager-to-please interns became showboating full-timers, became father-figure managers—all possessing a zeal for predatory economics and a flair for making it all seem cute and innocuous, perhaps even brave and noble. I fell in love with them at every stage and rooted for them. Most, if not all of them, were stunningly beautiful.

I got to know these boys because they'd saunter over to my desk with their fat asses stuffed in their tight trousers and ask me for special favors. They'd roll a chair over too close to mine, lean back, stretch, let me watch their pecs, their nipples hard under thin white shirts, and ask if an adjustment could be made. They would beg for it. Could a tweak be made here or there. It was sick how fast I would say yes. Oh yeah I can tweak a few things for you, Callum, I can insert something right there for you, Jack, I can fuck something—a number, a formula, a date—or not fuck,

Ollie, just gently nudge it, soothe it, try a different position until a new total came and everyone left satisfied. "Thanks, mate, I owe you one."

In moral terms, all I was doing was painting grayness over an already gray canvas of numbers. The companies, firms, and trusts we worked with were already hell bound and dirty to begin with, so whatever new arrangements I concocted of their sins was simply water made wetter. Anyway, in a world of trickle-down economics, what difference was I really making here, perched on my midlevel rung, pissing numbers? What was a misplaced zero but another pawn of speculation that ultimately gave everyone the same, satisfying result: a paycheck.

I knew the job would be a void but I didn't know the void could move. I didn't expect it to migrate like it did and become a void that was then inside me. Which was all the more titillating of course, because a hole was a hole, and I was the bad boy entrusted with secrets, aloof but worshipped by a lineup of reckless men wanting me to service them. And that was ultimately what I wanted. Those fat-assed banker bros—I wanted to be inside them. Not sexually (although yes, sexually), but anthropologically, observationally; assimilate enough to be accepted into their fold, to become one of them. And I did.

They took me out for drinks, dinners, some even shared their commission bonuses with me but nothing ever went far enough. None of the men were gay, as far as I could tell, but that didn't stop our interactions from building up layers of flirtation, a kind of straightness that ends up being gayer than actual gayness. We'd chat each other up—the banter!—nonstop over work, lunch, texts, drinks, trips to the bathroom, my voice mimicking their posh bellows, echoing off tile walls, peeing together, herd mentality, become one—become one so that I might be wor-shipped the way I worshipped their posh suits, hipster backpacks, ankles skinny enough to snip, snip, snip, their minoxidil hair, their fitness-corrupted bones covered in HGH-assisted slabs of muscle, beef, pork, their pissing dicks at the urinal, and me with my glorious peripheral vision, a stained glass window of their warm fleshy hooks.

I worried about how reckless I was being, how empty-headed, and about the growing distance between me and my boyfriend—a man who actually enjoyed my company and the extra money I was bringing in, but hadn't anticipated the kind of vapid Canary Wharf whore I was becoming, with my £300 gym membership, £300 lunches with the lads, the sloppy abandon with which I went about tinkering lines of code, fueled more than once by lines of coke. Little baggies turned up everywhere. I was in fearful awe of myself. If I was turning into this horrible creature, where was the me I had been before? That shy, sarcastic, jokey boy who took life in sometimes too-earnest stride, with a smile and a sense of charity—or at least a sense of law—where was he beneath these new layers of corporate circus orgy? The answer was left unfound. The void was left exposed, and into it went a rushing wind.

The boys, my apostles, they sensed this happening, this hollowing out of my core. I simply didn't have the guts. They sniffed it out and noticed my hesitance, my growing reluctance, and similarly to how a fever breaks, the bromances intensified. That whiff of rot turned them on, and they went further. The innuendos became more radical, more tempting—the hands on the shoulder, the bathroom breaks, boundaries crossed, drunken cheeky kisses, showers at the gym, the shape of a bulge between legs, and the financial dares became more risky in tandem, and my depression—which was what this had been all this time—bloomed into its formal, blackened flower, and it aged me, crisped me up like a weed. Suddenly I found myself having worked years at this job, becoming the kind of brain-dead charlatan I had always hated, dripping with lies and bitter venom, and as for the boys . . . when I began to wear this all on my face, they abandoned me. There is no better explanation than to say that I was simply no longer beautiful. I had lost something irreplaceable and I was finally left alone. I wanted to blow up Canary Wharf.

I became hateful in a typical way. Another year went by. Another crop of boys, each one paying me less attention than the previous. Of course I still wanted to be them. I still wanted to be inside them, but now I understood that that desire operated from a deeper, primordial place, not just to be worshipped. My lust was decrepit and cavernous. I wanted their organs. I wanted their eyes so I could see what they saw when they looked out at a London that no longer felt liveable to me. I wanted their hair, I wanted their skin, I wanted their ears so I could hear their phone calls with their mums and girlfriends, how they FaceTimed with them in the street, oblivious to traffic, how they spoke so loudly, so unafraid. I wanted their families. I wanted their weekend plans, their voice notes, their nude photos, their salaries. I wanted their brains because I no longer had my own. I wanted their faces because I couldn't recognize myself in the mirror. I didn't look like me.

Do I look like you?

◇ ◇ ◇

Pitter-patter remnants of rain finally stopped and Simon stood up. Slowly, I did too—Simon helping me, hands grasped, pulling me up. His hand didn't feel like a handshake, it didn't feel like it had been typing out emails all day, like a claw, like a vise.

Blue-blushing clouds tightened back up and sunlight appeared, filtering through leaves that were once again their splendid greens. The rustle of the forest reprised its tune that hinted of abundance—of gamey birds, goats, wild boar? I had no idea. There could be dragons out there for all I knew, and Simon didn't look like he knew either. He knew where the river was, he knew which direction was west, and he had been to London proper plenty of times before, but it felt like we were on equal footing now, our certainties only based on what was behind us and all the things we could not go back to. Simon looked back toward Greenwich, then looked at me, watched me rubbing my sores and aches.

"You good?" he asked, hesitantly certain. Ready to go but only within this one shaky minute.

I nodded. I walked a bit, testing my legs, which were fine, and I said, "Yes." Then I waited for something—a phone call or an airplane above us or the hum of an idling car, anything to stop and give me pause, but there was nothing, only a silence walled up by trees that would all one day be chopped down.

I said yes again, let's go, and it was decided, clear and resounding within myself, that I didn't want to go back. Not just back to Greenwich, to the manor, but back to *my* Greenwich, to my time, my flat, my life, my days of toil and ruin. I would not go.

I simply did not want to return.

4

We left the woods and the woods left us, the greenery becoming sparser, replaced with a muddy brown, muddy bricks, muddy people. We sold the pieces of phone to different merchants along the road to London, under little outposts, thatched roofs, some terra-cotta. Blacksmiths inspected the metal bits, tiny screws, and strange circuitry, estimated ounces and purity once melted down. A jeweler held the glass orb of the phone camera up to the sun and asked us how much for this . . . opal? jade? and we just smiled and nodded at every best price. Here the lines of economy were physical—money trading hands, spreading urbanization, becoming London with a sudden ferocity until all you could see was the mighty fortress itself.

We made it to Southwark by midday and to London Bridge, where the river below was a highway filled with more boats than water and the Tower on the other side loomed much more a tower than I had ever thought of it before. Everything was dirty but dirty in a way that was cleaner than anything in modern

London. The air was sweet with sound, manure, herbs, rot, fruity fragrance, animal hair. There was no car exhaust, no petrol fumes, no plastic waste lining the river.

Yes, there were decapitated, mutilated human heads on spikes hung across the entrance to the City—that was a shocking thing to see: their eyes gone, teeth bleached by the sun— but people passing the display all shared the same wincing, perplexed reaction as me. It was all still a shared humanity. Most people looked away with disgust, pulled their gawking children away. Others scoffed, frustrated and tired of the barbarity. Others pointed with almost casual awe as if to say "Oh, that's the thief they caught last week." But most importantly, people simply carried on. This cloud of brutality existed simultaneously alongside the regular shoppers, beggars, construction workers, day traders, city officials, and the mix was astonishing. I suppose that isn't any different from the modern world, the only difference being how easy it is to disconnect yourself from it all. In the modern world, you don't have to worry about running into severed heads, you just have to make sure not to google them.

We crossed the bridge and the metropolis bloomed. This London was smaller, but more overwhelming. There were fewer people, but also less space, corralled by imposing walls that echoed with noises denser and prickly with squish, slice, scream, bark, crash, spray, laugh. Things slammed and broke. There were coy little jingles. Roosters, dogs, cattle, kids. There were no phones, no noise-canceling headphones; everyone was enmeshed and implicated and it wasn't pretty, it wasn't ugly either.

The people simply were the same. I just couldn't get over it. The mask of "history" peeled off and every type of human in every type of predicament was in the street just like they were in the London I knew. Rich, poor, regular, diseased, clerics, beggars, swindlers, lovers, tourists, nobility, knights, and while some of the forms these varieties took were intense and new to me, mostly everyone was staid, plain, and simply going about this pleasant, overcast day. For every strange law, custom, or sign of brutality I witnessed, there was alongside it the ultimate leveler of humanity: boredom. We waited in a queue to pay our toll to enter the city. We waited in a queue to buy bread and cheese at a market stall. We shuffled through crowds. Any exoticism or thrill of seeing "history" in real life was dulled by the blunt politics of the meal deal, the endless search for an open table, and the people watching that only ever reveals their sameness, their shifting of mass from one place to another, waiting out the day.

There was a festival in town, which explained the long queues. There were more people than usual. And if things felt extra-medieval and cliché to me, then that was the point—there was a Round Table tournament being put on. Demonstrations, carnival games, and jousting were on at the Guildhall and stretched to Smithfield with all the cringe of a comic book expo.

"Don't you want to see the jousting?" Simon asked with a cloying, sarcastic tone. I was surprised by his knack for sarcasm. Wasn't he someone who lived by holy oaths and duty? His un-readability was constantly surprising.

"Not particularly," I replied, still unsure if he was serious or not. "Are they actual knights? Like, knight-knights? Like, they work for the king?" I knew nothing.

"Yeah, these guys are the real deal," said Simon. "They put on these King Arthur tournaments to drum up money and sup-port for the war. The contests and stuff are all fake though, just a dick-swinging contest at the end of the day."

I nearly choked on my food. I couldn't tell if it was my improved English inviting me into friendlier layers of communication or Simon's escape from bondage making him looser and uninhibited, but I welcomed it. We laughed and watched the crowd gathering at the entrance to one of the arenas. He told me about the one jousting tournament he had gone to as a child, how it had had the opposite effect on him and made him afraid of horses when one had gotten spooked and jumped into the crowd. An old man was kicked in the head and died. He remembered how disorganized and drunk the knights were, the crush of the crowd.

"The goal is to hit the other guy coming at you right here." He balled his hand into a fist and pressed it lightly against the side of my chest and held it there, then he unballed the hand and slipped it under my armpit. "If it slips right in there it'll lift the knight up without really hurting him, and the force puts their body into a spin so they can fall sideways and not get trampled. It kind of ruins everything once you notice it. You can actually see the knights lean into the motion like they've choreographed it before. I'm pretty sure they plan out who wins and who loses just for the drama. There's always a tie, then a sudden death. A good guy, a bad guy."

"This is coming from the guy who thinks dragons are real," I said, sipping mead from a metal flask. The liquid was grainy and had a slightly charred-sugar taste. It was delicious.

"That's a totally different thing. There's no comparison there."

"Yeah, but if you can see through this whole Round Table, King Arthur charade for what it is, why wouldn't dragons just be an extension of that? It's all just stories and fables."

Simon shook his head. "No, you've got it mixed up. I'm saying the jousting and these silly tournaments are just for show—but the knights are really knights. Chivalry is a real thing, just not very strong in these showboaters. Dragons are real. The Round Table and King Arthur are real things."

"King Arthur's not real," I said. That was the one useful thing I could remember from school. A snide history teacher telling our class how King Arthur had been completely made up, how he was the Superman of his day, just a propaganda myth.

Simon raised his eyebrows. "Well, he's not alive anymore, but he definitely was a real king a long time ago. I'm sure some of the stories about him and the magic and all that are embellished a little, but no more than these knights here with their fake jousting. If he were alive today he'd be ashamed of these guys."

Before I could say anything else, a woman sitting farther down the table shouted over to us. "Hey, how about you show some respect for our troops. These men risk their lives fighting for our freedom every day. The least you can do is show some respect at a time like this."

Embarrassed, Simon began to apologize immediately, but another man sitting on the other side of us chimed in. "Don't apologize," he said to Simon, but loud enough, clearly directed for the woman to hear. "You've got nothing to apologize for, son."

"Excuse me?" said the woman.

The man kept his attention only on me and Simon. "Deluded are the people that come to these things," he said. He was elderly and his clothes were in tatters. Bristly white whiskers were all over his cheeks, his ears, his eyebrows. It was clear he wasn't here for the festival so much as he was here because it was a place to be. "Deluded! Cheering on a war machine. Makes me sick to see."

"I wasn't talking to you, sir," said the woman.

"Wasn't talking to you either but here we are." He leaned across the table and trained his wild eyes on her. "Only thing you're cheering for is more dead children in the streets."

The woman eyed him the way anyone would eye the brusque unknown—her wariness felt modern and familiar. There was a nervousness in her voice, but a determination to snap back, her eyes were calculating for a moment, then decisive. "I'm just here with my four boys"—she gestured to four children sat around her—"showing support for their father who's in Wales as we speak, making sure you've got bread to eat and a roof over your head." The oldest of the boys glared at us and the old man, who continued barking his rant.

"You know King Arthur was Welsh, right?" he said. "You lot love to ride into London for the day and have fun at the games and all this blasphemy, but he was a Welshman through and through and you and your boys can rest assured that when he comes again he'll rip up all the castles your daddy and king—"

"Oh, so he's still on his way then?" The woman broke into sharp laughter. "Anytime now, right? We're all waiting! Typical for a Welshman to be snoozing while his country's being conquered. The lazy bastard couldn't even show up for Caerphilly."

"No lazier than an army-pension-sucking pig—that's what you are, aren't you? Showing up to the trough?"

And with that the oldest of the children sprang up from his seat. He couldn't be any older than ten, but his hand was on his belt, on the hilt of a small dagger. The old man got up as well, shaky but determined and seething.

Simon pulled my arm. "Let's go." He didn't want us becoming part of a scene. We ducked away just as the child lunged at the old man. Commotion rippled through the surrounding crowd, which we pushed our way through, making our way to a side street. Only a piercing, sudden yelp broke through the jeers, and whether it was the old man or the child, I didn't want to know.

The commotion made me nervous. If the lord of the manor at Greenwich came looking for us—and surely he would—there were few places he'd need to go and few people he'd need to ask. London felt, aside from its anthill-like density, like a small room. The anonymity it would one day afford its residents didn't exist yet. We couldn't stay, I decided.

"Of course we can," said Simon, and maybe he took my worry to mean monetarily because he patted his newly filled coin purse, then patted my back. And again here was the whiplash sensibility of Simon—of caution in the crowd, but oh look, another open market at the end of the side street, another extension of the festival, another rowdy party, and it was all too easy for me to be charmed and give way because this newfound freedom was just as sweet for me as it was for him. We bought apples cooked in butter, a venison leg, two silly hats. We watched a stage performance of King Arthur saving Guinevere from an evil knight. We linked arms and drank grassy, murky ale and wandered the streets, the clustered shops, ruddy pubs, the afternoon turning orange and blue. We bought beer after beer. We shat side by side into a communal midden. We danced together and with strangers. My head became overstuffed with circumstance and celebration, and where in my modern life we had the internet and texting and breaking news, here there was nothing but our own brains and what stimulations we chose or had foisted upon them—the music, the smells, the touching, the echoes of shouts and screams and songs.

The touching was strange. Maybe not strange, but I made note of it. I was comfortable with it because I was comfortable with Simon after our escape together and, before that, our months of waning interaction, but still I noticed the touching—his hand on my chest when we were talking about jousting earlier, the two of us drunkenly linking arms, his hand lingering warmly on my shoulder blade throughout the day and into the evening, sharing food and drink. It was friendship and trust between us, that was all, but my ever-drunkening brain granted more dominance to old paranoias and complication and while a greedy part of me didn't mind the extended touching—because Simon was physically attractive, I could admit—I couldn't help but read into it more than just anthropologically.

Simply put, I didn't know what Simon's intentions were. I didn't know him really, at all, I had to admit. There was a barrier. And the drunker I got, those differences and that gulf became more apparent instead of dulled. The natural affability in his eyes misdirected me, daring me to come closer but inching steadily backward at the same time—a clear strategy. I felt frustrated and stubborn, only plodding along because what was my plan anyway? As we cheered in crowds and danced and sang, I began to feel an unmistakable sense of alienation—a distinctly modern feeling—and though alcohol eased the harshness of this world, it gave way to a melancholic egoism, my modern-brain telling me that the miscommunication inherent to my existence here was a result of something everyone else lacked, that I was worth more than this. These are barbarians, I thought to myself. I'm in the midst of a musty group of bodies that are all technically dead. Simon is handsome and fun but not alive. These are the dark ages. I'm surrounded by dead, foolish ghosts and I don't belong here. My cheeks flushed red and furious. Still, I let Simon force me to dance.

I've always felt alienated, but it's not like that's an uncommon feeling. I grew up in the classically homophobic 1990s and early 2000s and this had throttled me in all the ways that are too commonly detailed now—the bullying, the name-calling, the lost friendships—so common it's almost embarrassing to give them credit for their formativeness, but I suppose multiplying layers of shame is what makes the injury so effective. It scars you and then you're embarrassed of the scars.

I remember when I was around eleven years old, I lost all my friends. I don't remember the details, but I remember having friends one day and then the next day not having a single one. I remember the frost-covered grass at the playground at school, how much of an expanse it was, and not having anywhere to go. I was shunned and I was devastated and this happened more than once as I grew up. I'm sure it was something effeminate in me that I could never quite taper to anyone's liking, or the best friendships that would turn too-best, or football—just everything about it.

Of course later I learned that the depression and anxiety disorders gleaned from those early years were universal, shared by a generation of millennials who all more or less went through the same ringer of gay-bashing and unrequited crushes, leading to pop culture hyperfixations as coping mechanism, sexual disfunction as trauma response, good relationships, bad relationships, no relationships. As I came into adulthood, came out, gained friends, finally gained a few gay friends—ones who shared a similar degree of malaise—I always felt like they had really made something of their childhood injury and I had not. They had overachieved in education, landed six-figure salaries in media, finance, tech; had bodies of the kinds of gods they were bullied by as children; were savvier and quicker than me. My success had been marginal: mid-five-figure salary, wobbly relationships with fitness and boyfriends, perpetually renting everything. I was still so unconfident, and this matured form of alienation was almost more dangerous because it was directed inward, it was a threat against my own core, as if my childhood loneliness hadn't been a result of my gayness at all, but that there was something intrinsically wrong with me that peeled me apart from even the other outcasts. I still so desperately wanted to fit in and I feared I wouldn't recognize the feeling if I ever finally did.

I met my boyfriend through an app, and maybe that was the first mistake because I've never believed in the idea of a chosen family. The definition of choice negates the nature of family (and also because there never seemed to be one that chose me). Yet, for three years I was welcomed into my boyfriend's fold of successful, curated men and I felt truly welcomed. My calendar became pockmarked with birthdays, weddings, Pride events, gallery openings, West End shows, and Sundays spent shirtless in parks, selfies, Frisbees, brunches, gossip, bad TV, and the denial of any sort of aging at all. Any suggestion that these "mannerisms" (I'll call them that) were becoming gauche as we all entered our mid-thirties had to be dismissed as one's own internalized homophobia. Our *inner childs* were wounded, so these raves, these vanity fitness regimes and drug dalliances were only our stunted rebirths. We were actually only teenagers, one could argue, rocking back and forth on whatever queer god's timeline we were on, delirious to see which age fit best, and so we had to dress up in our Hockney/Haring sludge merch and go to that concert, that club, that dinner party, that half-marathon.

I didn't feel attractive, I didn't feel reckless. My impressive job at the hedge fund helped, but I felt attractive only in the sense that I felt pulled along by someone else. I dressed up, I dressed down, I always seemed to be teetering and maybe that was what the banker bros at work sniffed out when they came calling. They knew simple brotherly camaraderie was easier for me to obsess over than the complicated mind games of my boyfriend and his ilk who were actually gay. It was easier to fantasize about enjoying football than about whatever I would look like in a swimsuit on a beach in Spain.

And I ended up looking good. One September we all went to Sitges. (I told the boys at work just Barcelona.) Ten of us—but it felt like ten thousand—rented a house on the beach and spent a week under the scorching sun. The sea was as purifying as old bathwater. The men that frolicked in it were skeletons plagued with varying degrees of bloat. My boyfriend had adopted a sneering fitness and fasting routine that had rendered him childlike and hairless, freakishly lithe in bed like an eel, but with a body that lay over me like a sentient pile of bone spurs. I struggled to come.

Every couple in our group seemed unbalanced in their wariness, one partner always sheepish about how they knew someone else in the group, every connection's origin story kept intentionally vague. I constantly felt like I was being roped into something, and anytime I got a grasp on what exactly it was—a nefarious tango, a curiosity flirt—I was roped into something else, my read on everyone completely thrown. But of course everyone made a grand show of stability. I missed my boys at the office.

These undercurrents flowed throughout the whole week, poisoning our days in the sea, haunting our nightly drunkenness at clubs. We'd stand in circles and bob up and down, drink and smoke, take cheap drugs, look at phones, look at strippers going about their lazy routines.

One night I became hyperaware of how surrounded by men I was and had some kind of allergic reaction. It wasn't a headache or the flu, but it was a kind of paralysis, a muteness. The way I had been acting was starting to piss everyone off. I was being too standoffish. I kept thinking about how I hadn't seen a single woman all week. It was as if women had been irradicated from the entire town and all that was left were these roving bands of gassy, balding men who prowled, searching only for one another, snowballing into pulsating swarms, and myself lost among them, smelling all this beefy red. There's nothing liberating about this, I thought, nothing revolutionary. At most, I could force myself to feel the same rotten glee I used to feel as a teenager when I'd bring a male friend (when I had one) home from school and my mum would be gone, my sister would be away, and there would be a chance—just a chance—that our video game playing might evolve, a sock-clad foot might slip into a lap, a loss might lead to a wrestle, a dare, a playful, beguiling begging at the knees. It was embarrassing, contrived, and vapid. It was titillating and I was dizzy, losing grip.

Amid the undulating sea of men at the club there were the nightly strippers, who performed on small raised platforms like brawny, naked lighthouses. The night wore off their clothes until they danced completely nude, with pharmaceutically assisted full erections, and as they gyrated, a chemical filled the air—their bodies emitted it and so did mine, intermixing against my will. These emissions hung low in the air and I began to struggle to breathe. I backed away from the crush, moving to the side of one of the platforms, but I found myself only inches away from one dancer who was slowly jerking himself off. His body was bathed in purple and red. Suddenly the inertia of the club zeroed in on him, sensing a hidden synthesis. I tried to get away, but the crowds were gawking around him. In fact I was gawking. The veins of his penis rippled and stretched with the rhythmic motion of his hand. A man next to me reached, grabbed, and felt. Others had their phones out. The cogs of power wheeled in everyone's eyes, pointing at the one single thing in the dancer's hand and I felt the gravity of a thousand white and red eyeballs watching, pupils dilated, irises black. I couldn't catch my breath. I couldn't stop smelling that musty smell. It was as if every boy was here, every childhood bully, menace, crush, office boy, beach boy, boyfriend had been secreted into the air and was wholly unfit to breathe.

The unthinkable everyone was thinking happened and the dancer in front of me ejaculated thick, splattering gobs into the air. He twitched and broke rhythm, suddenly afraid and off beat. The crowd cheered and filmed. I stared motionless at his hand unclenching, the mess on the floor, his eyes looking down and then up. We locked eyes. And that was the moment. That was the only other time in my life where I feel like I could have time traveled, like the fabric of the universe had been ripped open because the next thing I knew I was outside on the empty beach, alone. I was snatched from the static present and thrown into the darkness of a new void, a new timeless silence, an empty plane without men, without women, onto which only the afterburn of the dancer's eyes remained and the fear in them, the fear in mine.

The fear in that memory latched on to me now as I lumbered along the streets of an ancient London and I shuddered deep within myself. The unsexiness of it, the perversion, when people can be so organic and odorous, single-mindedly fixated on one modicum of honey. I vomited into a stone pit I didn't realize was a well. A man shouted at me and shoved me aside. I fell to the ground. Everyone seemed to want to fall to the ground. A man on horseback plowed through us with a stick, bashing our heads, clearing the way. A bell rang in the distance.

"All right get to bed, you bastards. All you lot. Make way, get lost!"

I rolled out of the way, narrowly avoided being trampled. A pile of us were on the cobblestones, men and women giggling, struggling to stand, another vomited, and I realized I was clutching Simon to my chest, my arms around him.

"Oh George," he said, laughing and turning. We pulled each other up and down, tripping. To feel his body against mine was to feel softness and safety after my days of endless brutality. We toddled to an inn. Flickering torches brought darkness, lightness, darkness. Gates shut, merchants packed up, long shadows enrobed streets, and a candle was a floodlight. A candle was a blaring diode. A candle was only needed in one place downstairs and one place upstairs above the pub, under the beam roof, where we lay down in a darkness that heaved with bodies. The world spun and I used that inertia to push aside the memory of my life before, the nastiness of it. This isn't what that was, I thought to myself. Here there was nastiness but no mind games, no greedy lusts, no rat race, or strategic ambiguity. Even as drunk as I was, there was a reasonable density to it, a heartiness that set it apart from the chemical tides of Sitges. Here we were children. Here our touch was of joy sparking between us. Holding hands up the dark stairs. Lying down on the shared cot, straw poking through fabric, cold feet under warm legs, curling into each other.

We were children, me and Simon. Me and twenty others, me and a thousand others. And we all shared this joyful single breath, this creaky floor, this October chill that lay softly alongside us like time itself, the calendar my only old friend amid a thousand new ones and suddenly I was no longer alone.

FIRST EPISTLE, concerning the wards and liveries of the city of London

Written by the hand of EDWARD by the grace of God King of England, Lord of Ireland, Duke of Aquitaine, Conqueror of Wales

The ninth annual Round Table tournament held at the Guildhall in the city of London successfully concluded with the appointment of eighteen new recruits into the Royal Levy. They were to be outfitted, solemnly committed, and sent to the battalion at Westminster, then to Wales the next morning after a sunrise consecration ceremony at Parliament restricted to immediate family members only. Meanwhile back in London the bone marrow fritters sold out and the chilled strawberry soup proved a sensation. There were no riots, no fires, but one mare broke loose, one protestor was hung, three assaults, seven thefts, one murder, but again no fires, no misadventure, two maimings, five assaults of vicious battery. Of note was a child who suffered a fit and died in the queue to view Arthur's chalice, whose parents considered it an act of God but the ward constable insisting on charges of woeful negligence and a jailing. Another constable reported acts of calamitous misadventure near that same queue, of an elderly man stabbed in a brawl outside the jousting, whose body was discovered later that evening in the

Thames. In brief: three horses died of exertion, two knights suffered bleeding head wounds, the wool exchange reported record losses, seven Welshmen were beheaded at the Tower, public works were completed on Cornhill Road, unsold meat spoiled, and everyone commented on the purple pansies that bloomed, so strangely out of season, in the churchyard at St. Paul's and how what a shame it would be in two weeks' time, when the first chill of November would clench its jaw tightly and not let off until it had bled dry the melt.

What went unreported that day was a solemn vow of devotion made by one Simon of Greenwich, in the upper bedroom of the Five Chances Inn, at midnight, mouthed silently and promised irrevocably to God, the contents of which would go neither mentioned nor confessed, ever, but could easily be surmised by the subsequent service of care he administered to his brother in Christ, his pledged bedfellow, George, also of Greenwich, of whom the informed have been made aware.

Few noticed George and Simon leaving the Five Chances in the silent morning after the festival, when the constables changed shifts and the breakfast bells had yet rung and the gulls fought for leftover leeks spilled from cartons and the cobbles were still wet with ale. Only the widow Marjorie of Goutter Lane could remember the discreet loitering of George and Simon in the alleyway behind her tailoring shop and the pleasant smiles on their faces when she agreed to let them in early, before working hours. She recounted to the equerry how easy they were to part with their money, and the awkwardness of the timid one, George, how he struggled to pair his understockings with his tunic, not understanding the correct knots for his cloak shutting, his strange accent, his strange manner, his insistence on better shoes with thicker soles, and his easy laughter. Flippancy was what Marjorie called it.

"No man can afford to sling money around like those two did. Sure, all I operate is a brokerage of linens, all secondhand, but you'd have thought they was purchasing new ones in full—wanting the garments tailored to fit snug, which of course I obliged for the extra penny as needed, not uncommon, but for so many purchases and in such a rush, and outside trading hours—I warned them of the penalties I could yet face—and I promise *you*, Sir, I did not tally the coinage until the proper time. Oh the strange tongue on the one—to be of such flippancy and softness, yet unsure, yet demanding in such a silly way. To be honest I'd confess he was a delightful company to have, 'specially so early in the morning, and my ledgers being nicely fitted for the day—nicely for the week, mind you—once I had tallied them in proper—but how queer, how freely they both was together, the two of them. If you'd have told me they was the two boys from Greenwich gone escaped, who'd caused the ruckus at the manor and run so afoul of the lord there I'd have happily reported them straightway to the constable, but I had nary the faintest idea. Their politeness, their cheery abandon. At most my thoughts was that they might be new recruits headed east—gallant enough, new money, albeit so excitable and prone to laughter, I know how that younger lot are. But they weren't going east, no far from it. North they said. Far north. And alone. Just the two of them. They both seemed so cheerfully unsure."

◇ ◇ ◇

George and Simon left London that morning and were far beyond the city gates by the time the sun finally warmed the landscape, colored the frost, heated the stains of sweat beneath their new garments and satchels filled with wares. A blanket, two porcelain plates, thread, a knife, brass buttons, a bow, a hatchet, netting, seeds—these clattered around in the rucksack George and Simon carried in turns, the contents of which were learned from receipts obtained at Duckett's Green, a blacksmith at Berkhamsted, and the keeper of the Inn of the Sea Mare, in Aldbury, who remarked on the openness of the boys, their ease and decorum.

"Two lads starved on the road all day and you'd have thought they'd be right fit for demanding all sorts, but all they requested was a roof, nary the bread I scraped together and offered, which they took with great thanks. And though the stew had gone cold, it warmed up roundly with a dash of next morning's porridge, and with the coals still warming they were indeed grateful more so than was worth the fuss. They seemed amateur but in good spirits, not full of themselves, eager to move as fast as they could. I recommended the carriageway northeast by a few farthings—if they could manage it in the morning, they'd catch the next caravan, albeit small, but safe and of a reliable guild, well protected. And if their silver was persuasive enough, there were older knights, hunting parties, and the like. If they were on the run from something, it was well enough disguised in their cheerfulness. They were not fearful but excitable as they spoke of the land they were heading toward—a homestead in the north—eyes misting in the one that spoke of the fells and trees, deep barrows of earth full of badgers and mushrooms, foxes, wet logs the size of houses and a stream running through the middle of twenty acres, of water so pure like blanketed glass and deer at each bend, beavers, ravens, squirrels, bees; greenery lush like a cake. So stirring was how he talked, that I had forgotten the trail of conversation, and hadn't noticed how little the other one—George, you say—had spoken. By the way he looked about his self, I saw a lostness, or a sense of thought too wide and great to fit through simple doors. Real feelings. Both lads had a rawness about them that I felt I was intruding myself upon. And that was the next thing I did in fact— excused myself. I left the two of them for the night before I could ask them exactly where they were going. I apologize I did not press them further."

Records of George and Simon's journey become harder to link together from here onward. We know a caravan was joined at Poynders End, bound for Peterborough. Of the land discussed with the innkeeper, a line of inquiry indeed found the reallocating of a smallholding by a judge at Malton, northeast of York, the recording of which is sparse, understandable given the nature of the land—it being just an old smallholding, untamed, gnarled, and tainted by ██████ residue. Whilst the boundaries had been claimed, then reclaimed, passing from hand to hand, nothing of permanence had been done to solidify a patch of woodland squeezed between the Moors and Scarborough, where talk of a ██████ had caused a desertion of industry and a pinch point of migration in an otherwise unnoteworthy realm. Even the old Roman roads had buckled and been broken by the strains of pure nature, the coastline unabridged, the rivers melting into marsh and yet still a land grant was granted, a seal broken and resealed, soil daring to be tilled in the most feeble of winters. Something was in motion. The helm of the earth seemed unfettered. It was the year 1300 and a time traveler was in our midst. And I rode out to meet him.

5

The road north was not some fantastical journey into a land that time forgot. It was simply a road. It was difficult—because walking any long distance at the onset of winter is a stinging, uncomfortable undertaking in any century—but it wasn't barbaric. Well, it was barbaric, but it wasn't ferocious. The road—for all its meandering paths, its grifters, its threats of snow and mud—was defanged. There weren't any wolves.

At times the "road" (a muddy line wrought through the dead landscape) felt like a long hallway. There was traffic. We'd shuffle along with everyone else, all of us fish with our own imperatives and internal compasses, sighing impatiently if we found ourselves stuck behind a group of slower travelers, glaring down those who could afford horses. We'd try not to waste too much time or money at kitschy roadside bazaars and we'd always avoid the watchful eyes of knights or anyone who seemed in a position of authority. Or at least Simon would. I was often too busy being agog at something: that child huckster with disturbingly adult facial expressions and mannerisms; that horrifically swaybacked horse, how its belly nearly touched the ground; that nobleman being carried on the back of a stringy, elderly manservant.

"I don't think we need to hide from him," I said as the nobleman passed us and Simon ducked his head. The man sat on a wooden chair under a tattered silk canopy. I thought to myself, How did that get made? How do you make anything out here without what my cloudlike mind had only ever understood to be: machine, invoice, shipping fee, plastic wrap, google instructions, commerce, *voilà*! The chair lay on top of his poor servant's ketchupy, calloused shoulders. "Surely they're not looking for us all the way out here," I said. "He doesn't seem to be paying attention anyway." The nobleman was slumped in the chair, asleep.

"I'd rather not find out the hard way," said Simon. "You were the prized Danish prisoner of the lord at Greenwich. They'd have put out a reward for you."

"But how? Do they send out letters or something about me? How would people even know what I look like?"

"They'd know."

I chuckled. "They wouldn't."

"They would." Simon was grinning. By now he was used to my rush to interrogate, not annoyed but amused by my ignorance and happy to explain this wild world.

"Be serious," I said. "If those policemen back in Peterborough had seen me, how would they have known anything? There's no photo of me. There's no, like, alert system, no criminal database. How would they know?" (When I said *policemen* and when I said *photo* and *database*, I cushioned these words with several minutes' worth of translating them to Simon's realm of understanding, explaining how a policeman was like a constable, but more omniscient, and a photo was just a miniature portrait, but witchy—"You have to believe me"—a one-to-one replica, an instantaneous miracle and a curse.)

"*Fo-to* is an insane-sounding word," said Simon.

"It's short for photography."

"You two are strange," said a woman walking behind us with her husband. By now the road had thinned out and it was just our traveling party, which was only five people. We had split the cost of a wagon with this middle-aged couple when we left Peterborough. A wagon driver and mule hauled our bags. The four of us trudged along behind it.

Simon turned around and said to the woman, "He's a time traveler." He grinned that grin of his and winked at me.

"OK." I gasped and gave him a playful shove. "You can't worry about police one minute and then out me in front of everyone. Your paranoia has to be consistent at least. Are we undercover or not?"

"What's a police?" asked the woman's husband.

"It's nothing," I said.

"It's a secret time traveler code word," said Simon.

"Hey, if you're a time traveler," said the woman, "then why can't you make this journey go any faster?"

"That's not how it works," Simon and I both said at the same time. We caught each other and broke into laughter, a laughter that was so generous I felt myself repressing it a notch, as if to shore up this easiness for a colder day, when the chill of winter wouldn't be so easily teased. November was disfiguring itself into December right in front of us and yet we were laughing, mud-stomping, and singing, embroidering cheeky grins across every second of what I can really only call rejuvenating, life-affirming chitchat.

The wagon ahead of us came to a stop. Simon, myself, and the couple caught up to it with all our lazy giggles still going. The driver held up a hand to silence us.

"What's going on?" said Simon.

The driver held a finger to his lips.

We were a two days' journey away from the city of Lincoln, on a route that cut directly through dense woodland, on a less-traveled road. Misty steam from all our breaths faded up into the white sky. Trees and frost surrounded our party, and through the white fog, cutting through our echoes of laughter, was a baby's cry.

The wagoner stood up on his seat and peered off into the woodland. All of us followed his gaze. Frost singed every brown leaf that dared to still cling to a tree. Nothing moved. I was the only one who had the naivete to ask aloud, "Is that a baby?"

The cry was sharp and distressed, more animal than I had ever heard a baby sound before, really wailing. It was the cry of an infant. Its pitch was high, its shrieks were breathless. I stepped off the road and tried to focus my vision through the tangle of trees and brambles. Some distance away, I thought I could see an unnatural bundle of cloth on the ground. I took another step.

"George, don't," said Simon.

"What do you mean?"

"Just don't. Don't go any farther." His face was stoic. Morose but not shocked. The older couple was the same, they could only shake their heads. They murmured something to each other, then the driver signaled to the mule. The wagon's wheels slid stubbornly in the mud for a second before rolling into their old momentum, moving on. But the baby's cries continued.

"Come along, dears," said the woman.

"George," said Simon.

But all I could say in return was "Simon," saying his name in periled awe as the most horrific acquiescence washed over me like the iciest of seawater, aided in part by simple disbelief. Was there really a baby over there? Why? The shock of nonreality once again rejigged me from the world, made me question my own ears and the screams knifing into them. A baby was crying in the middle of nowhere. I couldn't quite move. I was a bystander not knowing where to stand, and Simon, as if sensing this, came and put his arm around my shoulder.

"Let's go," he said. And finally my legs moved.

The driver decided we'd travel all through the night if everyone could manage. No one questioned the decision. At some point a nonsunset occurred and white afternoon turned to black night and we continued our journey in darkness, the joy of it gone, our movement powered only by unlit coals in our stomachs.

What was—I couldn't even think it.

Why would—I told myself it wasn't what I thought it was.

Maybe I had misheard it and it was nothing. Something was lost in translation and there was an explanation. I'd see this was just another strange custom I didn't understand, something that was done on the regular and not a big deal—and it wasn't what you thought it was, George. You don't have babies screaming in the woods where you come from?

We reached the city of Lincoln and paid our tolls, paid our fees for arriving in the middle of the night. We rolled through the beyond-midnight streets with only one torch guiding us to the massive cathedral where we would be sleeping. I marveled in silence at the spires that appeared like spider legs, which seemed to travel up until they disappeared into a ceiling of blackness, not a sky. How could there be a sky in a place like this? I could still hear the baby's cries ringing in my ears. We entered the cathedral and it was still cold. Clergymen welcomed us but I still felt like I was outside. I stared at the ceiling, wondering where it was.

"I thought you said you'd been to Lincoln before?" said Simon, seeing my wonderment. I could sense he wanted to ease the eerie grief that had stung all of us back in the woods.

"I've been to Scunthorpe," I said. "Farther north, but only to visit an aunt once when I was really little, I barely remember it. We took a train." Halfheartedly, I explained what a train was.

"You're saying you once traveled from London to Scunthorpe in just one day?"

"Just a few hours," I said. I smiled, but it felt sacrilegious. Still, it warmed my body. Simon smiled back, dipping his toe in too.

"What does it feel like to move so fast?" he asked.

I didn't say anything for the longest time, then finally, as if opening a trusted drawer only to find it empty, I said, "I don't know." Trains and hallways, waiting in queues, ticket checkers, sandwich boxes—that didn't feel like the same world as this. Physics didn't apply the way they applied here, where the air itself was heavy with damp, an air I felt I had to scoop with my palms. The silence, the stony cold.

Our traveling companions had all gone ahead to the guest quarters and only Simon and I stood alone in the center of the cathedral's nave. Only three faint candles were lit at this hour of night, spreading a low mist of dim orange across the empty wooden pews.

"Simon," I finally said. Once again, I could only say his name. I noticed how freeing it felt to say it, to have a friend. "What was that back there?"

Thick stone walls created a cocoon. I could hear Simon's eyes looking, watching, analyzing. "It could have been a couple of things," he said. "I don't know. It could have all been *fine*—it could have been there with its mother and we just didn't see her, with its family, and it was just making a fuss for everyone to hear. It could have been an animal, maybe. It could have been a trap. Bait. You have to be careful out there." He paused, searching for words. He exhaled. "It was probably what you think it was."

"And that's just something that happens?" I said.

"Yes," he said. "And I don't see how it couldn't happen, sometimes. Especially this time of year."

"I mean, we could have done something."

"I don't think so." Simon's voice was hollow like I had never heard it before. "We don't know what kind of state it was in. We wouldn't have been able to take it with us. I don't even know if Lincoln accepts foundlings. It's most likely that it came from here anyway. Stepping in and helping in those cases isn't . . ."

Reasonable? Meant to be? Simon didn't say and instead let silence drip and gather. I tried to keep my expression blank, tried not to seem like I knew any better or had some future-man, utopic vision of humanity because I didn't. I had delusions of a moral high ground I could have tapped into, something condescending and self-soothing, but I said nothing. I joined

Simon's unanswerable silence and in doing so, let my idea of human life—the brass tacks function of our bones and brains—recalibrate.

The chattering trill of a magpie sounded from somewhere outside the cathedral. Something smaller and braver chirped in return. The sun was already making its way back to this side of the planet. In silent agreement, Simon and I stayed where we were, there in the nave. We sat in the pews and over the next few hours watched the black stained glass windows fade to pure blue, their stains of red, green, and yellow slowly coming to life. Faces awakened and I realized my way of seeing had been permanently altered. With no TV, no films, no easy reservoir of human representation to tap into besides what I could see in front of me, I felt real fear as the figures in the windows came to life with daylight. Apostles, saviors, and virgins all awakened as sentient, shimmering creatures and I felt an animalistic sense of fear tickle me, right at the back of my neck, making me blush, skittish as if exposed, weak as if the stone walls were an imposing god's giant hands about to slap together and squash me—and the conflicting sensation of *wanting* this to happen, of wanting to be crushed. The only thing I can compare it to is a feeling I once had in Italy, on a trip I had taken with my boyfriend early in our relationship, where I had felt a similar, destructive awe.

"This reminds me," I suddenly said. My voice was a croak. I cleared my throat. The sudden noise jolted Simon awake and he looked at me with his regular eager self, eyes wide and blue. I didn't know what I was saying but I needed to say it, to let the pressure out of what I was feeling. "Back in my old life," I began, "I had a boyfriend." I let that drop. Simon had no reaction.

"And early in our relationship, we took a trip to Italy, which is a place—"

"In the Mediterranean," said Simon.

I smiled. "Right. Sorry." I decided to stop translating every little thing and continued. "This Italy trip was the only big trip we ever did together, everything after it was just beach holidays to Spain with his friends. But in those early days I think we were both trying to be something for the other, trying to show off." I tried to describe the overwhelm of expectation, both of us trying to impress each other—him with some DJ friend he wanted me to meet in Naples, me with my inability to be intimidated by Italian. I remembered old train station walls plastered with laminated signs, broken ticket machines, asking Americans for directions to Pompeii. "We did a day trip there," I said. "It was a billion degrees, I got sunburnt. We spent all day there and even stopped at Herculaneum on our way back to Naples, like we were trying to overculture each other, even though we had probably both watched the same travel videos to prepare the itinerary."

We were annoyed with each other by the time we arrived at the Herculaneum complex, hungry and hot. We argued about getting audio guides or not, why we hadn't thought about lunch, whose idea it was to go to Herculaneum the same day as Pompeii anyway. We blazed through the complex. I felt nervy about all the arguing we were having—we had been together less than a year, we were both about to turn thirty. I wandered alone to the very bottom of the archaeological site, to the boat docks, where hundreds of screaming skeletons frozen in volcanic ash had crammed the docks, trying to escape. I gazed into their empty eye sockets and felt the cheap horror, but what I remembered most was turning around and seeing the hundred-foot wall of solid rock they were up against—what their city had been buried under. Long grass grew at the bottom. The wall was pink and purple, stained in places with moisture. It was the purest form of hopelessness I had ever witnessed and it washed over me like a boiling wave.

My boyfriend came over and I pointed out the rock wall left over by the volcano, but he was more drawn to the skeletons. We took a tasteless photo together, we returned our audio guides, bought a chocolate bar, but I couldn't shake the presence of that massive wall. I felt it in the back of my mind for a long time after, almost like a hidden shame, like a desire. It had been such an anomaly of destruction, how could you do anything but surrender? I wanted it to envelop me.

"I swear," I said to Simon, "if Mount Vesuvius had been any closer, I would have thrown myself right into it. I wasn't upset or anything, I just felt the overwhelming impracticality of being there, being up against something so enormous. I wanted it to bury me. I guess it was awe." I went silent, surprised by how real the feeling was when I acknowledged it out loud. "Anyway, that's what this place reminds me of. It just feels like it's about to swallow us."

"Well, I hope not," said Simon. He put his hand against one of the gothic pillars and gave it a comical shove. "Seems pretty sturdy to me."

I smiled but my awe was not eased. I almost proclaimed this was the biggest building I had ever seen, but of course that wasn't true. I laughed at how acclimatized I had become, my where-withal no greater than any peasant scurrying under the stained glass gaze of angels.

We stood up and stretched, yawned, nudged each other along. We went to the guesthouse to find our travel companions and some splatter of breakfast. We ate and rested in the churchyard while magpies thieved about and the city thrummed to life. We gathered our things for the final stretch of our journey, and all the while I still felt that destructive awe, the gravity pull of the cathedral. Like light pouring through stained glass, I felt the eyes of monsters on me as I stepped further into their world.

6

We went north of York. We went near the coast, a few hours' hike to the sea, a day's journey into Scarborough, a long, blind step into winter.

We went under our blankets, under silence, under snow, under the abandon of the land—quieter than those early days in Greenwich, quieter than antinoise, than fog, than snow, than deer breathing out but never in, just out, their curly steam one vast exhale we swam through, all alone for weeks at a time.

It's a miracle we didn't freeze to death.

It's a miracle that actually I consider this time to be the warmest I've ever been in my whole life.

Being mapless was liberating and evened the playing field. I had no idea where we were. Simon had no idea either. I had been to York, once, years ago when I was a child. I had been to Leeds and Manchester and Scunthorpe to see my old aunt. I assumed I had driven through the Moors at one point or another, or cut across it on a train, or maybe not. It took me months to stop doing this—refer to future-spam still in my brain—and admit that any memories that were there (or would be there?) were useless to what was needed now, which was fresh water, more blankets, food preserves, firewood, warmth and dryness, fixed roof, rot avoidance, animal management, that sound in the night, that crack in the forest, a critter? A mouse? That man we saw. A neighbor? A tradesman? There were no neighbors—the concept of them. There were only people and when one of them was in a place that was yours you tensed up, you looked around, listened, stared until their footsteps faded away or they hollered a friendly greeting and you remembered the concept of community. Sometimes it was just water and your imagination anyway—the snowmelt! Dripping through the pines! That stream overstepping the banks! It would all need fixing in spring.

OK, there were maps, technically. There were beautiful ones, drawn with more detail than my twenty-first-century fool-self could have expected. We had relied mostly on caravan crowds and traveling merchants for directions for most of our journey, but by the time we arrived at York, we were truly on our own.

We arrived exhausted in the town hall, in the cathedral, where a giant map was rolled out big and gilded with a blue-painted sea, and I realized I held no intellectual superiority over these people. The map had no perspective or considered ratio to speak of (no satellite assistance), but things were more detailed: the squiggles of the river seeming childlike and crude until you counted the bends and inlets and realized that that's what was really there; and the astonishingly observed species of foliage, rocks, roads, cliffs, and hamlets that had all been drawn exactly as what they were: stacks, sticks, little tome-like boxes. A warden reached a long brass pointer across the map to indicate where Simon's uncle's smallholding was located. It lay in between a crisscross netting of forests and meadows awash with invisible claims of borders, our land included, which OK wasn't technically *our* land, yet somehow the manorial system felt more equitable than the rent system I was used to. Scrolls were stamped. Though illiterate, Simon signed his name. We paid three pieces of silver for a pocket-size copy of the map and I hoped this was all a good deal.

The endless journey north, the cold, the sudden snow—the snow that fell around us like powder, then sawdust, then like a thick lather of cream, the earth suddenly covered in it and trying to find our house underneath it all—we had a house, right? We had a roof over our heads? Simon assured me we did, his nodding head growing weary and delirious with each step, until finally, look! There.

Where?

White on white—what am I looking at?

Simon was already running ahead, opening a door in the middle of a blinding whiteness. A space revealed itself, a house. Darkness came alight, dust awash, critters all furry and leggy screaming and scattering from what we were going to call home. When I say house I mean hut.

I have to say I ceased to be human, or at least how I thought a human was meant to be. I worshipped fire, I melted snow, I ate once, maybe twice a day, placing rocks of roots into my frozen stomach, massaging my guts to ease their digestion. I vomited often. I drank milk from an ancient goat, I feared my neighbors, I developed a putrid, chronic cough.

But it felt exhilarating to be so baseline, to feel my body take advantage of every shift in temperature and calorie. If I had it in me, I had it in me, and it was queued up and spent. I finally figured out what year it was. It was December of 1300, then it was January of 1301. For the first time in my life, I knew what it meant to toil and to freeze.

"In the future, there'll be electric heaters," I told Simon. We were watching the fire in the hearth in our hut house. Despite my worsening cough, I inhaled its smoke like sniffing a warm summer breeze, grateful. Even as far out in the country as we were, smoke was inescapable, wafting in from neighboring homesteads, big swells of it from villages in the valley, and of course our own hearth, which we kept roaring day and night as long as winter lasted. I explained a radiator, underfloor heating, hot water taps.

"How can you know all of this without knowing how to make any of it?" said Simon. "What good is that?" We were huddled close together. We shared a bed, made from rope and wood, the mattress stuffed with hay and old wool. The fire was right next to us—coals and embers the most tempting blanket.

"There'll be electric blankets someday," I said.

"Then go make one, right now." He tried nudging me out of the bed with his knee, laughing. "What do you need to make one? Wood? Mercury? Copper?"

"I need . . ." I paused. An Amazon account? A mum who had one stored up in the loft? All I could do was laugh and nudge Simon back, tempt him to put another log on the fire.

By February and into March, the sun slipped into the picture more frequently. I gave little weather reports as we went about our daily chores, tilling the land, skinning rodents, milking

goats, sorting sheep, and I'd estimate the change in degrees—
the numbers meaning nothing to Simon of course, and nothing,
ultimately, to me either, but the sun was unburrowing itself and
I had never been so aware of it.

Our smallholding was on a slope, and when the snow
melted it caused flooding and puddles to form anywhere we
had attempted to tame. Whole crops were washed out, there
was mud and awkward spinoff streams that ran counter to the
actual stream that had broken its banks. The puddles attracted
the wrong kinds of wildlife and the land rotted, turning brown
before an approaching spring could think of turning anything
green. I set out one morning to do something about it—that was
how easy it was to live out here, you just woke up and decided to
do something.

Like all mornings I woke up and grabbed the kettle (or what
I called the kettle) off the coals and fed the hearth a new stick of
wood, then went outside. I mixed hot water from the kettle into
a larger basin of cold water and used this to wash myself as best
I could, grateful there was no more frost or ice at least. Then I
went back inside and ate/drank a cup of perpetual stew/gruel of
roots, grains, and old bones, which mixed nicely with eggs (when
our chickens laid any) or fish or what have you, which we didn't
have any at the moment, despite Simon's best efforts. Simon was
good with the animals (three chickens, two goats, eight sheep)
and an apt tradesman, but I was still mostly useless. Everything I
could do (read, write, execute Excel formulas, manage streaming
subscriptions, unsubscribe from newsletters, make pasta salads)
I could only do well in the world I had come from, not this one,
and I was always in search of ways to prove my worth.

I grabbed a shovel and trekked down the slope to the dip

in the land where the puddle had formed a muddy trench and a refuse catch. Birds scattered and flew up into the trees, which were just starting to hint of buds. Simon's footsteps came down the slope behind me.

"So what's your plan?" he asked. He was leaving for Scarborough for seeds, supplies, and a donkey. He touched my back and moved around me, almost slipping.

"Don't fall in," I said. "There's too much water to do a straightforward canal, but if I dredge this and feed it into a smaller system of switchbacks, that will divert any future runoff away from the house, like a funnel. Then I can feed it into the creek down the hill, and if I'm lucky enough, it will reach as far as the mill at Wykeham, which would be a whole other thing to deal with. But think of how nice it would be to have that mill running all the time next winter."

Simon nodded in approval. He looked at the slope of the hill and how it washed out into open meadow. "If it's able to maintain a steady current, we could use it as transport. Float things downstream. We could sail a barge down it."

"Don't get too ambitious. That would have to be pretty wide."

Simon smiled and winked. "You'd better start digging."

"You'd better hurry home and help," I said with a laugh that tripped over my throat. I cleared it.

"Be careful with your cough. Don't overdo it and have another fit."

I assured him I'd be fine. The cough flared up every now and then but felt like nothing more than a common London smoker's cough, except that I wasn't in London anymore, and I wasn't smoking. The air out here had to be cleaner than anything in the modern world, and maybe this was just my body's way of shedding those last vestiges of London-stain, that poisoned world of microplastics and methane. Simon worried because coughing out here meant mortal peril. There were no thermometers, blood analyses, CAT scans, Google. A cough could mean anything.

"You smoked?" he asked.

I said no but my friends did, my boyfriend did, and I guess yes, sometimes I did too. Kind of. Only when I drank, which was usually every weekend. I explained how pubs, clubs, brunch, and wine gardens would all evolve over the coming centuries.

"That sounds like what we've got out here," said Simon.

"Noooo," I sang. I insisted like I always did that it wasn't the same. (I didn't admit that they were actually better here than back there.)

Simon shook his head and smiled, then sighed at the task I had given myself. "Just come with me," he said. "We'll go to a pub and you can compare."

I laughed. "You could have offered that before I told you all my plans for today."

"I didn't think you were serious," he said. "I'm impressed and I like it, but it's a lot. Just come, the water will still be here when we get back."

"That's the problem." I dug the shovel into the ground and stuck it farther with my foot. I told Simon I'd go with him to Scarborough next time and he made me promise. "You're very conniving," I said as he headed out on his way.

"Just with you." He smiled over his shoulder and left.

This was how we had survived the winter together. We'd giggle and poke at each other like this, both of us clearly enjoying the life we had somehow managed to find out here together.

But what was this life?

I didn't understand who Simon was. He was devoted to me, we enjoyed each other's company, we shared a bed by sheer winter necessity, but there was a distance there, something unknowable. We seemed attracted to each other. I was attracted to him, definitely, and he was, I think in a way, to me. Sometimes I felt him watching me, waiting for something to happen, but our friendship stayed rote, as if we had been driven asexual by all the land tilling and hard labor. We were spent, physically, by the end of each day, and any serious conversation that didn't revolve around survival simply melted away into the comforting depths of slumber. We would just sit and watch the fire every night and nothing more. During some of the harshest winter days, we would stay in bed all week, only leaving to eat, feed the animals, and go to the toilet, jumping back in and huddling together, laughing and shivering like kids. We loved to watch the fire together. Those were actually the best days.

I was attracted to him, but it was like I didn't know what that meant anymore.

I began digging my trenches with barely a clue of what I was doing. I broke the earth with a hatchet first, chopping deep cuts down a long row, then shoveled everything out. Eventually I'd need gravel, or cement, ideally, to line the bottom but I didn't know if any of that existed. I also didn't know if this was how canals were dug in the first place or if this was even good land management, but looking at the row of topsoil I had removed and feeling the exertion . . . I felt like I knew exactly what I was doing. I felt like this movement, this disciplining of the land—

this was purpose. More purpose than I had ever felt before. Hours wiled away like this. And then my cough started up.

It came not like a regular cough. There was nothing caught in my throat, but there was an irritation. I had had bad asthma as a child, relying on an inhaler daily. At night I would stand in the kitchen with my mum before bed and she would watch me as I inhaled two puffs of albuterol and she would count to ten slowly—I thought about her. I thought about my mother as I stood on the side of the hole I had dug, doubled over and wheezing. It was a barking, asthmatic kind of cough that brought no relief, just an exhaustion of the muscles of my chest and a pulsing in my larynx. I coughed and it only made me cough more. My ribs hurt.

I miss my mum. The thought passed through my mind for what I hate to admit was the first time. The general idea of a mum, of care at least. I kept coughing. My head flushed red as I tried to slow my breathing and bottle down the spasms. Tears pulsed naturally from my eyes and maybe this spurred the feeling, the memory. Counting to ten, inhaling, holding my breath, getting better. As a kid, I would instinctually hold my breath whenever a lorry or a bus drove by me on the road or if someone at school wore too heavy a perfume.

My asthma went away by the time I was a teenager, and my mother did too. My asthma was replaced with more nebulous, existential problems and perhaps more accurately they closed me off from my mother, she didn't go away. It was me who turned and faded. In a way, the stability of her—of standing in the kitchen, her focused healing—had made her seem as if she would always be there, and maybe that was why it took me only until now to really grasp that she was gone from my life forever.

She was gone.

Or rather, I was gone from her. I had no way of seeing her again. It was shocking how plainly that fact surfaced and I accepted it. I kept coughing. Tears pulsed, excising emotions I didn't know I had. She had been there, but so had all the weight of her expectation, her chatter and glazed surface. Constant prodding and questioning, tinged with guilt.

I didn't *want* to go back—first of all.

I coughed.

That was the hardest emotion to admit: not wanting to not say goodbye—purposefully clouding that up with double negatives. I didn't know what I wanted, but I knew I didn't want any of the things that were back there, which presented themselves now like phantoms of what I had never had.

I coughed.

I let myself not miss my mother only because a part of me believed there was a version of me who was still back there. The me who hadn't slipped through time. If a part of her was still back there standing in the kitchen, counting to ten, then a part of me had to be back there too. No need to do anything about that.

I kept coughing and when I breathed, I tasted acid, pure smoke. Something was really wrong. I rubbed my eyes and they stung. The tears I was crying weren't from memories, they were from smoke. I opened my eyes and suddenly the land was awash with it. Long tentacles of smoke wrapped through the trees of the surrounding woodland and for a moment I was completely blinded by it. A thick fog enveloped me—clearly from a fire somewhere—but there was a chemical flavor to it, it didn't smell like regular smoke, like firewood or burning rubbish. It made me stop thinking about Mum at least. I got a grip. I ran to the house—it wasn't on fire, thankfully. I ran to the animals and considered letting them out of their pens in case there was a forest fire or something. I scanned the treeline, looking for flames, but saw none. Then somehow, as huge as it was, the wave of smoke passed and the air began to clear out. The toxic cloud continued moving across the landscape. I tried to think of a scientific explanation, something about weather inversions, trapped emissions, maybe the environment here was actually worse off than it would be in the future. The smoke moved like a sentient being, crossing through neighboring fields, pressing through hedgerows until it was completely out of sight.

I walked back to my digging site and counted my breaths with each step. The air cleared up. I thought about those dragons no one seemed to be able to form a consensus on. They existed, they didn't, they were huge, they were tiny, they spoke English, they spoke Welsh, they were in Yorkshire, they were in Scotland. No one seemed to have actually seen one because of course no one ever lived to tell the tale—convenient. It was always someone's cousin, or in Simon's case, his uncle.

A dragon had landed on him, squashed him to death. And these rumors came from people in town—in Scarborough, in York, or down the coast in Filey—silly, inconsequential people. I shouldn't think like that. What a modern form of judgment to have. I wished I could commit to something. Did I want to live out here or not? I thought about my mum one more time and waited for any lingering emotions to come blaring back. They never did and I scolded myself for thinking dumb, modern thoughts of grief and family. My cough never came back and I continued my work without interruption.

I saw Simon's torch ten minutes before he was anywhere near me. I watched it squiggle its way through the woods. He pulled a gray donkey behind him, and strapped to the donkey were bags of food—grains, roots, some leafy greens, seeds, and bundles of herbs. Most of this would have come from neighboring tenants within our manor on his return trip (selling goods on his way, buying goods on the return, netting an even, feudal zero), with the more rare and bulk commodities like salt, herbs, and the donkey coming from Scarborough.

"I got you a nettle and yarrow salve for your cough." He showed me a little ceramic jar. "It's supposed to work better than the mullein but you have to apply it directly to the back of your throat."

I looked at him questionably but said nothing.

"You'll be compliant," he said with a mock seriousness. "I heard you coughing all the way down the hill."

I waved him off. He complimented me on the trench. I didn't ask if he had seen or smelled the smoke from earlier and maybe I should have, but truthfully it was completely out of my mind, I was too exhausted from the day and happy he was back, eager to laugh and get the news of the day, to think up names for the new donkey (Steven, Maurice, Donkey Kong) as we walked back to the house together.

For dinner we ate the rest of a bone marrow we had been cooking off for three days. The fat slipped warm and buttery down my throat, soothing it. A tight grip squeezed its way through my arteries, little bubbles of energy burning off, warming me up. To be so aware of the world working within and without was a thrill and so much of my day was occupied with this, the simple study of sensation. I couldn't help but smile.

Later, when we were getting ready for bed, Simon came to me with the opened jar of gloopy herbs he had bought.

"I'm not eating that," I said.

"You're not eating it. You're coating your throat with it." He sat me down on the bed and sat in front of me cross-legged. "Open up."

"I'm fine now, honestly. Can I drink it as a tea or something tomorrow? I don't want that right before bed. My cough is gone."

"George. I'm your doctor." Simon smiled. "You just put it in the back of your throat, leave it for a minute, then wash it down. Here's some water. The lady at the apothecary said if you gag, that's good, that's what's supposed to happen."

"Fine. I'll be compliant," I said in a mocking tone. Simon stayed in front of me and watched as I took the mixture and gathered a scoop of it with one finger. Carefully, I stuck it in the back of my mouth, which was hard to do without gagging or involuntarily swallowing it all. I caught a taste of it off the back of my tongue—an acidic, tart pepperiness—and winced and choked on it. It went down worse than the bone marrow. The beeswax used to thicken the salve stuck to my tongue. I reached for the water.

"Here—" Simon took the mixture and moved closer. I resisted but he leaned in, close enough that I froze, defenseless. "Keep your mouth open and don't move." He peered down my throat, dipped his finger in the jar, then slowly put it inside my mouth. I flinched but didn't pull away. His finger was steady enough that no part of it touched me until it was all the way at the back and I felt a warm, single impression on the back of my throat.

"Slow . . ." he said. He held it there. My eyes watered.

"It's supposed to sting a bit," he said, but I felt the opposite. A numbing coolness radiated slowly from where he was pressing. My breath warmed the rest of his fingers, which touched against my lips. We locked eyes with each other. We were used to physically tending to each other—like monkeys picking fleas from each other—but never quite like this. There was such a calming vulnerability, a delicate invitation, an entrance.

Something unlocked inside me, something I had been meaning to say—something that was more than anything I'd have been able to say if Simon's hand hadn't been inside my mouth. A silent address passed between us. Seconds of chance, doubt, and hope ticked by. The smallest of smiles was on Simon's face and that was all I needed to ease into one daring, blind leap, and slowly close my lips over his finger. Our movements were symphonic: my mouth closing around his finger, lips puckering and sucking as he gently pulled it out. I tasted the herbs again and finally got their notes of sweetness. Tip of finger touched tip of tongue. Simon's mouth was open in awe. We said nothing. Only continued to stare at each other. Two locked sets of eyes. Simon broke away first, he looked down.

"Here," he said, handing me the water. I took it and drank slowly. My throat felt chilled and I closed my eyes. I couldn't believe what I had just done. When I opened them, Simon was looking at me again.

Looked away.

Looked back.

Took the cup, set it aside.

Looked again.

"Let me see again," he said. I opened my mouth and gave an exaggerated *ahhh* like a patient. Simon inspected and nodded, content with what he saw. "Good boy," he said and gently patted my cheek, then caught himself, as if this was a step too far, and looked away. He quickly added with a chuckle, "This makes up for the last time I had my hand in your mouth."

"What?" I said.

He froze. His smile twisted and turned. He hesitated and frowned. "Come on," he said. "I shouldn't need to remind you." He made a fist with his hand and held it up to me. He watched me nervously and immediately I knew, I remembered. A vale of shame went over his face. That first day. The men who had beat me, tied me up, and taken me in. He and Wulfric. Simon had been the one who shoved his fist in my mouth. The way I had choked, bit down, fought back, and been hammered in return. My jaw was sprained and stung for days. I still felt a pop every now and then where something had been dislocated and healed strangely.

I didn't know how to react. I could see the vexing guilt in Simon's eyes as he realized I had never completely made the connection between him and that moment. I knew he had been one of the attackers of course, but the violence had been so extreme it was like it was detached from specificity. I had forgiven him and Wulfric for the incident as a whole, but that was back before I knew him like I knew him now, as a man sitting across from me, the only man in my life now.

Maybe I was too quick to appease him and sounded dismissive. "You were only doing what you were told."

"I shouldn't have been."

"You *should* have. Otherwise none of this would have happened." My words were feeble because what was *this* anyway? A stone hut on a muddy hill?

Simon wanted to appease and deflect as well. We both wanted to get beyond this, get back to something else. "Well, you took a good chunk out of me." He showed me his hand—there were small scars across his knuckles and thumb.

"Is that me?" I took his hand and marveled at the glossy little stars etched in his skin.

"Yep, all of them." He laughed to break through the shame. We slo-mo reenacted what had happened. He put his open hand across my mouth. I felt the warm calluses against my cheeks, the determined, eager fingers. I had bit him there and in retaliation he had balled it into a fist, forced it in with his other hand and held it there from behind my head. He held the closed fist right against my lips now. Tiny wisps of hairs on his fingers tickled my nose. My lips fit perfectly between the peaks of his knuckles.

Playfully, I nipped his hand. I tried to line my teeth up with the scars. He laughed. We did this slowly in wonderment. Then I closed my lips.

We froze. Simon's hand relaxed. His fingers loosened as his knuckle stayed between my lips. We stared at each other. Waiting. He held his hand there, then rotated it, running it across my lips, presenting his index finger now, unequivocally, which I took inside my mouth. He moved it deeper. I wrapped my tongue around it. He felt along the inside of my cheek, then out and around my lips. We both exhaled at the same time and instead of the air expanding between us, it was as if it contracted, bringing our faces closer than they had ever been before and his lips coming over mine and closing as easily as hands over mouths, fingers between teeth. We kissed. Sensations I thought had been left behind in modernity came flooding back and I needed him, I pulled him closer, his hands already slipping under my clothes, gripping, grabbing, I could have cried, tears threatening to pulse and break with the thrill of a man becoming exactly what I had wanted him to be. A man of my own. But there were already tears, a saltiness I tasted. The wetness was not mine.

"I'm so sorry, George," was all Simon could say as we pushed ourselves together, over and over again, as we kissed necks, lips, cheeks, crying eyes. And I was so sorry too—that all this could have been done earlier, the long winter that had been so long—as I rushed him out of his clothes, out of mine, interlocking our bodies and snapping together but pulling apart, wanting to see every inch of his chest, the soft nipples, tight stomach, hard penis, arms reaching, legs wrapping, heads together, bodies forcing a conjoining, a closeness that had been obscured by so many layers of clothes, of suppositions, unsaid dares and whispered prayers.

Oddly enough, I felt loneliness as we sucked each other off—the sensation of loneliness lifting in and out of me, in and out, of it breaking like a fever and realizing the imprint it had made across my whole life and how for all its weight and terror, it instantly went fleeing into the past, into the future as I came and filled Simon's mouth just as he did so in mine, feeling the warmth coat our throats.

7

I t became suddenly clear that this was what we had been working toward all this time, inch by inch. We had escaped Greenwich and saved each other, but there was more to it than that—there had been this unspoken longing, there had been a goal all along. After all, Simon seemed to know exactly what he was doing when we made love again in the morning, both of us spread out wide and open for the other, a complete newness transforming everything. We had spent every day of the past six months together, only now for the first time we were spending time inside each other, fingers interlocked, sweat on backs and chests, our grip on the day inverted, and everything I thought I knew needing to reestablish itself through unclouded eyes.

The world of Simon opened up to me and the thrill felt nostalgic—our desperate clawing for each other a feeling I didn't think I would ever find out here, yet here it was. We inspected each other's naked bodies in the brilliant light of day. We fucked on the banks of the flooded stream. There was a meatiness to all of it, a brutal humanness that had us both in strangleholds and the thought crossed my mind that maybe this actually wasn't gay at all, just an excise of pent-up maleness. We had spent an entire winter together, hardly seen another soul. More importantly, Simon's sweetness and chivalry seemed in diametric opposition to the concept of gayness and the bitterness it creates in a person—there was no shirking, there was no squeamishness. We held hands in public.

We went to Scarborough together a few weeks after this new dimension revealed itself and we walked the streets arm in arm, hand in hand. Vague fear crossed my mind, but fear was always crossing my mind; I followed Simon's lead. We traded bundles of flax for two sheep, we bought rosemary, lard, a sharpening stone, and rope, and the whole time our glow was showing, a pheromone flagging our coupledom, yet nobody batted an eye. We even attended a mass at the church there and while I felt the natural homophobia of decorum, Simon still slipped his hand inside mine. He held his arm around the small of my back when we were greeted by a cheery vicar before the start of the service.

"Look at you two," the vicar said. He was simple and round, draped in plain robes with minimal adornment like a snowman without a face. He touched us both on the arm. "Strapping young men. Lovely to have you here today."

"We were just passing by," I said, wary—wary right from the start and regretting coming inside the church. (It had been my idea to pop inside because, well, because I was gay and appreciated aesthetics, but there was no such thing as *pop inside* in this world and a church was not an empty tourist attraction. Simon had taken my suggestion nearly as important as our first kiss, nearly as commonplace as boiling water before drinking it.

Yes, of course we needed to take the eucharist, we needed to be blessed, good idea. The flippancy of popping in and taking a picture of a stained glass window with a phone would not exist for hundreds of years.)

Simon took command of the pleasantries with the vicar while I waited for the penny to drop at any moment. The cold water would be thrown over me and all this would come into context. This was Boy Scouts, this was a heightened bromance, this was a Masonic Movember arm wrestle, this wasn't—

"We're lovers," Simon told him.

Maybe he had said "brothers." Maybe something completely different. Maybe the English I thought I had gotten my head wrapped around was all wrong, but whatever he said was enough for the vicar to touch me on the arm again and say with praise, "A budding romance." He winked. "A regular David and Jonathan we have in our midst. What a blessing."

There's a clear misalignment here, I thought. "Budding" as in buddy. "Romance" as in romanticism, as in the glory of the individual's emotional truth, not something shared. We were pals—surely that was the interpretation. The church service itself wasn't even church—not that I had much of a preexisting context, but this was more like a census taking. We worshipped, I guess, but only in the sense that we declared ourselves *present*, we recited prayers, we were blessed and given a sacrament but it felt purposeful like indication, not ritual, like something was being absorbed, physically, into my body, not in a New Agey, superstitious way, not even in a pseudoscientific, born-again way, but like a shampooing of my hair, a stethoscope on my chest, a section of my brain unfolding then recreasing.

It was half in Latin anyway, nobody understood a thing.

But it was novelty, it was mystery, and these things felt accumulated and weighty, pressing down. Any tangible checklist about Jesus and what he did or didn't want us doing was irrelevant in a world where I had spent the past weeks digging holes and making love. It was all just chemicals living this way. Endorphins and hunger, hot and cold, the fever of expenditure and its rewards. Emotions—if you encountered them at all, even at church—didn't nip and gnaw at you like they did in the modern world. They came and went like smoke. I watched the saints in the stained glass windows and it was more entertaining than a film, no longer as terrifying as they had seemed in Lincoln. They moved with the sun. Simon and I discussed them like superheroes. That's Saint Bartholomew, that's Saint Francis, that's the Virgin Mary.

"They look like astronauts," I said. It was true. They each had a perfect circle drawn around their head, painted gold. The halos looked like helmets you would wear in space.

"What's an astronaut?" asked Simon.

"Someone who goes up into the sky," I said. "Beyond the sky, far out into space where there's no air, so they need special helmets to breathe."

"That's what you need."

I paused, raised an eyebrow. Simon added, "For your cough," but somehow my mind had already raced ahead of him, thinking yes, that's what I need because my breath catches on itself when I'm around you. The spark, the quickness, the smoothness with which he could just touch, press, and kiss. Who he was in private was exactly who he was in public. I didn't know how to be like that and I was in fearful awe.

◇ ◇ ◇

What worried me most was that Simon's eagerly honest sense of self reminded me of Callum, a man from the worst (or best) of my days at the financial firm in Canary Wharf. Callum had come along like all the other sales boys selling themselves for favors. Crisp shirts, tight trousers, thick hair cropped close. Callum's "performance" with me was the most successful of all the men, so much so that I can't look back on what it turned into without feeling a flash of severe shame, a disconnection from my own self thanks to what I had contorted into being for him. That feverish anticipation, performance, praying—I recognized too many of those ghosts in how I felt about Simon. Our lovemaking was love making, sure, but so many other things can be that too.

With Callum it started with small things. Pure fantasy on my part. Then real fantasy—fantasy football, which the office ran every year, and Callum, out of all the boys, was the one who finally got me to join in. He got me to treat it seriously, helped me set up a login, cutting through my self-deprecation and irony. He got me to wager serious money.

"You're a stats guy, that's all it is. I need you to help me figure out my team at least."

I need you. I need you. I played it over and over in my head at night.

I wasn't a "stats guy," but I made myself into one for him. My number-crunching hell-job wasn't maths-whizzy in the slightest, but I loved the impression it gave him of me and the power dynamic. I was meek and lowly, he was high and hot.

What I hated—what I absolutely hated more than anything—was how much my boyfriend saw exactly what was happening, counting each one of my tiny self-manipulations, and never did anything about it, never called me out; seeing me watch a match on TV—something I had never done before outside of maybe the World Cup or the Euros—and how my phone would blow up with each goal, my group chat with the lads, my private chat with just Callum. *Gwon that's my stats man! That's it baby! Get in!* He called me man. He called me baby. And I didn't care what he called me as long as I could be just the one word that mattered most: *my.*

Was that all I wanted? To be owned?

I knew it had gone too far with Callum when I started to feel an old familiar childhood craving to hear him say that I was his best friend. Like an itch, I wanted it said out loud, each way, me to him and him to me. We had hiked the Pennines together, we had shared a tent, I had been to his wedding, become friends with his wife, helped him avoid financial ruin at work—he hugged me for the first time that day, then hugged me often, all platonically and I understood that, but we both knew it traipsed on the edge of something else, and that in some moments, all it would take was a certain route, a special formula, where things could be persuaded into something more, some discreet new dimension because the deepness was already there, the emotional fuel was there. I wanted to throw psychology at him: men have sex with each other because they're gay, they're not gay because they have sex with each other—so nothing to worry about, buddy. Easy-peasy. Ease him in. But I never did because that'd be perversion to a tee—yes, much better to crave in silence, boil myself to bits while he danced with me and toed the line, daring me to call him out because calling him out would only prove a thousand points. I couldn't call him out because I couldn't bear to let it stop.

I compromised myself a thousand times, told myself that it

was completely platonic even on my end, that all I wanted was to be his best friend like a chocolate cake with a cherry on top and for him to say it back—just say it, Callum—I could cry how much I wanted to hear those words, which had to be some bizarre emotional fetish left over from not growing up with a brother or an absent father or too much American TV. I wanted my subjugation rewarded and named. But the one thing I swore to myself was that I would never say it first, Callum would have to. Down on one knee. We were so close. We knew each other's birthdays. We knew our star signs and checked in on them often.

Now I found myself lying under those same stars with Simon in my arms—this new friend, this boyfriend? this *lover*?—and I had to tell myself to let it go. Relax. But our hungry physicality for each other had dug up my same old fears, those unsayable words, and I felt the need to pull back. I needed to slow down. One night, we lay out in the field of our smallholding and watched the stars at night and I remained deliberately passive. I collected kisses like clues. I didn't dip into easy ecstasies. I didn't even bother trying to say something impressive about astronauts or the moon landing or satellites and simply relished the fact that nothing was more thrilling than having Simon's head against mine, his voice in my ear, as he pointed out constellations. I clung to the edge of every word—those affirmatives, those directions—in awe of how a man could be so confident and exactly who he was.

He laughed.

"What?" I said.

Simon said nothing, only smiled. His eyes were cheery shadows in the moonglow. I asked again and kissed him like the peck of a bird digging for more.

"I was just thinking," he said, "about how I wished we had figured all of this out sooner. And I was about to ask you: If you could go back in time and change anything so we could have come together quicker, would you? But then I remembered you actually *have* traveled back in time. It's silly."

I smiled. "I've thought the same thing—about how long it took."

"I wish I had said something. I wish I had done something sooner."

"You could have busted me out of that cell quicker." I laughed, and Simon tried, but there was a falter at the corner of his mouth. There was still guilt there.

"I was so scared," he said. "I waited too long."

"No, how could you have known?" I said. I kissed his forehead and looked up at the forest of stars above us, more stars visible than I had ever imagined possible. Night was practically a purple daylight. And there was a silence that suggested every human on the planet was looking up in similar wonderment, all of us so few in number compared to what would someday be billions. "I don't think I'd be able to go back in time and make this any more perfect than it's already been. I wouldn't change a thing."

"Even to avoid all that pain you went through?" Simon asked. "If you had to do it all over again, you wouldn't change a thing?"

I thought for a moment in silence. I had a vision of a thousand copies of myself, all the branches my life could have taken, looping through time. A thousand Georges beat to a pulp, brought to the brink. It had been unlike anything I had ever experienced. I sighed, searching for words. But before I could give an answer—some paradoxical mishmash about how if I had wanted to go back and fix something, I would have already known about it, by meeting myself already doing it, so there wouldn't be a need, which all suggested that the initial instigation came from something external, beyond our control, like all this was *meant* to happen, both the good and the bad—Simon nestled his head closer and whispered into my ear, all too shockingly soon, "I love you."

I did not mishear it. As much as my stomach dropped with unprepared shock, thrilling rush shot through me up and down and the temptation to overindulge was right there. Simon's eyes were too open, large, and blue, asking for nothing, just pouring pure giving, and I said, "I love you too," more as a reaction, like an umbrella for what was pouring out of him. Here was the affirmation I wanted—but I didn't know what *I love you* meant, at least not here, not in this context.

"I've devoted my life to you," Simon continued, and all I could do was look at him. He said this like he expected to hear nothing in return. Maybe he sensed my shock because he took my head in his hands and cradled it to his chest. Each pectoral was perfectly formed and taut, skin smooth beneath his loose shirt, smelling of charcoal and wet stone.

"What does that mean, exactly?" I asked, as abstractly as possible.

"It means exactly that. I love you, and I've sworn my life. I would lay down my life for yours. I would have done so even before all *this*." He ran his hand across my back. "Although this is a nice development." He kissed the top of my head. I looked up at him. I didn't know how to say what I wanted to ask, so I kissed him first. His tongue enveloped mine. I smiled and so did he. No need to pull back and take this slow, George. I sat up and tried to remember what I wanted to say.

"But how does that work?" I asked. "What does that look like out here?" I gestured wildly around the field, at the whole strange reality around me. "Like, are we a couple? I remember you told the vicar back in Scarborough we were lovers, but is that what this is? We're in love and we'll just live here together? Forever? And that's OK?" I didn't know how to avoid sounding rude and completely too modern. Abstract feelings didn't compute in this world. Everything was about satisfying immediate ends: survival, food, shelter, and now there was sex and not just sex but real feelings—amorphous, shape-shifting love. He'd said he'd *devoted* himself to me.

"Are there even gay people? Is that a thing?" I asked.

"Of course it's a thing."

"You're gay." (I said this in as specific a way as I knew how, using all the vocabulary that existed here.)

"Yes," said Simon. "Very clearly, I am."

"You're a man who has sex with another man and falls in love and lives with him as a couple."

"As a companionship," he clarified.

"As a union," I clarified.

"As a union."

"As a marriage?"

He demurred. "Well, not as a marriage because one of us would have to be a woman for that, but theoretically—"

"There, see! That's what I mean." I tapped on his chest. "Where I come from two men can get married."

"What for?"

I balked. "Well, I—don't know actually. Because they love each other."

"Plenty of people get married without loving each other. And plenty of people love each other without getting married."

"I know but I'm just saying there's a difference. Between us. And this." I pressed against him, ran my hands over him. "We each have this idea about the two of us and I worry it's two different ways of thinking—thinking in opposite directions or something—and I guess I only say that because it scares me. Because . . ." I let my voice trail off. I toyed with letting my mind dive fully into this feeling—devotion, melding, giving myself fully into someone else, into the love—but pulled back like a face from cold water. I thought of Callum lying there, feet propped up on my desk, nudging me. I thought of him at the pub, holding court among a hundred devotees just like me, a hundred thousand texts on his phone from a hundred thousand Georges. I rolled off of Simon and stretched. Midnight gnats flew up from the grass. Sleeping sheep nearby swatted their ears reflexively. I helped Simon up and we went sleepily back to the house, where we readied for bed in the dark, not wanting to waste a candle, undressing nude and blue. We kissed, felt, squeezed. I sighed. I looked at the ceiling above us, the bars of shaved timber. "Like, isn't sodomy a thing? A sin?" I asked.

Simon laughed. "Of course it's a sin!" he said and pulled me into bed with him. We wrestled each other and he playfully slapped and shook my backside. "It's a really nice sin. So nice even straight people do it sometimes." He nibbled on my cheek and after more laughter, some flexing and strain, added, "But so is envy, so is laziness, so is dishonesty. So is not showing love to someone as much as you know you could." He traced a finger around my lips.

I stared into his eyes. "The fact that you even say that means you're coming at this from a completely different place, so how do I know that any of this—"

He shushed me with his lips, kissing me deep and slow as if to slur. He kept his forehead against mine, curls sliding. His eyes were closed and he said, "Just listen."

I watched him and listened. I waited.

He said nothing for the longest time, then repeated himself. "Really listen."

I listened.

Outside our stony hut, an antler rubbed against a tree, a fox coughed, and in the thick, voluminous gulf of the sky, stars vibrated, the moon hummed. Before Simon had a chance to say what he wanted to say—that the world out there and the placement of ourselves within it, whether together as a union or apart, was all that mattered, and that if sodomy was a sin then it was a sin like all the others in the sense that sin was a sign of caution, a warning that served as a guardrail between our world and whatever greater thing lay beyond it, both in unknowable great joy and unattainable great peril, and the timeless, crushing responsibility of devotional love—but before he had a chance, he had fallen blessedly to sleep.

His body sunk against mine like a smoldering hearth, logs shifting, embers sizzling. My craven lust for the boy eased into loving splendor and I tried to fall asleep in that contentedness, ignoring the ruckus of second-guessing, the visage of Callum, the longing for signs—the hoot of an owl, the bleat of a goat.

By the time the sun rose, I had reasoned with myself enough to accept that this was pure living, purer than anything I could have imagined in my previous life, and I had to just live, for the first time in my life. I kissed Simon's arms and pulled them tighter around me, moved my lower half closer against his, felt the warming, hardening response, and together we greeted the morning, just as there came a loud and forceful knocking at the door.

8

The knock at the door became a banging at the door. Something hard and metal pounded on it, upending the entire facade of our secluded Eden. Suddenly this all felt like camping, like we were in a tent and had overstayed our welcome. Voices called for us outside. Through the gaps around the doorframe, shadows shuffled in the morning sun.

Simon and I leapt from bed and threw on clothes. I looked at Simon for direction—I had never answered the door in this century. We had no windows to peek out of. Simon grabbed a knife and demanded the person on the other side of the door identify himself.

"John Abbenhale of the Crown Equerry," said a man.

Simon looked at me with bewilderment and shrugged. He slipped the knife under his tunic and went to the door. He slowly unlocked it, then pushed it open fast and wide. Both Simon and the man on the other side stepped backward from each other as it swung open. The spotlight of the morning sun lit up every inch of rustic squalor around us. I squinted.

"Don't move."

Five men surrounded the door with bows and arrows raised. We froze.

The men were richly dressed in decorative armor, which had been strapped together over thick layers of colored fabric. Muscled, stoic horses stood behind them. One man with a sword (the one who had knocked) cautiously approached while the others kept their bows raised and pointed at us. He kept his hand on the sword's hilt and with the other raised a rolled piece of paper.

"Which one of you is George Green?"

I took a second to reply. "I'm George," I said, stepping forward. "Not Green, but from Greenwich, yes." My head was tilted instinctively toward the ground, wincing at the arrows pointed at me.

"Your presence is requested at an audience with His Majesty the King Edward on the evening of the fourteenth of June, in the twenty-ninth year of His Majesty's reign. You will be allowed one horse, no arms of any sort. You are to be escorted into his presence by Piers Gaveston, an equerry to the Prince of Wales, who will meet you in Kirkdale and bring you to the royal caravan stationed at Thirsk."

He handed me the scroll, which was tied with red string and a wax seal. I opened it but could hardly read the handwriting—I could at least make out the date, the village name. I had never been to Thirsk but I knew it was a day's journey west, north of York. The messenger and the other men were already back on their horses.

"Wait, but why?" I said. "What's this for?"

He looked down at me with haughty surprise. "When you're summoned, you're summoned. You can bring your squire if you wish, given current wartime mandates. Believe me, if we knew what the summoning was for, there'd be no reason to summon you."

The men rode away, leaping over our half-built canal. Mud splattered under hoof. It all felt unreal. The richness of the colors in their clothes had made the men look more costume-like than anything I had encountered here. The horses looked like show ponies. I looked back at Simon and he was in a transfixed state of whispered, panicked prayer, eyes closed, head bowed. He was actually jolted by this. "Simon?" Only when the sound of the men was far away did he finally exhale and stop reciting. That old sense of unreality came back to me again—this just didn't feel real. I looked down at the scroll, the thick red wax seal, the expert penmanship. I realized this had to be just as out-of-this-world for Simon too.

"What wartime mandates? Who are we at war with?" I said.

Simon shook himself from his reverie and stepped outside with me. "I don't know. Wales, Scotland, France, everyone." He looked supremely worried. "Let me see that."

I handed him the scroll. He examined it closely, even though he couldn't read. He marveled over the royal seal.

"This has to be about me, right?" I said. "How'd they find us out here? Is this for real, like from the actual king?"

"Yes, it's from the king," said Simon.

"Well that's a relief," I said. I brushed away the indent of a horse hoof on the ground. "I guess . . . we have to go? Do you think we'll actually meet him? How long do you think it will take us to get to Thirsk?"

Simon looked at me perplexed. "Are you not terrified?"

"Well, I'm not *terrified*," I said. "I'm surprised maybe. Intrigued. They probably didn't need to point bows and arrows at us, but it could have been worse. My first thought was they were going to take us back to London or something, so I'm actually feeling quite relieved." I still knew so little about anything. I knew the king was King Edward—the First, although they didn't call him the First because how would they know about the next ones. I knew he was old, that he was on his second wife, that he was tall and ruthless, a warrior king—that's all I had learned about him in my time here. Most people were reverential, almost pious when they spoke of him, but in quieter moments, at pubs, after a long day of work, I had witnessed people joking about him like they would in modern times. Simon was still white in the face, worried and pacing.

I tried to think concretely. "There's some travel implications. We'll need someone from the village to come up and feed the animals while we're away. Other than that I don't see—I think we should be fine . . . I mean, I have nothing of value to offer them, so there's nothing to fear. I'm not afraid of doing something that would upset events in the future or rewrite history or whatever because if I'd have done that, I'd probably have already done it, or something, however that paradox works." I tried to think of what the modern equivalent to something like this would be. A summons from a king would be, well, a summons from a king. But a scary king, a dictator, or something. I felt completely inadequate.

Simon walked away from me, shaking his head.

"What?" I called after him. "Hey, what?"

"You don't care."

"What?"

He turned around. "You think this is a joke."

"Not at all. Simon—"

"Something like this happens and all you can do is think about it with your time traveler brain. You think this is all beneath you. I've seen it in your face before, when we go to Scarborough. You think you're cleverer than them. You're doing it now."

I was completely taken aback. "OK that's not true at all. I don't think this is beneath me." Now I was annoyed. Where was all this coming from? "I'm just saying I'm relieved it wasn't something worse. I thought they were going to shoot us. And I don't know—I don't understand why you're afraid. We get to meet the king. That's exciting, isn't it? Scary a bit, sure, but we'll be fine? Maybe he'll know about Greenwich, or maybe he'll think I'm some foreign whatever, but the second he meets me he'll understand. We probably won't even get that far—we'll meet this Piers Gaveston guy and he'll call it all off."

Simon came back to me fast, right in front of my face. "This is a man who kills people, George. Who tortures people—personally. Pulls them apart into pieces. I know you have your nice friendly old king back in future-land, but that's not what we have here. This is a man who banishes entire races of people—wipes them out. And we're gay, I'm an escaped slave, you're an escaped prisoner and a foreigner. He'll kill me—that I'm certain of. He'll get what he needs from you, then he'll kill you. He'll make his son fuck our corpses."

"You're being ridiculous."

"*You're* being ridiculous!" Simon grabbed me by the shoulders. I tried pulling away, weirded out, but he pulled me closer. "I'm looking in your eyes and I can see it right now—you don't get it! I know how you think, George, I've seen it in how you look at things out here. You're constantly bewildered by regular people out here, you're so in your own head, and yet I'm the one overreacting by—"

"Stop." I put my hands on his arms and held him still. We stood like that for the longest time and stared at each other. Panic and nerves coursed through us. He was right, there was a difference there. His blue eyes were manic and darting all over the place. We shared a common bewilderment at the king's summoning, but bewilderment translated into terror for Simon; only lostness, maybe even bemusement for me. Searching each other for an opposite reaction only made things worse. As I held him, I'm sure he felt the same crude cap, wanting to pull away from me now. Weirded out.

Simon stayed on edge all night and the next morning. No matter what I said I couldn't convince him I was taking things seriously enough. I was—really, I was—but I couldn't summon a fear of death to match whatever he was feeling, I just couldn't. I had nothing to hide and felt we had no other recourse. What else could we do besides comply?

As the weeks ticked by into June, a buzz began to swell in the nearby hamlets—which we visited more frequently in order to keep track of the date, as our own timekeeping methods were never strictly maintained. The royal caravan was coming and each day there was gossip among the villagers about routes the king might take, manor houses he might stay at, and what this all meant for the war—a war no one had really known anything about in the first place, except now was a topic they were all experts on. We didn't tell anyone about our summons.

I began to feel a sense of seriousness—not that I hadn't felt it earlier, but a new kind of hysteria I couldn't square myself with. I felt flashes of it, and anytime I mentioned it, I felt Simon close off from me, assuming I was just doing it for his benefit. Our differences seemed magnified now. Those early days we had spent in bed, that love we had unearthed with such emotionality—it felt like a mistranslation—and when I clung to Simon now, I clung to someone I feared I had completely misunderstood. I looked around at the stony shack we lived in with the dusty roof made of straw, the untamed meadows and impenetrable forests, and wondered really, honestly, was this it? Was this—and I hated how much I needed it to be—normal?

Maybe what I had with Simon was an oddity in this world after all. There were no relationship models around to look to. There was a fraction of the number of people on the planet than where I came from, so there was a fraction of the number of gay people here, which was already a tiny fraction. Even in modern times, all the gay couples I knew still seemed so searching and undefined. If any of them were defined, it was always forced— the most confident-seeming gay couples only the product of hijacked heteronormativity, with their Same Sex Weddings and matching classic rings, their GMO-children calling them Daddy and Papa, cosplaying this life as a Lifestyle in the most derogatory sense. It was either that or the hijacking was inverted, the committed roles reverse engineered into a nonbinary gray soup where nothing mattered, where there were no rules, and tradition was blended into a fluid of purposeful blasphemy—the purpose being so glaring and obvious, the tongue planted firmly in cheek to the point of cringe, and yet it was the whole crux of the union. Prove them right and prove them wrong. I wanted neither. I wanted both. They were nothing and everything. Either way, I felt excluded.

The king's men in all their finery had flagged all the things I wasn't. There was no outside validation. Could a life like ours be so unmarked and simple? *Simon says yes*, I heard in my mind— easy for him to say when all he knew otherwise was slavery. And what about Simon anyway? He had escaped his station in life, but pointedly with me, thanks to me. He had chosen me, some- one who could read and write (kind of), who possessed a capital- ist instinct and Protestant work ethic this world wouldn't see for at least a few more centuries, and maybe to him I was this prized oddity he could continue on with to greater things, sex just a surprising new form of nudging me along. He'd be my "squire" just as the messenger had surmised. I hadn't even thought to correct him.

No—I knew it wasn't like that, I knew it was love—or not knew, but at least felt. There was love, but also there were his eyes, so wide and open, that sense of him pouring into me. A substance like that has to have an end, doesn't it? And a reason. I couldn't help but view it from afar—from London specifically—measure its value, project its quarterly dividends. We had nothing.

"You know you could just stay home," I suggested one night. The summons was only for me, only my name was on it after all, and if Simon was so worried about torture or death, he should stay home. He looked at me blankly and almost laughed me off. It was as if I had suggested he get on a train to Heathrow, board a plane, and fly somewhere else.

"I'm bound to you," he said in reply. He said this without a hint of romance, irony, humor, passion, without any emotion at all. It was a statement of fact and nothing else, like a physical string was tied between my head and his and he was merely recognizing it. It made me feel the complete opposite of assured. I loved him and I knew he loved me, but whatever this thing was—the way he had tied himself to me—I couldn't compete with that. It was such an incompatible way of thinking that yes, in that moment, I couldn't reason with it. To me, that mindset was as much an existential terror as the approaching warrior king.

On the thirteenth of June we packed a small bag of provisions. Early on the fourteenth we tied it to the donkey and embarked on our six-hour trek to Kirkdale. Simon was stony and morose, walking slowly behind me and the donkey. I didn't know how we were going to last the whole journey like this. But before we were too far from the house, Simon stopped walking. He asked that we say a prayer.

I said sure of course—trying my hardest not to sound flippant or ungenuine—and I joined him, on my knees, side by side, while he prayed, which was something we had never done before. He did so silently. I wasn't sure what to do. He said nothing.

We knelt in silence. I listened to the woods surrounding us. I thought back to that first day I had arrived in this strange new world—nearly a year ago. That was the last time I had prayed. That nonsense, primal cry to no one. Well maybe not to no one, I thought, because I couldn't deny that it had worked, that I had been saved. Then again it was still 1301 so maybe I hadn't, but maybe that was my own fault and I should have been more specific, all I had done was sputter and cry. I wondered now, with fear and trepidation, if I should ask for it for once. What if I just wished myself back to modern times? Did I want that? I breathed out and shuddered.

"George, I have something I need to tell you," Simon said. He had finished praying. I opened my eyes and looked at him. He was looking away, into the forest. "I have to tell you about something that happened to me before I met you."

"OK," I said carefully. He was trembling.

"It happened the day before you arrived in Greenwich. It was the night before. And I know how this is going to sound to you, so I'm just going to tell you exactly what happened and what I saw. That night, in my room . . . an angel appeared to me." Tears formed in his eyes as he looked straight ahead. I felt a shudder run through me. I had no other choice but to take him seriously.

He continued. "An angel appeared in my room that night and told me that you would appear the next day, that I would meet you, that you would be my new lord and I should pledge my life to protect you. It said that we'd escape together, that we'd love each other. And that one day you'd receive a summons by the king and that would be my sign—my token that all this was real, that there really was an angel in my room, and that all this was meant to be and I was on the right path. I swear to you, George, just like I've sworn my whole life to you, that this really happened, that there was an angel dressed all in white, a brilliant halo of light—and it told me all of these things that were going to happen and now they're happening and I've reached this point where I don't know what's going to happen next, George, I don't know what's going to happen and I'm afraid." He began to shake and cry uncontrollably. "It's like I don't know who I am. I don't know what's happening to me." He grabbed onto me and I held him there, both of us still kneeling on the ground. His crying made me start to cry and I felt the rush of the unknowable, the mystery of life in all its majesty. I hated how callous I had been about the summoning.

I kissed the back of his neck. I stroked his hair.

"I love you, Simon," I whispered. "I'm devoted to you. I love you and I believe you."

He shuddered in my arms and whispered a heartbreaking sound. I barely heard it. "You don't," he said.

"I do," I said, but through my own tears my voice was warbled and unsteady. I didn't know what else I could possibly say. I wiped my eyes and was resolute. I did love Simon, truly. And I knew we would be all right. "We shouldn't be afraid," I said. "If everything's happening just as this . . . angel said it would, then we're on the right track. We're doing what we're supposed to be doing and God or whoever is going to help us. We just have to love each other and keep going. We know that's what we both want. I love you, I love this home we've made. I'm not going to leave it. We'll be all right."

Simon nodded and rubbed his face, but his upset didn't seem to have reached a clearing. I tried to wipe his eyes and he tried to stand up and pull himself away from his fear but he couldn't. He shook his head. "I just—" His voice broke all over again. "I'm worried. I'm scared. Because, George, I'm beginning to think— I'm beginning to worry—that maybe it wasn't an angel."

9

We made it to Kirkdale at exactly three o'clock in the afternoon, and I knew it was three o'clock thanks to the sundial above the doors of the small church on the banks of the creek where we met the man named Piers Gaveston. If it were any other day, Simon and I would have marveled at the sundial, amazed at such simple tech, and wondered if this church was the same church whose bells we could sometimes hear ring from the top of the hill behind our smallholding, but this wasn't any other day, because this was the day we met Piers Gaveston.

Piers was youthful, clean, and breezy. There was a concerted styling effort in his whole look—the waves in his hair, the buttoned linen shirt, the jewelry—that seemed wholly modern and out of place. He looked like a teenager, actually—the first teenager I had seen out here that I could honestly say looked like a teenager, not some prematurely aged, ruddy thing. He looked soft and faux-gallant, bratty, yet somehow in possession of authority over a cavalry of twenty men who had accompanied him.

His accent was laced with a French inflection and he had an easiness about him, a pseudo-intelligence that I instantly felt the need to measure myself up against. He seemed clued in to something beyond everyone else, with eyes that cut through circumstance, and I guess what I'm trying to say is that I felt, for the first time in nearly a year, self-conscious. Earlier that day I had been crying on the ground with Simon, who had been praying for our lives, but here everything seemed business as usual: you're late, let's get a move on, leave that donkey here, take this horse.

Piers briefed us on the king's movements. His Majesty's time in the county was short, as he had an audience at Durham the next day and couldn't be delayed. His son, Prince Edward, was coming up from Manchester to join with his own battalion, everyone grouping up and heading to the border at Berwick. "So whatever the king wants you for, it must be important. Don't waste his time." We were briefed on formalities and protocol. Piers was serious enough in his speech with us, but also let out a huge, cloying yawn. This was just another day at the office.

As we rode out, people gathered on roadsides to watch us pass. Simon and I had been so isolated, spending most of our time at home, going into the nearest hamlet occasionally or quick trips to Scarborough, but essentially anonymous. Now I felt the buzzing sensation of being perceived. Onlookers watched us, noticed the men we were with, noticed our ragged clothes—clothes I didn't know were ragged until now. I was certain Piers Gaveston and the other well-dressed men escorting us didn't have terrified visions of angels or sloppy theories about time travel. They all seemed to have an insular self-assurance powering their cores, which made them stable, unbothered, eerily modern. I half expected to look over and see Piers scrolling away on a phone, smirking at something on the screen.

Simon had calmed down a bit but remained stoic. He was quick to subjugate himself, obeying our handlers while still taking care of me—helping me with my horse, carrying my satchel—and not in a chivalrous, romantic way. There was an element of debasement to it and I wished he'd stop. Where Piers and the men felt modern, I felt clumsily stuck in the past.

We reached Thirsk late at night. An encampment of canvas tents had been erected on the outskirts of the town and everything glowed orange from within. Soldiers visited and ate around open fires, others were readying supplies and horses for the next day's continuing journey. It was the largest crowd of people I had seen since London and I was reminded again how completely on the outside of things Simon and I had become. Not that there was an "inside" I could be privy to, but in another life it was easier to see the world passing me by on a more regular basis. Here it was a shock all at once.

We got off our horses and Piers took us inside a private tent. We were brought food and ale. Simon and I ate in silence until the tent flap opened and in walked another unmistakable teenager. This one was equally handsome, blond, and his skin was the smoothest skin I had ever seen.

"Piers!" he cried the moment he entered the tent. Piers got up and ran to him and bizarrely, the two of them kissed. Passionately. They kissed each other on the lips and embraced. Simon looked up and watched this just like me but expressed not as much surprise.

Piers composed himself and turned to us. "Gentlemen, I present to you His Royal Highness, Edward, the Prince of Wales."

Simon stood up and I followed. He bowed his head. I did too.

"Prince of Wales. It feels good to say that," said Piers. He kissed the prince again.

"It feels silly," said Prince Edward. He conversed for a moment with Piers, then motioned for Simon and I to come with him out of the tent. Despite his youth, his sense of command was inherent, with no second-guessing. Simon and I did what we were told and followed him.

The prince locked arms with Piers as we strode through the encampment. He spoke over his shoulder to us. "I apologize for the disruption to your lives. My father can lose himself in his fantasies and tends to overdo things. You're not the first unsuspecting peasants he's pulled from the muck for an interrogation and you won't be the last, but you've nothing to fear. He'll chat for a moment, hopefully not accuse you of anything, then get depressed and send you on your merry way. Just don't play into it."

"Into what?" I said.

"Well, the whole King Arthur of it all. He's paranoid about these resurrection stories from the Welsh and his suppression tactics haven't been the kindest. He dug up the king's grave and reburied him in England and that's only made things worse. My new title didn't help things either."

"He thinks King Arthur's real?"

The prince smiled. "That's good! Keep that attitude and you'll be fine. Just don't say anything crazy or agree to anything. Don't mention Scotland. Don't say anything about my dead mum. Don't be Jewish either, and if you are, don't say you are.

Just be normal. Try to speak a little better English too. Hell, French if you know any."

Prince Edward led us to the largest tent in the center of the camp. It was about the size of a circus tent and inside we entered into an expansive chamber that was a far cry from standard military barracks. Torches and silent guards lined the canvas walls and there was sleek wood flooring. The space was mostly all one room, but there were curtains and dividing walls that could be repositioned as necessary to create privacy. There were chests and beds in the corners, rugs and desks. I was overwhelmed.

In the center of the room was a large table, and standing at the table, watching us as we entered, was the king. There was no mistaking who he was—he was the most naturally occurring instance of a king you could imagine. Of course he was king, he was the tallest man on earth. His face was long and weathered. His nose was smashed and crooked but artfully, like a battered Greek statue. His eyes pierced mine with purpose and mission and I felt the orchestration all around him, the machinery of his days filled with appointments, wars, traveling, ruling. It was hard to believe that Simon and I had been huddled up in a stone shack through the dead of winter while all this was going on. All these other ways of living.

The four of us bowed—Piers Gaveston and Prince Edward kneeling, Simon and I crouching hesitantly, unpracticed. I heard Simon's breath catch on itself. It was like we had approached a sentient hundred-year-old oak tree. The king spoke.

"Clear the room." His accent was more modern than anything I had heard before. His voice was low and grizzled. Quietly, the entire perimeter of guards filed out of the tent. As they left, King

Edward reached under the table and retrieved a polished wooden box with gold hinges. He placed the box on the table and looked at me and Simon, then looked at Piers and held his gaze. "I said clear the room."

The prince stepped forward. "Father, Piers has been appointed my personal protectorate and I don't think—"

"OUT."

Piers Gaveston ducked his head and fled the tent without a word. The prince was left aghast and brattish, revealing every one of his few years.

We were invited to sit at the table. The prince plopped down next to Simon and me. The king surveyed each of us.

"You're all children," he said. "George of Greenwich. Your age?"

I had to think for a second. "Thirty-four, sir."

"Your Majesty," the prince corrected me.

The king waved him off. "A man of thirty-four and yet by appearances you must be the youngest thirty-four-year-old I've ever seen. Or perhaps the oldest child. You seem sheltered and protected. Magicked upon or a con man."

"He's not Welsh, Father."

The king raised his hand again to silence his son. The prince flinched and recoiled. Simon and I, for the first time, were able to share a glance.

The king continued his examination, looking me up and down. "Miraculous generation of wealth. Unseemly, impervious youthfulness. Predilection toward sodomy, or so I assume based on the feyness—another sign of magicking." He shook his head. "You're not from here."

"I am from England, yes," I said. "But I'm not exactly—"

"I've studied your relics," he continued. "The clothes of your people, the fabrics. I know the Lord of Greenwich personally. I write to his parish in Ghent and he keeps me informed of the goings-on in his manor—I have an altar on the hill there, you know, a favorite of my wife before she passed. I try to visit whenever I can. I go there to feel peace. To be with her. But suddenly the last time I go to visit, I'm alerted to a cacophony of complaint, about the sudden appearance of this man-child in the wilderness, his strange speech, the foreignness of his clothes, his health, the signs and rumors that have caused such perplexment amongst the townsfolk."

"Father, he's not what you think he is," said Prince Edward.

King Edward closed his eyes. "Child, if you speak one more time—utter one single extra sound—you'll be unhesitantly smitten by a hand that has held clenched all the day's fury."

The prince closed his mouth and sank low in his chair, blushing red.

The king turned back to me and studied my face again. Silence passed among all of us. Then he said one single word that shot violently through me. A word I was completely unprepared to hear.

"Plastic."

It was a jolt. My eyes widened. I took a sharp intake of air, which triggered my cough. I tried to clear my throat, but suppressing it made it even worse. I coughed twice loudly, then tried to ease my breathing and the tension in my chest. Simon touched my knee under the table.

"That's what it is, correct?" King Edward continued. "Plastic woven into the fabrics, mixed with other fibers. You call it plastic. Polyester."

"Yes." I coughed. "But how did you—"

"You've heard the stories, I presume, of the dragon attacks along the eastern coast? You should know, as they're happening in your own back garden."

I said nothing but Simon nodded.

"Have you seen one?"

"No," said Simon.

"Interesting," said the king. His voice was raised. "And interesting that your journey from London has led you up here, of all places, right into the very territory where the dragons have been sighted."

"I'm not sure I understand what connection you're trying to make," I said. "We've been here six months and never seen or heard anything about dragons." I thought about the sudden typhoon of smoke that had engulfed me that day in spring. I glanced at Prince Edward, who was looking at me aghast that I would address the king so brazenly.

Simon cut in. "With respect, Your Majesty, it was I who brought us here. I have an uncle who passed away and left me the smallholding we currently reside on."

"An uncle who was killed in a dragon attack."

"Well I—yes. The nature of his demise was never confirmed, but that was what I had been told. There are always rumors, but nothing we have ever seen."

King Edward nodded, impatient, then stood up from the table. "One of my most difficult, recent tasks is making sure that the rumors of dragons remain just rumors. I've got a war in Wales, now one in Scotland, and always the French, the Jews, revolting Londoners, money nowhere to be found—the last thing

I need is mass hysteria over the supernatural, or worse yet, some symbolic cause for rallying. But lately I fear things have gotten too obvious to ignore." The king looked at me while he spoke. He was contemplating something. He stood silently and watched me.

"Why did you say the word *plastic*?" I asked quietly. "How do you know what that is?"

He smirked. Then he reached into his pocket and retrieved a small brass key on a chain. Prince Edward silently observed this—gone was his attitude, instead he was merely perplexed by what was going on, evidently out of the loop. The king inserted the key into the wooden box on the table, which unlocked with a click. He opened the lid but I could not see inside from where I was sitting.

"The dragon appears when there is no moon," said the king. "And no stars. Sometimes during the day, oftentimes at night. It masks itself with smoke—with a thick burning cloud that covers the land in darkness, washes the earth with an acid rain. That cough you have—that's an unmistakable sign you've been exposed to it already, to the whiffs of its fires, which pour across the country from its Satanic bowels. The magma is unstoppable— the few who've lived to record their testimonies speak of whole villages washed away by it, whole hillsides flattened and rivers split, all mixing into an ashen murk that eventually cools into a barren earth. And inside that earth, inside that filthy regurgitation, there are tiny revelations. Strange metals, glass, melted formulations that suggest a curious diet not of this world."

The king scanned the room, then finally reached into the wooden box. From it he retrieved something foreign and strangely shaped, translucent and twisted, but which only took seconds for me to realize were the unmistakable, charred remains of a plastic bottle of Diet Coke.

I recoiled in my chair, made a guttural sound of shock. I felt ill. Simon and Prince Edward leaned forward and looked closer. The bottle was a mangled mess on the table. It had been twisted, was half melted, and looked like a washed-up jellyfish, but the label was still there, with the red lettering, white and gray, a gray bottle cap, black nutritional facts, recycle me please, a slogan and a promotional contest. I couldn't believe what I was seeing.

"You seem disturbed," said the king.

I felt the same shock of displacement I felt when I first arrived in Greenwich. Chills ran through me.

"You recognize this object?"

"It's a Diet Coke bottle," I said, fighting nausea. The old words were like forbidden incantations. "Coca-Cola. It's a drink—it's. It's unbelievable." I laughed from disbelief. "It's a beverage. A fizzy drink."

"From where you're from."

Simon spoke up again. "He's a time traveler, Your Majesty. George appeared in Greenwich nearly a year ago. He's from the future and I believe him. I've sworn my life to protect him as his servant and helpmate, and I know him to be a decent man, he has nothing to do with this. I love him."

The prince, who remained obediently mute, raised an eyebrow.

"Time traveler," repeated the king. This threw off his rhythm and he didn't know how to proceed. He scowled and looked back and forth from Simon to me. Then he broke into a wry smile. "And whose reign did you time travel from?"

"King Charles," I said. "The Third. And before that there was his mother, Queen Elizabeth. The Second."

The king looked amused more than anything. "Do I capture Scotland?"

"Yes," I said. "Kind of. Well. I don't really know if you do it, but eventually yeah, kind of. I don't know my history very well."

He laughed. "You're too indecisive for this party trick to be believed. Time traveler or not"—he grabbed the Diet Coke bottle and pointed it at me—"*this* is all I know. This matches the materials retrieved during your capture, materials that up until now had only been linked to reports of a dragon. Netlike fabrics that melt into black tar, that emit a noxious blue smoke, that poison the air. Now whether this dragon takes the form of a conspiracy by revolutionaries, Danish invaders, French warships, I really don't care, but what I do know is that I have you, George, and now I find myself in the curious predicament of having tracked down a man who seems innocent enough not to have tried to hide his whereabouts. My men were able to follow your trail of traded goods in a matter of days. They've been observing you for weeks. And perhaps because of that, I'm going to allow you to return to your homestead."

Prince Edward, Simon, and I were all surprised at this. I felt a wave of relief.

The king continued. "You'll return there with my son, the Prince of Wales, who will watch and observe, along with an encampment of troops. And on the night of the next black moon, you will hunt this dragon down and bring it under your control. I'll know this is done by the silence of Yorkshire and the word of the prince. And if I so much as hear a rumor about another dragon attack, then I'll know who to bring my sword down upon."

I was lost for words. Prince Edward seemed surprised as well, as if this was his first time hearing of his father's plans. I tried to reason with the king—I truly had nothing of value to offer. Simon and I had established our little pocket of agrarian peace, and the sudden appearance of a Diet Coke bottle, while truly unnerving and bewildering, had nothing to do with me. What help could I possibly offer? Was there another time traveler out there somewhere? And if there was, what was I supposed to do about it?

"You'll find the dragon and put a stop to its attacks," the king repeated. "And if the slightest foot is stepped out-of-bounds, believe me, my son and his men will dispose of you, your boy, and raze your land to ash."

The prince spoke up. "Father, I will appoint Piers Gaveston to the head of my cavalry to accompany—"

The king sprang immediately across the table and threw a cruel backhand that connected squarely with the prince's face, knocking him back in his chair, nearly tipping over. The prince recoiled in shame, covering his face and blaring red, trying to suppress tears.

"The Gaveston sodomite will not be accompanying your party. He'll be joining me at the front in Berwick against the northern invaders."

The prince got up and stepped a safe distance away from the table before yelling back at his father. "You recognize the union between these two peasants and yet fail to respect the oath of mine own!"

"I respect courage. I respect the devotion of kin and land—

not that of two battle-bored bedfellows. I respect one England, one rule, and men who understand that, not opportunist charmers, and so far before me"—he looked around the room, from his son, to me, to Simon, suddenly realizing his age—"I've yet to see such easy miracles. I'm running out of fools to waste chances on."

He put the plastic Coke bottle back in the wooden box and slammed it shut, then called his guards and servants back inside, dismissing us. Men entered the tent at once. The meeting the king had called—which had intercepted Simon's and my life, sunken it into a month of preparation and fear—was now over. He was ready to move on to the next. I had the vision of a showboating CEO who parachutes into the office for a blitz of town halls, spouting thought-leader clichés, then moves on before anyone can ask what he does all day.

"George," the king called just as we were being led out of the tent. Everyone froze and waited. I turned around. The king sat at the table alone, a gaunt, stretched-out man of a thousand years. He stared at me with an expression that suggested he knew and had witnessed all the world's capacity for folly.

"If you are what you say you are, then erase this history from whatever future awaits us. You ride at dawn."

10

My head was a swarm of nonbelieving thoughts. There was first the rush of living history: seeing a king of England. Then the nonreality of my reality: a medieval warlord holding a bottle of Diet Coke. And there were dragons. No, there was *one* dragon. One dragon and somehow it was connected to the Coke bottle. It didn't make sense how the king had explained it. The dragon was breathing fire and leaving behind plastic bottles from the future? It was littering? And the plan was for me to be used as a sort of bait to find and slay the dragon—but not slay, "bring under control," and what did that mean? It was possible the dragon might not actually be a proper *dragon* but something more abstract, enough of a threat for the king to hear about but not enough for him to get involved directly. What I felt more than anything was my outsider status. Surely I had missed some key opportunity back there, I had misheard something, and now it was too late and I was caught up in this uncontrollable swirl.

I tried to think. I tried to think out loud. But Simon was making himself more subservient than ever, which made me feel more on my own in my thinking, and I was irritated. Still he wrapped his arms around me in our private tent that night. Still he assured me we would find a way through this, he would stand by me, God would provide. He was delusional. God was a clown—that's the only thing I knew for sure now—complete with a honky red nose and an earth full of balloon animals, squeaking and squealing, popping in and out of time.

"He threatened to kill us, essentially," I said, laying out the facts. "To kill us over something we have no control over, something we don't have anything to do with. And we don't know what his son's going to do. We can't have him and a bunch of soldiers coming back to our place. They'll trample the land, terrify the animals. And there's no dragon—there's no such thing as dragons! How are we supposed to satisfy that? It feels like we're being set up."

"What would you like me to do?" Simon asked.

"Stop. Don't be like that."

"I'm here to help you."

"You're not," I said. "What was that back there? 'Servant and helpmate'? That's not how I want you to be. That's not how I see you and you know that. You're not my servant."

"But I am. I've sworn to help you—"

"Then help me understand what we're supposed to do." Our heads were pressed together. "We're getting wrapped up in something I don't want us to be a part of and you've barely said a word. You were terrified of all this before we left and now it's like you're checked out. What changed?"

"Nothing's changed," said Simon. "It's just, in this kind of world, I think whatever you think is probably the best move. This is your territory."

"Simon." I looked into his expansive blue eyes but only saw my darkened reflection in them, the glow of campfire outside the tent. Again I felt that strange distance between us, like our relationship—his idea of what a relationship should be—was completely foreign to mine, and here I was on an upward slope looking down at him, paces ahead of him but lost, completely out of my depth. I didn't want to be served. I had spent so much of my life doing that, lost in the same role Simon was now immersed in—I didn't know how to suddenly be on the receiving end of that kind of devotion. I couldn't be. I refused. I had been the servant so many times before, with all those men, and I would not let Simon become the same. I thought of Callum from work, the way I had melted for him.

"You're too nice." Callum called it out one night.

I had sublimated myself for him just like Simon was doing for me. All that yearning for something I could never put into words, dying for it so many times. *I've sworn to help you*—I had practically said those same words myself.

"No, c'mon, mate. You've done so much for me, George, tell me what I can do for you." Callum had said this to me at dinner with a twinkle in his eye. We were out after work. This was during the zenith of my devotion to him, my servicing, my worshipping. We had been to work, been to the gym, and now we were at a cocktail bar. Eight a.m. to eight p.m. I had spent twelve whole hours with Callum and suddenly with these words, with this look in his eye, there was the potential for something concrete to be announced, a stamp beyond approval. "Tell me what

I can do for you. For once," he said. "Seriously." He reached out and touched my arm.

I froze. Involuntary nerves fired throughout my body and I couldn't speak.

"I've actually never said this to anyone . . ." Callum began.

My heart leapt. I tried to harden the maturity of the emotions I felt clamoring up from inside me. He had recognized my inability to let out my greediness, and he was going to reward it himself before I could even ask for it, before I could plead for it.

"This is kind of personal, so don't tell any of the lads, but . . ."

My breathing stopped completely. I waited. Best friends be damned, we would become something more. I watched his parting lips.

"Alex's dad owns a hotel out in Tenerife and I think I'm going to go help set up and run a second location."

A valve somewhere inside me snapped shut. The waves of intimacy backfired and soured too quickly.

"Who?" I said.

"Err—Alex, my wife. Her dad owns a hotel in Tenerife and wants to open a second location. He's in Costa Adeje now but he's just bought a property on Lanzarote." Callum went on to explain that he was quitting his job at the firm to go run a hotel—or at least thinking about it, or at least, like, maybe, "Depending on our bonuses this Christmas. If I triple my commission after these next client trades, I can pull it off. I've already doubled my target this year, thanks to you." He winked. I stared. "Just kidding— well, not really—seriously, thank you for your help. And that's not to say I don't want any more special George-favors, because I might need some more coming up."

George-favors?

"You're moving to Lanzarote?" I said.

"Tenerife. I'll take over the old hotel while my father-in-law goes and starts up the new one. Eventually I'll get to start up my own if it's a success, and I don't see why not. Location is perfect, right on the beach, and it's only going to get hotter there—warmer winters. Alex is already looking at condos. We'll rent out our place here."

I don't remember what I said next or if I said anything at all—just sort of mumbled a burp and looked around. Glass and steel was all there was. Canary Wharf, the ugliest place on planet Earth. A spreadsheet of empty buildings dolled up with shitty Instagram-slut-hut cocktail bars. Mini-golf and £30 salads.

"Of course I'll miss you," he said. My heart soared and I hated it for doing that. "You've been my best mentor here." It deflated just as quickly. "But hotels is what's always been my main thing, my goal. That's what I was doing at uni before I came here. Remember? We talked about hotels before. George? You OK, mate?"

Best mentor.

"No," I said. I didn't remember. He had never said anything about hotels. What was there to possibly say.

"Ah, maybe I was telling Ollie." So then he started telling me, about how he had worked at a hotel in Dorset growing up, starting in the kitchens—they served fresh seafood, he'd go fishing every morning with his pops you see—working his way up, cleaning rooms, coordinating with tour companies, working the front desk. It was there he learned his charm, he said, his ability to make anyone fall in love with him. He said those words exactly. *I know how to make anyone fall in love with me.* He mimicked his routine: "Good afternoon, darling, let me take that suitcase for you and help you out of your jacket, too nice of a day innit, where've you come from today, you don't look like you need a holiday, you look like you've just come back from one, all fresh faced, you're a cheeky one—you're going to be the cheeky one this week aren't you, you're going to get me in lots of trouble, mind the step, let me help you, take my arm." They would fall for him hook, line, and sinker. Thousands of people are already in love with him, George, what are you thinking.

In the bowels of the fake-flower-adorned cocktail bar, I felt mummified. A glaring neon sign behind Callum read in a swirly font VIBE SHIFT BITCH. He was a blinding pink eclipse. I wanted to close my eyes and unbend my spine, flip backward, and push myself out from under the weight of the Earth and all its gravity and the LOVE that I had let harpoon me.

This empty pang was what I felt as Simon held me now, in this tent dripping with condensation, in this bed unimaginably softer than the one we had at home. It was always Simon holding me, not me holding him. Simon giving me his body's bare warmth and me absorbing it like a cold stone.

In the morning, we rode back home as changed individuals. Prince Edward and ten men, all on horses, rode out with us. The next new moon was a week away and if a dragon was really going to appear, then fine, let it appear and eat us, I dared it. I had no reason to believe this world had anything more to offer than the vacuousness of the one I had left behind, with all its boys and banter. We arrived at our smallholding and the prince sneered at the state of our land.

"If you really are a time traveler, someone should inform you there are much easier ways to live than like this." He dismounted his horse and inspected our stone hut, tested the creaky front door, sidestepped the divots in the clay ground. The fine hem of his cloak was already taking on dirt and dust. He made an adjustment so it wouldn't drag. He surveyed our empty meadows, the canal we had dug, our skinny animals.

"Right then." He sighed. "I'll have my camp in that far corner. Two men with me—my scribe and my messenger—plus three men in the opposite field." He snapped his fingers left and right. "You remaining five, head to Scarborough for supplies. I'll have the constable summon a patrol along the coast. I'll write a letter. I don't want the king thinking we haven't done our due diligence."

Five men rode off and the remaining five unpacked and set up tents. Already they were trampling and slipping over the banks of the canal. The footpaths and trails Simon and I had hewn were meaningless to them. Their horses were shitting everywhere. The prince laid claim to our house, pulling his scribe and messenger inside, slamming the door behind him.

This left Simon and I on our own and at a loss. Any sense of strategy or way ahead was gone. Again that pang, that yawn of grief. Simon looked at me with that look—that nothing look, where had I seen it before?—it was beyond how I had once looked at Callum, it was more like the way my ex had looked at me when we first moved in together: a shrug of empty-headed happenstance. That's what it was. We had arrived at a place, unaware of the finality. Maybe we moved in too soon, maybe we moved in too late. A set of expectations had not been laid out. We had been giddy and freewheeling when it was all decided—am I thinking of now or am I thinking of then?—when we found the place in Greenwich, the place outside York, the view over the river, the creek, the easy commute, the seclusion of the forests, the sunsets, the bathroom battles at bedtime that are so fun and cute at first until the dreamscape erodes into something uncanny, something gray and unclaimed; the goats need milking, the plants need watering. By the end of it all, it wasn't a flat, it wasn't a building, it wasn't a home. It was a hut. A roost for seagulls and spiders. A warren of unpaid bills and now a sneering, snotty prince.

Every year there's at least one suicide at Canary Wharf. A morally bankrupt banker hits pavement, train, marble floor, and for one day a billionaire somewhere in the world has trouble getting in touch with his account manager.

Mine was a slow-moving, deathless self-combustion. It was limbo. It was the sudden realization of the barren earth I had been pouring myself over until I had run out of myself. There was nothing left of me. Callum had taken it all.

But the thing about Callum was that he had a blind spot. That night at dinner, as he detailed his hospitality tricks and how he could make anybody fall in love with him, he couldn't see that he was confessing to all the wool-pulling tactics he had used on me—and that had to be the ultimate sign of a master, that even his confession could still be so charming. This was a cheeky chap striptease of vulnerability and it forced me to reward him even still, to fawn and say, "Nooo, I think Tenerife's a great idea, it makes total sense. I'll make sure the commissions pay out the way they should"—out of control of my own words. I paid for the meal. I felt tears sting the corners of my eyes as I hugged him goodbye and said I had left something back at the office and had to go back. "No, no, you go on ahead," I insisted, and I left. I hid my face as I walked back to our building alone, strode through the lobby, took the lift up. I went to my computer and logged on to our billing platform, the creaky old system we used for commissions and legal money laundering. I pulled up his accounts. I clicked here and there. And I fucked Callum as hard as I knew how to fuck someone. The way I had always wanted to.

I avoided Callum at work for a few days until payday, when his commission was half its usual sum. It took him another week to figure out it was me and what I had done, the avalanche I had started. I was already dead to myself so being dead to him came as no shock. There was no confrontation—there couldn't be one because there was no "right" way to do the wrong I had been doing for him and all the others. Callum simply evaporated like rain on Tenerife. There was no goodbye.

It took another month for a compliance officer to come for me next. A security complaint was raised—a serious one. I was invited to a disciplinary. Several. The clucking henhouse of HR did their song and dance, mental health terminology bandied about like hot pokers. My systems access was downgraded. I felt oddly at peace as my world fell down around me. There was a bizarre comfort in never seeing or speaking to Callum again, how it confirmed my suspicion that I had been used, that these people would never amount to anything more than the amusing little fantasies they projected of themselves onto the walls of the dark empty room inside me.

When everything was over and done, I found myself with the dogs, with the boyfriend about to leave, with the days that never amounted to anything more than a sequence of time and breaths, all while I felt the oddest, strangest sense of contentedness. As wrecked and ruined as I was, I felt like I was exactly where I was supposed to be.

11

There was no plan. There was direction to obey, but no plan. And as the days wore on, it became clear this was the unspoken, agreed consensus among the soldiers and Prince Edward. Dragon or no dragon, we had all been given an order by the king, and here we were, sitting and doing the thing, trying to occupy our time with meaningfulness, but really just watching the sun roll across the blue sky. The upside was that it was finally summer. The surrounding fields shimmied green waves of alfalfa. Our chickens praised the warmer weather and cooed more like joyful parrots than chickens. Crickets, grasshoppers, butterflies, and all the songbirds that feasted on them were sprinkled across every vista like film grain and the only thought I could keep in my mind was "This place . . ." like a sigh. This place, this place, this place.

The first two days, there was an attempt at appearances— ignore the nature and get to wartime work. One of the soldiers tutored Simon and I in sword fighting and how to improve our aim with a bow and arrow. The prince watched us struggle, amused. We'd run military drills, practice combat stances, memorize the weights of different weapons, and avoid the issue of what exactly we had been tasked with going up against. The strictness quickly devolved into lightness and the drills became more like camp games, and everyone looked forward to the nightly meal from Scarborough, which would arrive with great ceremony. Pheasant and chicken and veal—often all stuffed inside each other. Dark liquors over steak-like cuts of grilled vegetables I didn't know were available out here. Wine and mead, wine and mead. This place, this life.

Nobody dared talk about what *actually* the dragon might be. The soldiers seemed to have varying degrees of credulity about it, happy just to be here and not at a battlefront. The prince seemed to have forgotten what we were here for too, distracted by worry more for his absent lover, Piers. He spent most of the days inside, reading and writing letters with his scribe. By late afternoon he'd march around with on-the-fly orders ranging from the position of a tent flap to the stacking of firewood. One day he made us all skinny-dip in the canal, which then became a daily ritual. There was an erotic, masculine charge to everything—the physical exercise, the endless preparation and riling each other up. There was the stiffness of formality and discipline, the wonderment at the exotic mystery of what was to come, and finally the liberation of laughing it all off, stripping down and admitting one's insignificance, jumping into cool fresh water. Inside these rhythms were spaces where even Simon and I could relax, forget about any supposed terror, and enjoy each other. We swam in the canal and wrestled each other, wrestled the soldiers, played games, and lounged. Sunsets danced on the narrow water.

"Look at the vortex," I said. I clung to the side of the canal and stopped swimming. I let the pull of the water take over, stretching me out. "I don't know what causes it." Simon on the other side was pushed in the opposite direction and a shallow swirl formed between us. His face was adorable as he marveled at it.

"We dug the switchback too deep here, so there's an undercurrent," he said. "The water can't complete the turn." He reached his arm like a hook over the vortex and dipped a single finger into the water. "It's kind of beautiful."

"You're kind of beautiful," I said.

Simon smiled. Beads of water glistened off his shoulders and dark curls. Between his eyes, the water, and the sky was an unbelievable blue beyond all blues, and on his cheeks, faint summer freckles had begun to appear like tiny dots on a pear. He swam through the vortex and we kissed. We fashioned a boat made of twigs and watched it sail down the rest of the canal, hypnotized.

By the end of the week, all discipline was lost. The day of the new moon came and we acted as if there would be no dragon at all. If anything, we'd see an environmental glitch like a geyser or a rare spotted owl and all the hearsay would be explained. The dragon would be a vibe more than anything.

Only Simon kept up the combat training, wanting to master the regimental weapons he had been given. On that last day, he stood in the meadow alone with his bow and arrow doing target practice. Everyone else lazed about, binging on leftovers from the night before, watching the day's long shadows continue their slow turns.

"Do you want to fuck?" Prince Edward asked me. His messenger had just left with another letter for Piers. We were lounging in the grass watching Simon practicing farther away. None of the other men around us seemed surprised by what he had just said.

"What?" I said. "No."

"Why not?" he pressed. "You and Simon fuck. I heard you last night. I've seen you running off into the woods together for your private moments. You kissed in the canal the other day. Why don't you fuck one of my men? Or me?"

I laughed. "Aren't you like seventeen?"

"All the more reason to want to fuck me," he said. "It's military strategy, you know, it's good for morale. The Romans kept boys like me as pets back in the day, little trophies to take with them on their battles. Or *you* can be my pet if you want. I take good care of my pets when I'm on deployment." He reached back to a soldier behind him and grabbed his leg. The soldier obediently leaned forward and kissed the prince's cheek, tousled his hair.

"What about Piers?" I asked.

The prince's face dropped. His tone soured. "That's different."

"He's your boyfriend?"

"My what?"

I tried another combination of words for what I meant: lover, romantic companion, helpmate. The prince shrugged but nodded slightly. I didn't have the heart to tell him that although my knowledge of British history was negligible, I knew for certain there had never been a King and King of England.

"You write to him every day?" I asked.

The prince nodded again. "My father sent him to the front,

which means he's trying to get him killed. Pathetic old man, playing toy soldiers like its Anglo-Saxon times. He's looking for formal war where there isn't one, or at least not how he expects it to be, not one he can drum up money for. These Scots are grunts and rogues, compulsive gamblers beholden to barons more than anything else, they don't care about military formations and ceremony, which actually shows they've got something worth fighting for. That's what will get Piers killed—an ambush while my father wanks off to a war dance from his Crusader days."

"He's expecting King Arthur."

"Exactly. That's what I thought he wanted you for, but I suppose he's found a new mythical beast to chase. Giant lizards. You know King Arthur's tomb was empty when we dug it up? We sparked riots across Wales all because of an empty hole in the ground, and for what?" He looked out across the meadow. Simon was pulling arrows from a hay bale. "I feel bad for your little squire. He's cute, getting all worked up for nothing. We'll drink all the mead tonight, look up at the sky, and have an orgy. Then we'll send a messenger to my father in the morning and let him know his precious Yorkshire is safe from dragons and we'll be off. You'll get a commemorative letter at the new year if he remembers and your squire can use it to get your roof fixed."

"He's not my squire," I said.

Edward laughed. "Right. I've seen the way he looks at you. I know that face—I see flashes of it in Piers sometimes. You can spit in it and he'll still call you his man."

"We don't have that kind of relationship."

"I'm not saying anything about your relationship. I'm sure you love each other, but it's a nonstarter with a squire. I get it with Piers all the time. We fight, he bolts, I call him back.

He pisses me off, I send him away, I call him back. He says something out of turn, he pisses my father off, he gets sent away, I call him back. He comes whimpering back to me. His obsession is in his blood. It's sick but that's what I love, that's what I'm looking for. I'm Prince of Wales and I need that. As king I'll need that. The unconditional love I'll have to give to this country—I expect it in return just from one person, one man, that's all. Now for you—a man who doesn't even get to be king? I can't imagine the difficulty. I wouldn't be able to get it up."

I opened my mouth to tell him he was wrong but stopped myself. I sighed long and hard and stayed silent. Swallows and finches chased gnats and mosquitoes. I watched Simon draw his bow back, let go, and hit a clean, pointless bull's-eye. Then I spoke.

"How do you stop it?" I asked quietly. I looked at the prince.

He leaned back and stretched, put his hands behind his head. "If Jesus Christ himself appeared to us right now and told us to stop worshipping him, our belief in him would only be stronger. You need to find someone who's not been raised like an animal, who has his own mind, not just yours."

"Simon's not like that," I said. "He's been spooked by all this, sure, but he's not like that. He's his own person."

"You love him, so you don't see it, but it's there, it's hardwired. Sadly the only way out the other side is to break his heart, really destroy it—which is your heart—shatter his reality and hope he's able to put something of it back together on his own and then maybe, possibly still love you again. He'll come back to you like a dog one final time and hopefully won't bite."

I considered this for a moment, then scoffed. "You don't

know a thing about love." I stood up and felt the eyes of all the prince's bored soldiers watching me.

"I never said I did," said the prince, giggling. "And I've got no reason to know. Love is a peasant's game."

"Is that what you say in your letters to Piers?"

I left him there and walked out into the field, to Simon, who was readying another arrow. He stopped and looked up as I approached. He smiled at me and I smiled back. I paid careful attention to the order of initiation, how Simon reached out a hand first, how he beckoned me close, and I only reciprocated, following his lead, and how serendipitous it felt, as I placed a hand on the back of his neck, and him with a hand on my lower back, and in full view of the prince and all his men and the setting sun, we kissed.

Then the smoke came.

The change in the environment was faster than an eclipse. The setting summer sun was there and then it wasn't. A veil of white smoke spilled across the land as if from a glass. It came from the north, spreading down the slope of the hill, thicker than snow, quieter than silence.

My first instinct was to grab Simon. We held each other at the elbows as the rush of opaque encompassed everything around us.

Prince Edward sprang into what I assumed was legitimate action, yelling around as convincingly as any soldier. He and three other men had already mounted their horses by the time Simon and I found them in the blinding smoke.

"What is this?" the prince demanded. The four of them on their horses surrounded us. One of the soldiers had a bow raised and pointed at me. Suddenly I felt my disposability and cursed myself for not having tried harder to win the prince's favor all this time spent sitting around. Smoke continued pulsing through the surrounding trees and filled the meadows.

"I don't know, I've never seen it this thick," I said.

"So you admit this has happened before?"

"You heard what I said to the king—I know just as much as anyone else. I don't know what's going on, I swear. I always thought it was smoke from our neighbors down in the valley. It might still be that, just burning rubbish, I don't know. It should pass soon."

"This is no rubbish fire. We have to track the source." Despite his quick jump into action, there was an accusatory strain of panic in Edward's voice. He commanded Simon and I to share horses with the two other soldiers and our hands, he commanded, were bound with rope. All trust was gone. Whatever boytalk we had been having only minutes ago was forgotten.

The flood of fog and smoke turned from a dome of muddy orange into a bluer, deeper hue as the sun continued setting, followed by a sullen, darkening gray. We could only see twenty feet in front of us, then only ten. Edward shouted orders that sounded convincingly tactical, guiding the soldiers into a spread-out formation as we rode around the side of the hill of our smallholding to where there was a modest peak on the other side. The idea was to get above the smog, to have a better view of the land and see wherever it was coming from. The prince shouted through the blinding smoke, his voice farther and farther away. The soldier I was bound to followed the slope of the hill, but the horse was spooked and going too fast. Visibility was down to barely five feet. I told the soldier to slow down, that we were nearing the other side of the hill, but suddenly there was no peak and not because I couldn't see it through the smoke. The peak was gone. The ground was going.

Where the peak of a steep hill had once been was now a sudden drop into a vacuum of moving, sinking earth; the land was crumbling, scattering. A wall of sound rang out as if the earth itself was roaring. The soldier I was with had run our horse too fast. It was too late to stop. Suddenly I saw the horse's legs as if they were my own, splayed out, pawing at the air as we went right over the disintegrating, crumbling lip of the ground and went down, straight down. The soldier heaved back, pushing me forward, pulling on the reins, horse screaming, all three of us falling in a somersault into a foggy orange void. The gray fog was orange then red. The ground—the peak that was now a downward slope—came at us startlingly fast. The horse hit first, then me colliding with the horse, rolling over it, with the soldier right behind me, his armor rattling, tangling up with me, all the ropes, hooves, rocks, and the scrambling and tearing of skin and limbs.

The pile of us reached the bottom and came to a final, fatal stop. The soldier was under the horse and both were unmoving. I had been tossed a few feet away and was bleeding—I couldn't tell from where, my clothes were a mess, I was covered in debris, I struggled to right myself. The gummy maw of adrenaline-diverted pain stung throughout my body as I stood up. My ears rang. There was a thundering, roaring bass line. The sound of sliding earth. The smoke was darker and harsher, more saturated with red and deep purple, violent flashes of orange. Smoke gushed, but inconsistently now, varying in opacity with rushes of wind, steam, and particles because I was here, I was at the source.

Clouds of smoke swirled and broke. *It* stopped and started. Something was breathing, something was clearing. There was a parting, and I saw it.

I can only say exactly what I saw, which was first: a spine.

A black jagged spine moved faster than seemed possible only because it was larger than seemed possible. Each exposed vertebrae was the size of a horse, moving and bending as part of a sentient whole being. Earth washed around its frame like tidewater. Its long neck wormed across the ground, with its angular viper head alight with eyes and veins of orange and spilling orange, spilling bright orange molten lava from its mouth, opening and closing, the detritus splattering.

It was a dragon. As clearly as I could understand such a thing, it was that.

I couldn't scream. The air was too scorched. My throat was seized in tight retraction, as if to reject this wild falsehood. My mind flipped through scenario and conundrum like flash cards: snake, lion, man, owl—nothing befitting the creature in front of me that I could only call ginormous, Babylonian, this apocryphal stain.

Black charred lips opened and closed around gnashing teeth, clearing the last of the lava from its mouth. It didn't just breathe fire, it spit hot magma from its mouth like a volcano. Plumes of smoke flooded out from its nose. Then it saw me. Its eyes widened like full moons. Its neck sprang upward and backward into an alert position with startling speed. I don't know how my brain knew to say *move* but I moved right as the dragon pulled back, inhaled, and spewed a new river of destruction right at me. I tripped into a sprint as fire and sparks ran after me. Fire and rock, fire and molten debris—it wasn't a simple line of fire, there were breaks to it, rocky fireballs and liquid lashings of flame. There were seconds where it nipped at the back of my legs and seconds where the flow broke. The dragon stopped. It closed its mouth. I reached the pile of dead horse and dead man and through the flames that now engulfed them, I pulled out the soldier's sword. It was heavier than anything I had expected—nothing like the regimental swords Simon and I had been training with, nothing like a machete or a baseball bat, which were things from a previous life I also had no experience holding. I gripped the hilt and held the sword like a baseball bat—was that what I should do? All knowledge and logic went out the window. The dragon approached and words finally formed—my throat allowed it—but all I could say was "No, no, no!" like chastising a dog off the furniture, a slobber of lava dripping from its mouth. "Go away! Get back!" Still the monster crawled after me, slithered over. I noticed its wings for the first time, batlike and retracted until the dragon suddenly leaned back on its hind legs and both wings unfurled wide. The lake of lava illuminated the leathery screen from behind. The dragon beat them and embers spun in the air. I shielded my face. Like a black swan, the dragon held its neck back and beat the air with its wings, leaning backward and exposing its stomach, which expanded. It was inhaling again. It took a sharp intake of nearly oxygenless air. Its stomach muscles contracted, a groan sounded from deep within, sparks flew from its teeth as it slowly opened its mouth. I had seconds to either dash out of the way or think my last sweet thoughts of Simon, but did neither, wasting them instead on sheer terrorized awe at the size of this thing, at the horror of the mouth as it came down, screaming, exhaling, lighting, ejecting.

But nothing happened.

No fire was produced, no lava spilled.

Through a wince, I opened my eyes and found myself looking straight down the empty hangar of the dragon's open throat, through its sharpened reeds of teeth, and there was nothing. Bits of ash and dying embers fluttered on a faint, hot breeze, but there was no flame, it was a darkened, empty funnel.

A strangely human moment passed between the dragon and I where we shared a cautious, questioning look. Then the dragon sneered, or reconfigured, or rolled its eyes—I don't know what to call it because I don't know what dragons do, because *dragons don't exist*, but this one did and whatever it was doing wasn't any less threatening, flames or not. It was angry now.

I dropped the sword and ran but tripped. I backed up. I crawled. I held up my hands in a plea for mercy, or an acceptance of futility as the dragon lumbered forward, claws and teeth at the ready, just as there came a flash of new metal between us. Something ran in front of me. A soldier and his steed. A blinding slice; or a cut, sliced blindly. The dragon whipped its head around. An arrow flew through the air and missed. Arms enveloped me, grabbed me like I was the last thing on earth. I grabbed Simon back, both of us suddenly barreling away, neither one of us able to speak or cry, the air having evaporated all sound, and our muscles, so feeble and spent, faltering as we scrambled up the crater's slope, avoiding stray flames and pockets of magma, avoiding a man's body as it flew through the air and crashed to the ground, clawed and bitten, blood like I had never seen before, dragon behind us again. I felt the pulse of displaced air, the snapping at our heels, the frustrated breath, bottled snorts of disgruntlement and strain, the dragon wheezing, then the shouts of the prince over there, flagging us down, the monstrous footsteps behind us growing slower, quieter, almost—in some strange way—contemplative, like it was deciding it had something better to do. Then its footsteps disappeared altogether. I dared to look behind me and with just as much disbelief as when the dragon had been there, the dragon was now gone, lost in the vacuum of smoke and sinking earth. And just as resistant to breath and life as this moment had been only seconds ago, there was now only just that: the inflation of collapsed lungs, a last gasp of hope, a getting the hell out of there. We fled.

12

I don't know what I would say to someone in the past. I don't know what I would say to someone in the future. I thought myself a rarity up until that point—that singular moment of solitude I had experienced in Greenwich, when I first arrived in 1300—how like a coin I had felt, slipping through some impenetrable fabric all on my own, the terror of that loneliness and how it was edged, I'll admit, with the smugness of being chosen. But later, in 1301, in the summer, in northeast England, all of us had seen it. Simon, Prince Edward, three soldiers—two of them now dead—and myself. We had all seen the dragon. The world I thought I knew had tilted by another degree.

We all retched and mourned privately for our ideas of reality that were fracturing and splitting open, but we confronted the impracticalities together—namely the lapping lake of fire the dragon had left behind, the magma it had been spitting. We needed to get out. The lava was spreading. We ran across the border of the crater's crumbling lip, away from the sliding rock and ash, feeling the earth still making adjustments. I felt like a bug-man, a pitiful shrew with no legs to stand on, not a time traveler who had slipped through the fabric of the universe but an idiot who had tripped, a glitch in a system that had made him permanently its mite, of which there were already millions, scattering, sprinting away like fools, passing out and coming to, then passing out again.

The four of us woke up to a deathlike white morning along the shores of a smoldering pyroclastic flow. We nattered and stuttered, paced, but mostly sat on the ground, exhausted from the adrenaline that had petered out and put us to sleep. We wondered how long we had been out. We poked at the ashes with our swords. Two surviving horses stood shell-shocked and black against the rising sun. No one mourned the other horse. No one mourned the two other soldiers.

Simon and I were the most levelheaded. I had time traveled, so I already knew what sick surprises the universe could pull, and Simon was the innocent who already believed in such easy magic. I thought about the angel he'd said had appeared to him back in Greenwich. I thought about the dragon's hulking frame in the middle of the lake of fire and magma. I didn't know how to prioritize my levels of disbelief.

We all took turns vomiting.

The lava flow cooled and hardened into a thick black scab across the landscape. I scraped the skin of the ground with my sword and it ripped open, spitting bright orange magma from the vein. It took my breath away—literally sucked the oxygen from the air, leaving a dense sulfuric scent. My lungs burned and I coughed.

In other places, the cooled magma was already flaking away into ash. Reams of gray fluttered into the air like paper, and for a moment I thought it actually was paper, or plastic, or some kind of man-made material, and when I looked closer: I saw that it was. Butterflies of something unnatural. Something wasn't right. I dug my sword into the ashes. Black broke into white, into uneven chunks of material. Burning things. Metals. Dripping puddles of—

"Look," said Simon. He raised his sword. Speared on the end of it was still-burning, melting and deformed, but very obviously a plastic bottle, dripping into ribbons like tipped wax from a candle.

My stomach dropped. I riffled through the ashes with my sword, coughing and spitting ash. Flames sparked anew, smoke flowed and cleared. The magma was not completely viscous. Parts of it were thicker and broke apart in chunks, melting slower. Materials burst into flames, thinner plastics melted and seeped, fibers and wires bent and stretched, but all of it—the entire pool of flaming earth—was junk.

"It's rubbish," I said, out of my mind. "It's . . . a tire?" I noticed the pattern of the treads in a thick slab of rubber that curled and smoked in the air. Over there was a broken bicycle. And a toasted, cracked computer monitor. There were metal buttons, nails, plugs, iron and copper and steel. And a kettle, a fan, a storefront sign, chair legs, screws, scaffolding, LED panels, bells, pill bottles, food packaging, little plastic baggies, plastic bottles, plastic forks, plastic shoes, plastic watches, plastic phone cases, plastic remotes, plastic pools of goo that dribbled red, purple, translucent, fluorescent, silver, and gold.

"This is all just someone's rubbish," I said. "It's like the dragon was throwing up garbage. It's rubbish from—from the future or somewhere and it—hey, where are you going?" I looked up. Prince

Edward and the surviving soldier were mounting their terrorized horses. I ran over to them, dragging my sword, which was coated in melted rubbish.

"I'm not built for this," said the prince. "Dragons and sorcerers and lakes of fire are all good ploys for politics, metaphors, whatever—but this—this is something else. Yes, I would deem this a legitimate inconvenience." He gave his horse a reassuring pat.

"So you're just going to leave us? After all that?" I said.

"I'll ride to Scarborough and inform my men."

"Can we go with you?"

"No. But I'll ensure a battalion is raised immediately and sent here, I'll also write to the king. You'll be in safe hands, trust me, I'll put in a good word with the regiment. You'll be treated with the highest regard."

"Wait, stop—I don't want to stay here," I said. I tried to step in front of the horse but it kept moving forward. "Don't just leave us. Take us with you."

"And have two more witnesses drumming up hysteria? No. This thing, this whole misadventure, needs real sorting of a kind I'm not equipped to provide. But believe me, it will be dealt with before my father rides south again. And if it's not, well then . . ." His voice trailed off. His face was white and gray. The horse sped up, looking straight ahead. The other soldier followed, leaving Simon and me on the banks of the smoky bog on our own.

The dragon was a giant dragon. The dragon was spewing molten piles of what appeared to be rubbish not from this world—or maybe from this world, but from a world I thought I had given up.

It was in the fire. It was in the lava. I thought about mummifi-cation. I thought about bog people—about bodies buried in peat and acidic mud, preserved for thousands of years. I remem-bered a trip to the British Museum as a child, my face pressing against a display at kid-height, breath steaming the glass be-tween me and the dark-orange skin of a man curled up, mouth torn like a nightmare, eyes missing but watching me. That same millennium-spanning gaze watched me now as I dug through branded litter. Coca-Cola, obviously. Apple, Estée Lauder, Tesco, Shell, Pepsi, Intel, Sony, and a host of others I didn't recognize, their functions more or less the same, in plenty of different lan-guages. Arabic, Spanish, Korean, Chinese. Some languages I couldn't recognize at all. I was losing my mind as I dug, and the only thing that kept me from coming completely undone was Simon's almost nonchalant mentality. He was shocked by the dragon and the magma, sure, but only shocked in the way you would be after seeing a tsunami or a train derailment—something horrific but ultimately grounded in reality, something you wouldn't struggle to recount to someone who wasn't there. He just didn't get how it felt for me.

"So these are things from where you came from?" he asked. Something in his voice sounded hollow and staid. Even though Simon believed who I was and where I had come from, the future didn't factor into our daily lives—and now that it very clearly did, there was no way of negotiating the gulf of perspective between us.

"They are, but they look different," I said, trying to distance myself from the distance between us. "This looks like a micro-wave, which is something that cooks things without fire, but I don't recognize the brand—the company that made it—and the style is weird." We watched it sink into the boiling slurry. The ground was still hot and angry and we stepped back. Our clothes were drenched with sweat. The edge of the hardening lava touched up against a blackberry bush, instantly catching it on fire. The flow was finally slowing down and stopping its expansion. The crater was settling. The ring of the surrounding woodland was like a silent, staring stranger, the edge of reality. And where was the dragon in all of this? Had it flown away? Had it vanished off into the future? Was it coming back?

"Why did you want to go to Scarborough with them?" said Simon.

"Don't you?" I said. "It makes the most sense. We spent a whole week with them, I thought they'd still need us. The least they could do is give us a place to stay or something."

"Our house is still fine, we're miles away."

"I know, but who knows what will happen when that thing comes back. I thought they'd help us get away from this at least."

"And abandon our home? You think we've earned their favor and now we're good to go? We'll just pack up and move to Scarborough? Become members of court?"

I looked at him mystified. "I don't know, Simon. But I know there's a dragon now."

"We knew there was a dragon before. I knew, even the king knew."

"Right, but now we *really* know. And I know for sure that Scarborough exists in the future more or less how it exists now, so I know we'll be safer there than staying here and doing nothing, and it seems more beneficial to stay with a prince than not. If a prince ever got killed by a dragon—if *anyone* ever got killed by a dragon—I think I would have learned about it in school."

"My uncle was killed by a dragon. You knew that." Simon looked at me the same way he had when he very first encountered me on the road to Greenwich. A look of complete foreignness. Disbelief at my speech, at my disregard.

I exhaled. "Yes," I said. "You're right." Ash blew between us and the two separate worlds we inhabited. Spurred by Simon's unexpected snippiness, something hesitated inside me before dropping out all at once: "But we also knew there was an abandoned baby in the middle of a forest last winter and we did nothing about it. The world's full of surprises."

"What?" Simon's eyes darkened. "That has nothing to do with any of this."

"It has everything to do with this—we could have done something, but we didn't." Emotion burned the back of my throat. The words were too far gone to take any of them back so I kept talking. "We left a baby to die. I was too shocked to realize that's what it was, but it was. We could have done something. Well now I'm doing something."

"We couldn't have done a thing." Simon came back with fighting words. "It was winter, we barely had any food. We could have died ourselves and it's a miracle we made that journey alive, don't you dare put that on me, George. You don't get to play your little routine and pretend you didn't know any better, or you didn't understand what was going on. You chose to move along, just like you're choosing to move along now and run away to Scarborough. You're just as guilty as you think I should be, but I'm not, because that was about survival."

"Going to Scarborough would be about survival," I said.

"It's not," said Simon, "and you know that. Going there would be giving up. Which is something I know comes naturally to you."

Hot, angry tears stung my eyes. We had never spoken to each other like this before. A sick part of me almost enjoyed getting to see this new part of Simon and I felt a wicked expansion of my heart. I didn't know what else to say or do besides shake my head and hear Prince Edward's words repeat in my mind: *You need to find someone who has his own mind, not just yours.* He couldn't have been any further from the truth. Clearly Simon had one.

We trudged back home through the ashen wasteland. The direction of the wind had saved our neighboring hill and woodland from complete decimation and slowly the greenery came back, the air freshened up, the sky became blue again. Once we looped around the hill, down the slope, our house was the same as it ever was: the mossy rock walls, the slow evaporation of steam from the thatched roof and how it caught the morning sunlight, our animals in their pens, which were all fine—if they sensed some new, fire-breathing beast at the top of their food chain, they didn't let on. The only noticeable intrusion was the space Edward and his men had occupied in the meadows, where the long grass had been trampled down. Their tent was still there, abandoned. Who knew who would return to occupy it again, and how soon.

Simon and I spent time apart over the next quiet days of recovery—apart only because of the distance I had thrown between us so quickly, so blindly.

I worked on fixing up the banks of the canal that the men and their horses had trodden over. I cleared ashes and leaves out of the water, reestablishing the flow. Then I went across the meadow and tended to the hedgerows that bordered our plot and had been neglected for days. I marveled at the speed with which they had turned unruly. I had spent all spring tucking their woody tendrils inward, weaving a wall of branches that didn't follow any formal pattern, and now I regretted it. A summer explosion of offshoots and leaves cluttered the whole hedge, threatening to strangle itself. I needed a saw but we didn't have a saw. I needed a hatchet but our hatchet needed sharpening. What I needed was a motorized hedge trimmer. What I needed was a phone with an app I could use to hire someone with a hedge trimmer to come take care of the hedgerow.

I tossed aside the blunt hatchet and instead went and got the heavy sword I had taken from the dead soldier. It was still coated with tentacles of melted rubbish from the dragon, but I knew a sharp blade was still underneath. I swung it at the hedgerow blindly. I swung hard, not like a baseball bat or a golf club, but like a sword, whacking at branches while making a note in my mind that this was something I would need to be able to do—I needed to train these muscles. I needed to accept that this was a reality that required holding swords, gripping and slicing, feeling the strain across my back. This was my world and this was where I would be. Stay, George, stay.

Why was I so beelike and distracted, even out here in man's most natural state? Look how easily I could be swayed by modernity, by fine clothes, clean bodies, logos on bottles. I had let one week with a dumb, horny prince distort so much of what I had held dear. I had let self-consciousness—a relic of another age—still be the driving force of my inner compass, even when I had everything I could ever want and nowhere I would rather be.

I have everything I want, I said to myself, as limbs of the hedge went flying. I said it again. I knew I wanted Simon. I wanted our land, our life together. If anything, *I* was the one tailing Simon, clinging to him for my own advantage, not the other way around. But the arrival of the prince and his men, the dragon and its force-fed memories of the future, had discombobulated me once again into a shame I didn't know what to do with. I hadn't been paying attention.

As I butchered the hedgerow, bits of charred debris broke off the sword. Rocky gray chunks fell apart, revealing rubbery veins more stubbornly adhered to the metal. I went and got a knife from the house—ignoring Simon and Simon ignoring me—came back to the hedge and carefully sliced and unpeeled the remains of what appeared to be a long white extension cord wrapped around the sword. Jesus Christ. The white rubber had melted and hardened into a flat smear across the blade and on the underside were glimmers of hairlike copper wires like the bones of a fish—all it was missing was the nubby head of a USB or a charging plug, ugly and incongruent with the greenery of the hedgerow. Someone, somewhere, was looking for their charger. Hah. I choked on a sad laugh that stung with vomit in the back of my throat. This triggered a coughing attack and I hacked up a clot of wet gray ash across the goldenrod ground. Tears pulsed behind my eyes as I held the extension cord aloft, my brazen serpent, so despicably easy, so antithetical to how the world was supposed to work. Who needs the oath-like balance of exertion and reward when all you need is a charger, free Wi-Fi, free refills, annual leave. What chance does the miracle of a hedgerow have against the splendor of an EasyJet flight to Spain, an arrow shooting across the sky chock-full of manchildren plugged in and streaming—airplane not just an airplane but a flying phone charger. Did anyone give a flying fuck? That right there was obliteration. That was blue hands grasping across dirty sand.

Pure magma. Pink and orange lights cutting across sandy divots of shadow. Nightclub wails muffled by crumbling stucco walls.

Back in Sitges, in Spain, on that boys trip from hell, on the beach outside the club that awful night decades and centuries ago, I smoked a cigarette and wished I was drunker, wished I was more numb and on my way to forgetting the whole city existed at all. I felt the filth of it—the litter across the sand, clubgoers stumbling along, every drink just a warm dreg or a broken bottle, a crushed can. I sat on the beach alone. I assumed the ocean was out there somewhere, but probably with its back turned, just as embarrassed of everyone as I was. I felt shame. I felt internalized homophobia, which actually felt good and self-soothing in a way. Then I felt shame for being ashamed of things I wasn't supposed to be ashamed of anymore. Some imaginary voice in my head saying, "Umm that's internalized homophobia, you should get that sorted out."

My boyfriend and our friends were still back at the club with the strippers. They had seen me leave and probably assumed I was just stepping outside to smoke a cigarette, which I was doing, but through bewildering tears and with no intention of going back inside, no intention of anything but sitting in the middle of the beach and waiting for the ocean to come crawling back, pull me in, and pummel me to its depths.

The throbbing music behind me grew louder—a side door opened. A shadow cut across the orange streetlight-stained sand and I watched it grow longer, nearer. Smoke joined mine. Vapor, actually. Fruity flavored. I turned around. It was the same stripper I had just seen come onstage. He wore a pink thong now, and took a long drag from a disposable vape. A dire peach-vanilla scent washed over me, which he made no intention of blowing in any other direction. I raised my eyebrows but nothing else. I had seen all there was to possibly see of this stranger, and I had nothing to say.

"You didn't like my show?" he asked. He remembered me. We had locked eyes back there but surely I was just another lost soul in the crowd, just as empty-eyed and vacant as he had looked to me.

"You got cum on my shoe," I said.

He smirked. "Workplace hazard."

This eked out a smile in me. I wiped my teary eyes as he stepped closer and sat down beside me. Up close his body lost its stagecraft splendor. There were razor bumps on his thighs. His muscles were impressive, but like rocks in a plastic bag, like they weren't quite adhered to his body properly. A few stray wrinkles near his eyes betrayed the whole act. I stopped myself when I realized the same critiques could be made of me. I hated myself.

"Sorry," I said.

"For what?"

"I don't know. For walking out on your grand finale. It's been a weird week."

The dancer shrugged. "It's all right. It's probably not fun to watch something like that on your own."

"I wasn't alone. I was with people there, they were just on the other side of the stage."

"You're just lonely then."

"Sure." I flicked my cigarette into the sand in front of us. It landed filter-side down so the fading ember kept burning. It looked like the beach itself was smoking. The dancer finished his disposable vape and tossed it into the sand as well. I thought nothing of this. What was one more vape tossed into this litter box of a beach, where the sand itself was litter, imported from some foreign quarry. The dancer stood up and brushed sand off his butt cheeks. He stretched, knowingly, and made to leave but I suddenly wanted him to stay.

"Do you do that every night?" I asked. He must have sensed the tone of desperation in my voice because he smiled and spun around. He stepped back so he was standing right in front of me, looking down at me. I watched the tight bundle between his legs.

"Just sometimes," he said. "I usually get a little *assistance*, if you know what I mean. But tonight was all natural, if you can believe it." He looked down and adjusted himself, revealing for a moment the smooth base of what I had already seen. "That's probably how it was able to hit your shoe. The jet propulsion of willpower."

We stared at each other in silence. He knew my words were all backed up in my throat. Words that had been sliced up and held in reserve, from days and years of conversations cut short or mis-said. He possessed a conniving kind of patience, that smirk on his face, the tilt of his head, when I looked him in the eyes and asked, "What does it feel like?"

"It. Feels. Like . . ." His voice held on to every syllable, making each one last as long as each slow step he took toward me. When he was right at my feet, between my legs, he knelt down. "It feels like the very edge. It's the brink." He placed his hands on my knees and ran them slowly up my thighs. "Everybody's watching you but you're up there alone, practically anonymous. You could be anyone, really—even though every part of you is on display. Your very DNA is up for grabs. And maybe that's what it is: hell. You get that horrible shame feeling, but it's a curtain that comes and goes and before you know it, you're through it and:

ahh, bliss." He grabbed me, up through my shorts. "You were in heaven all along and nobody bothered to tell you."

"But that's what makes me so sad," I said through a moan. "That nobody bothered to tell me. I'm out the other side but I've brought all the muck with me. I can't push through it and pretend it's not there—like it was never there to begin with." The tears were back in my eyes, pulsing in rhythm with his moving hands.

"Oh, but you can push through it," he said. "You must." He pulled my shorts off, lifted my shirt, lifted my legs. His thong was off and tossed away into the sand.

"I can't."

"You must."

He tasted repugnant. The hint of peach-vanilla on his breath was like a chalk drawing on the wall of a cave, a horrid representation of beauty. His body was just fists under slippery seal skin. Both he and the music throbbed inside me, growing louder. Shadows crossed the beach and he was lost in me and my vicious loneliness. I knew a crowd was gathering and it made the thrill of it all the more intense, the shame all the more heavy, the curtain whipping me left and right. My boyfriend's voice. Laughter and cheers. Then applause as I came onto stinging, sand-rubbed flesh and I can confirm that what the dancer said was all wrong. We were always and still in hell.

SECOND EPISTLE, concerning the contents of a foreigner's wardrobe

Written by the hand of EDWARD by the grace of God King of England, Lord of Ireland, Duke of Aquitaine, Conqueror of Wales, Hammer of Scots

ighty-six percent recycled polyester. Fourteen percent spandex. Made in India. Machine wash cold. Tumble dry low. Keep away from fire. Wash dark colors separately. Do not soak. Do not iron printed part. Color may rub off."

That was what the writing on the small white square sewn into the lining of the garment said. This was among the evidence sent to me by the Lord of Greenwich, leading to my tracking and summoning of George and all the madness that ensued. It took four days for a translator to decipher the characters and make the translation, making no reasonable interpretation beyond what I could easily surmise on my own. I knew of greater India and had seen garments of similar brilliance among traders during my pilgrimage to the Holy Land in my youth. The multi-deity beliefs of those in the Hindustan regions would account for the word "polyester," with *poly* meaning multiple and *ester* a derivative of ether, the unknowable substance of God. "Spandex" could be the joining of *span* meaning the span of time and *dexterity*, giving credence to

George's assertion of time travel. I know George did not hail from Hindustan, but religious inference seems a legitimate line of inquiry, given the circumstances—but why such markers would be plainly written and sewn into a garment makes no sense other than an aim to intentionally dissuade. And I don't believe there's a single man on this Earth who hasn't the predilection to deceive me.

When the Prince of Wales returned, he ambushed a meeting of my war council in a grotesque display of emotion, barging into the room, clothing soiled, his frame like that of a rattling waif, more insult than son of mine, demanding his crusted rag of a lover before all else:

"Where is Piers? Where is Piers? It's real. It's real, Father— Your Majesty. Apologies." He twaddled into a bow. I stared. "It killed two soldiers. Its tail stretches through fields and fields. Its eyes are like meaty discs. Its face, a small planet, the weight of its body, heavier than our own, it crushes through the earth, and the fire. God almighty, Father, like heat, like sweltering, like I don't even know. And Piers? Where is my Piers?"

I banished the prince and ordered silence. I ordered the rug where he had stood cleaned. I ordered a censuring of the council and a full testimony to be taken from the soldier who had accompanied the prince and also borne witness to the beast. He was more coherent and of a sound mind and recounted the creature's appearance, its destruction, all with admirable articulation beyond his rank. He was a natural believer, unlike the prince, his steadfastness keeping him on the faithful side of hysterics, and I applauded him. I noticed a scar stretching from his ear to his temple and remarked upon it.

I said that if he had managed to survive whatever Welsh demon had given him that injury, surely this English one could be brought under similar submission.

The soldier replied, "Aye, this? No, Your Majesty, it's not from beast or man, Welsh or English. It's from an unfortunate incident when I was small, back in Lancashire. My sister had hoisted me up to tie a bale of hay and when I jumped down upon her in jest, we both failed to see the scythe resting there on the ground, improperly stored. Just the unlucky business of children, I'm afraid, nothing remarkable—still something we're both lucky to be alive by. And even still, I'd have been just a wee lad during the Welsh campaigns, barely fit enough to strip arrows let alone accompany Your Majesty in a vanguard."

I asked the soldier his age and he confirmed he was only twenty-five, saying the number in such a way as all youth do—no one more obsessed with being young than the young themselves—and I felt every single one of my sixty-two years. A reflexive fury pulsed through me and the soldier took note of this, apologizing for his forthrightness and excusing it by saying it was only because we had spoken before, actually, at Falkirk. He had been a spearman behind my archers.

"It was after Falkirk that I was awarded the patronage of your son," he said, "for my bravery and the great success we had there. And whilst the Prince of Wales is no Scottish horde, some nights when he calls on me to his chambers I can attest to a fear not unlike what I felt as a spearman." Again he apologized for his forthrightness before my anger could boil over, but I was more stunned at the gall that possessed him to speak in such a way. Before I could react properly with anger, my sensibilities turned neutral and staid—a first. I tried to summon the memory of this soldier at Falkirk but saw only wanton rivers of blood, the leaves and grass they mixed with, how the eyelids of boys wouldn't close.

I dismissed the soldier and returned to my battlements, thinking not on the Prince of Wales's hysterics, nor the soldier's report, but on the image of the soldier as a child, climbing and falling from a bale of hay, thinking on my own children's travails of youth, the majority of which go unreported to me, my long separations from them, how this must have warped them for the better and the worse, again feeling the solidity of all sixty-two of my years.

All abated rage reignited days later at Lindisfarne of all places, on that holy island, where I discovered the Prince of Wales once again in the arms of the Gaveston sodomite as if the pair were on a bridal tour. I flew into a deserved fury against the both of them. Gaveston fell in line immediately, of course, shielding his modesty, groveling. Of the prince I tore clumps of hair from the scalp, pulled his neck and throttled it, feeling my own line of succession falter beneath my grip—and let it be so: I have Thomas now, and Queen Margaret again with child, and plenty more heirs to come. I forced him to look at the way his lover had so quickly filed behind me, how his filthy allegiances swayed and teetered by mere proximity to rank. I shook the boy like all of the boy he was and he wept and wept.

My intention has always been to temper the boy, to cease the hysteria that only pushes him further into those duplicitous arms that know nothing of sacrifice, nothing of valor, nothing of brotherly love, only the romantic. I told him love was the last thing that would save us. And love drawn like blood from a stone, well that's just humiliating. I spat.

My Eleanor, the boy's mother, died when he was but a child and it's as if a child he has stayed. I mourn for the nation the lasting indentation this must have made on his psyche. My new dear Margaret, though a worthy wife and mother, is more closer in age to be the prince's sister than mother, and is no guide for his lack of wit, his inability to think linearly, his mind too amorphous and dyeable by the mores of others. "Color may rub off." That's what Gaveston has done, the legal thief, the heart stealer. He has tainted my son not with the spoiling pleasures of sodomy, but with the constant taking, the ruinous humanizing, the desecration of our calling, making this all but an adornment to masturbate. He has taken my heir's heart before he has had the opportunity to consecrate it for another, let alone a nation. "Keep away from fire." When I mourn at the cross for Eleanor, I mourn for that loss. The loss of a goodness the boy will never know, and the sharp pain, that intake of stilted breath I feel, of knowing I am not blameless. For if my son will one day become me, then what have I been that hasn't been enough? What have I not been that he will also one day become?

13

I became an archaeologist of the future. I began taking trips out to the lava field alone, scavenging, and for what, I was afraid to really say. I broke our shovel breaking ground. I went to the nearest village and bought a new one and spent whole days out there with it. Not that there was much to dig up. But if I dug deep enough, clunked hard enough into the burs of magma, they would crack in half and reveal an etching inside, some petrified barbaric logo or a screw, wires or the remains of wires, coat hangers, melted engines. If there was copper or any sort of refined metal, I'd take it home so we could sell it. If there was plastic or something strange, something I couldn't put my finger on but was sure it was a shape, a semblance of something, I took it home as if just to say *look. My people.*

"How about you take the donkey with you next time and bring back some of the rocks," said Simon, sounding like the apotheosis of everything I never thought he would be. "It's volcanic. It'd be good for the soil here."

"I think I've found an entire car," I said. I was lying on the ground in the middle of the wide-open yard.

"I don't know what that is," said Simon.

"It's like a donkey but made of metal. Up to five people can sit inside it. You can fill it with your groceries."

Simon was performing operatic busyness behind me, sweeping dust out of the house through the open front door, moving misplaced cups, stools, cushions, making a racket while the rest of the summer pulsed around our little snow globe of a life. He chewed on a skinny birch twig while he worked. He moved it from one side of his mouth to the other, annoying me. He asked, "How would five people get inside a donkey?"

I didn't respond, just stared at the sky, at the sun still up there. It was July? August? It was late in the evening but the sun was still smack in the middle up there. I had once loved these long days of summer back in London—Pimm's and lost Frisbees, men running around half naked in parks while their girlfriends watched and wore, inexplicably, prairie dresses—but out here these days were sixteen hours of haunting stasis, filled with labor, endless labor, pointless labor, digging and digging. I picked at new blisters that had formed on my hands and wondered when we would see a dragon come soaring across the sky.

There was a whole-ass dragon out there. Wow.

I worried about how much I cared. My reaction to the dragon had initially been that of shock, but as these empty days of recuperation continued with no news from prince, king, or dragon, a cognitive dissonance took hold of me where I knew I wasn't feeling the right kind of terror. Part of me wondered if whatever the dragon was doing—did it matter? Even if the dragon was some kind of time-traveling monster, I knew it had no bearing on my life because I knew that in the future there were no dragons. There had been no world-ending invasion by a dragon in 1301 because there simply hadn't been. There was a dangerous freeness in the inconsequentiality of time travel and it made me feel too loose with everything else. If dragons were a problem, then I would already know dragons were a problem just like I knew Oliver Cromwell would one day be a problem, like Henry VIII and Brexit and cars, nuclear weapons, pandemics, the internet, and confusing internet bills would all be problems— these would be things of more consequence than a giant dragon appearing for a few hours in the remote English countryside once a month. I felt a sense of security in knowing nothing mattered. I didn't know how to convey this to Simon without it sounding like a horrific, nihilistic gasp.

"Don't pick," Simon said now, watching me inspect my blisters. "You didn't want gloves, well now your hands are growing a pair on their own."

"Will you bring me my cough syrup?" I asked. Again, we spoke at each other like buses on mismatched routes, flashing broad black and yellow words, no answers, just questions and demands. He brought me the jar of nettle and yarrow, but took a pointedly long time, exhaling loudly. He tossed it to me on the ground and then finally sat down, only not next to me, in a pile of hay instead. He rubbed his face and looked straight ahead at the treeline beyond the meadow. I wouldn't say things were icy or irreparable between us but there was this distance, and boy did it look like a chasm when the never-setting sun hit it like this. On my side of the rift there was my place in this world—and consequently my place in Simon's life—and whether I truly belonged in either of them. On Simon's side—well, I don't know. He was too far away.

I coated my finger with the green slime and shoved it down my throat. I tried not to trigger a wave of coughing, which had gotten worse since the dragon attack. There was a permanently wheezy, ashy taste in the back of my throat, and I struggled to catch my breath if I exerted myself too much. Simon still helped with it, keeping me well supplied with herbal concoctions, but the romance of his care was gone, replaced with rote tenderness, tossed jars. We still made love and shared a bed, but Prince Edward's warnings reverberated in my mind with every act of reconciliation.

You need to break his heart. You need to shatter his reality and hope he's able to put something of it back together on his own.

I continued my trips back to the lava field to dig, spending whole days out there, where lay all the reverberations of everything that had fallen between me and Simon, all of the things I thought I had left behind, entombed in rock and ash, and what choice did I have but to excavate them, to make use of them.

The land didn't look like England anymore. The ashen plane had taken on a pale gray, almost lavender hue, and the hardened ribbons of lava looked completely alien, which helped me accept my own foreignness here, my helpless self-pollution.

The "entire car" I thought I had found was more of a hunch. It was the outline of a windshield, then the frame of some kind of sedan, a place for a door, another door, a few podlike rocks in the shape of what could have been wheels before they had been eviscerated in flame. I cracked one of them open to reveal what looked like, if I held it at the right angle, the outline of a hubcap. After three days of digging I had exhumed the whole perimeter of what I thought was the car. Sweat coated my face, bringing relief from the ash. No birds or insects accompanied me and there was hardly any wind. Even the thwacks of the shovel sounded hollow and muted, not echoing out across the crater. By the time the sun was a notch lower than the great height it maintained all day, I knew I had worked too long and would be late getting back home.

Home. Hmmm.

I sighed.

"OK," I said to no one. (I hadn't brought the donkey like Simon had asked.) I filled a satchel with some of the aerated rock, but it felt too heavy to drag back on my own, so I left it over by the shovel. One of the rocks rolled out of the bag and hit the shovel, knocking it over. When I went to stand the shovel back up again, the ground around me sunk. It was as easy as that. The ground impressed itself deeper by a few inches—not dramatically, but enough to startle me. Dust flew up. There was silence. I didn't move. Then, with complete disregard, I fell through.

The ground had been deceitful, a brittle roof caved in. I landed painfully, ten feet below onto a new plane of earth under its crust. All the parts of what I thought had been a car shattered and rained over me in chunks of pumice and stray metal. I held my breath and waved away the dust and ash, coughing.

I had fallen inside a shallow lava tube. The ground here was smoother, less possible to break with a shovel, and black with a moonlit sheen despite the sun overhead. The tube continued into a twisting, downward slope, opening up into a larger cavern, which I entered, amazed. As the lava had cooled and hardened and the landslides settled, these deposits of empty space must have formed, sealing themselves up. The walls would have been cool to the touch, but now exposed to the sun, they were warm.

I realized I was bleeding. Not from any one place in particular, but I felt soreness and stinging pain. I had landed poorly. I wiped blood off my leg, then wiped blood off my hand onto the obsidian wall. Then I realized I was crying. I was crying because I had wanted to call for Simon, but he was miles away. I was weak. I had had so many things wrong all this time. We had survived because we were together. But now I was out here and he was back there and he was so far away. And just when I thought I could wrestle my emotions onto a sturdier plateau of reason, the ground, once again, fell out from under me.

Black obsidian shattered. Gravity pulled me gracelessly. I plunged even farther into the earth, sliding along with an uncomfortable mixture of rock, glass, metal—as close to a liquid as those solids could be. I landed with an unsettling plonk, triggering nausea and blurred vision. I braced forward in a prone position as real pain flared out from within me. Droplets of tears and blood mixed. Everything was dark and spread out wide. Sunlight only trickled into this new space like fine grains of sand dashed across a black expanse until in front of me—right there—two fiery orange eyes opened. Awakened.

Each pupil was a narrow slit as tall as me, each horn, claw, and tooth the size of a dead tree. Its mouth was ajar, half open like the folded remains of a sunken battleship—not as if to eat me but as if to pause in thoughtful repose before speech, because after I cried "Oh my god" the mouth moved. Lips closed and opened. Teeth shone. A tongue shifted. Noise emitted. Actual words.

The dragon spoke.

It said, "Now how did you end up here?"

I shrieked and cursed. Echoes of my screams bounced off the cavern walls. The dragon said "Shhhhh," like a steam engine. Smoke poured from its pursed lips, and I broke into a flurry of hacking coughs.

"Let me see if I can guess," said the dragon. It unfurled itself and moved closer to me. It bent its head down. It sniffed me. My clothes and hair flew upward, sucked in the air. "I would guess early 2000s. Definitely post-1950, but the smell of entropy is strong—you've been here a while, haven't you? Over a year I'd say. How've you managed to survive for so long? How've you found me?"

"You can talk?" I gasped.

The dragon rolled its boulder-size eyes and leaned back. Its body was doubled over itself, rolled up in folds of craggy, armored skin, so rocky and worn it wasn't clear where dragon ended and earth began. "These conversations are always tricky," *he* said—his voice rumbled with a devilish, male baritone, deep and throaty. "I know I'm probably causing a certain emotional reaction right now, but please understand that this is just as novel an occurrence for me. Don't spoil it with shallow quibbles. Yes, I can talk. You should hear me scream." His mouth didn't move much when he spoke. I imagined some organ the size of a house deep inside him, punctured with intricate flaps and holes, emitting such a booming voice.

"You've been here this whole time?" I surprised myself with the question, but it had been over a week since the dragon's attack and I had been out here every day digging things up. I remembered how the dragon had disappeared into a void of ash and smoke—we had never seen it fly away.

"I try to get a few weeks of sleep between feedings," he said. "And I prefer the underground, where I won't be disturbed. When I was smaller, I used to sleep in trees. I could perch like a bird and no one would be any wiser. Now tell me, where did you come from? What's your name?" Gone was the dragon's ferocious violence from weeks ago, all of that energy was condensed into a leering, sniffing eagerness. Despite his size, he squirmed around the cave with ease. His tail moved like that of a cat, snaking around me inquisitively.

"My name is George," I said. "I came from over there." I pointed vaguely over my shoulder, disoriented and overwhelmed. "On the slope of the next hill over, a smallholding a few miles away."

"No, no, no—your time. You time traveled. I can smell it on you."

"What? Yes. Right. I time traveled." Adrenaline coursed through me. I felt my forehead and it was ice-cold. My ears were hot. "I came from here." My mind blipped for a second. "But not originally. From London before. In the future." I struggled to find the words that would give an accurate account of my story. Breathlessly I told the dragon about the moment I had time traveled, waking up in Greenwich in 1300, spending a whole year here. He was stoic the whole time, nodding along. He was a terrifying, horned monstrosity, but he was calm and listening. It was like I was speaking to a travel agent about a holiday that had gone horribly wrong. It wasn't clear if he had ever had an interaction like this before, but he didn't seem shocked or surprised by anything I said.

"Spontaneous time combustion," the dragon muttered to himself—but even his mutterings were loud enough to reverberate in my guts. "Mental torture, emotional duress, heartbreak. Any number of combining factors can create ruptures and random collapses, which unfortunately only helps prove theories about entropy. You're just a bunch of dust mites at the end of the day, so what if one of you flies through the window."

I noticed the dragon's accent. It was unplaceable, but it was clear and modern, that was the most notable thing about it. There was a calm, orderly tone to his voice, almost like a customer service rep explaining a tech issue. It gave me chills.

"You can time travel too," I said.

"I can," said the dragon. "I can come and go as I please, though I try to move sequentially when I can. I'm five hundred and fifty-five years old and often lose track of where I've been. Sometimes I've run into myself—have you ever talked to your literal self? It's uneventful. It gets paradoxically boring because of course it's a conversation you've already had with your other literal self who said the same things before you, to you, ad nauseam. Still, it's refreshing to have company, seeing as I'm all alone."

"You're the only dragon?"

"Only one there's ever been. I've seen my own birth, no brothers or sisters. I've seen it all. But not often a human in your predicament."

"But you have before? There have been others this has happened to?"

"Very rarely. Spontaneous time combustion can occur only once in a human, organically at least. My own father was a human, actually. I remember an egg breaking and a man's hands. I would sleep outside his house in a tree." The dragon paused here and exhaled a ponderous line of smoke like from a cigarette.

"Hey, I can take you back if you want. To your own time period. Name the place and I'll take you there, go on, I'm dying to know."

My breath caught on itself. Through all the shock, I hadn't considered this. "How does that work?" I asked. I was weak and unsure. "You can just time travel whenever you want? How does a dragon show up in the future and not cause chaos?"

"Future? There's no such thing as the future." He chuckled. The cave walls shook. "And I have agreements with the places I travel between, at least, with the places outside the entropic zone. My agreements are mutually beneficial, so nothing is disrupted. We're harmonized and recyclable."

"That rubbish you spit out, the fire and the lava—it's all stuff from the future."

"Yes, but there's no such thing as 'future' in the way you're thinking of it, George. You imagine a clock ticking by—I can think of no worse invention than a clock. In reality, time is its own living beast. It has a space which it occupies. Think of it like me—time has a head, time has a tail, time has appendages that branch out from its body and grow, it's always growing, always moving forward." The dragon extended an arm and flexed his claws. One clench of his fist could pulverize me.

"And you're able to travel across this body of time," I said. "You can travel to a place that's more forward in time than here. And what do you do there? You go and eat their rubbish, then come spit it out here? You're some kind of bin collector for the future?"

"I have my feedings and I have my expulsions, yes. They create a system of balances across time for all parties. I fulfill a need that the world would be missing otherwise."

I shook my head, unbelieving in this practicality. "You took out a whole hillside the other day. The people here are finding bits of trash from the future—the king knows about you. Doesn't that cause problems? Where I came from there's no such thing as dragons, but I'd imagine if you keep doing what you're doing it would cause some kind of reaction." I was drunk on a delirium I had never felt before, words just slipping out of me. The threat of very immediate danger—the dragon's tree-trunk fangs, its rocky hide and slithering tail—couldn't be disguised by the trickery of his more humanlike personality.

The dragon furrowed his brow. Large reptilian platelets folded upward and he shook his head. "No, no, no, that's not how it works, George, because there is no future. That's what I'm trying to explain without causing you too much distress. What we're in right now, this is called the *past*. While your survival out here is commendable, it's slightly misguided because you're only an echo. Time has a head and a tail, and this is the tail. Imagine a shooting star hurtling through space: there exists, at only one point and time, the present. This world, even the world you came from, it's all just the afterburn image of the present. The present is all there is. That's where it's all happening."

I had the sudden remembrance of stale coffee, dry cleaning, and industrial air-conditioning. "You came from the future?" I asked. "How does a dragon—"

"I came from where I came from." The dragon smiled a devilish, fanged smile. "I'm also half a millennium old. Time itself is where I'm from. You're wondering how a dragon could exist in the modern world—well what, George, is a modern world? I could ask the same of you. Why would a man willingly send himself even further from the present?"

"Well, it wasn't willingly," I said. "And I think what's considered present is pretty subjective. This is the world I'm living in and I'm very much alive."

"I think you'd be surprised by all the ways you're not," said the dragon. He winked. The wink failed at being "knowing"— a pinkish, translucent membrane slipped horizontally across his eye, under the main eyelid, reminding me just how much of an animal he was. My cheeks flushed with warmth as blood rushed through me in different ways. I felt dumbstruck and without any words to say. Well, I did have words to say—I wanted to ask, "So you're saying nothing in the past matters?" but the words felt too unreal to utter. The crisp modernity of the dragon's speech had struck something inside me, knocking me off-balance. His mere existence seemed to denigrate everything I had built in the past year. Everything was up in flames.

"So tell me," the dragon said, "I can't wait any longer. What year have you come from? I want to see if I've guessed correctly."

I actually had to think for a second. I shook all weariness from my head, how clouded I was with disbelief and exhaustion, and then I said it: "2026." My voice cracked. The number sounded like an epithet.

"How queer." The dragon—the enormity of him—smirked. "And what a shame. Right on the cusp of the entropic zone." He moved toward me. The bluntness of his pointed snout, the sharpness of his jagged teeth, his snake eyes, all of it made me back up, but his tail was in the way. A wall of leathery skin hedged me in on every side.

"What's the entropic zone?" I asked.

"I think you already know," the dragon said. His eyes did the opposite of twinkle. "And I think you'd better get back to your smallholding."

Suddenly I was lifted up. Ten, twenty, fifty, one hundred feet in the air. I was taken upward in the fastest lift in the world, even though the dragon must have been moving comically slow in comparison, carrying me with both hands as you would a prized piece of glassware. With his tail he broke a hole in the weakened roof of the cave, and the sun, for once, was not shining. The horizon was awash with dwindling pink. Simon would be worrying about me, and I thought to myself almost as if in the voice of the dragon, *how pedestrian of a thing to do.*

The dragon set me on the ground. "I'll be leaving for my next feeding now," he said. "I'll return to this place in a few days' time and I'll have to do my expulsions again, but after, if you catch me before I fall asleep, I can send you back to your own time. I'll speak to my people and we'll get it sorted. Twenty twenty-sixxxx—what a mouthful. Delicious." Only his craggy, twisted head showed above the surface of the earth, like a smiling, eager crocodile.

"If I want to come, what do I need to do?" I asked.

"Come to this cave after I've finished with my expulsions. Come alone. It won't work on anyone who's never time traveled before."

"But what do I do? What happens? We just disappear?"

A jet engine took off: "HAHAHA." The dragon's bellows stormed the sky, dashing pebbles and rocks away from us in pulses. "You're too naive for a time traveler," he said. "If only you could be so lucky as to simply disappear—no, that's a luxury reserved for me. For you to be able to time travel, my new little friend, well . . . I eat you." I flinched. The dragon's forked tongue flitted in between its needle teeth. "I slurp you up like a noodle in a soup—like a noodle stuck in a—what do you call them? A straw? Like slurping through a straw. I gobble you up. I swallow you whole."

14

"What is George going to do now?" I heard it said in a thousand voices as I ran from the crater. I had to scramble up the slope to get out of there but it felt like everything was downhill, like I was fleeing some almighty mountaintop, banished from on high, legs flipping over each other, hips out of socket with the speed and momentum of divine terror. There were a thousand questions I should have asked the dragon—*asked the dragon!* the idea was absurd—questions that bordered on pure admin for this insanity—about diet, time management, environmental factors, where the hell does a dragon actually come from?—but nothing was enough to distract from the throbbing pain in my stomach, the nausea tinged with an immense sadness that had opened up with the dragon's offer.

"What is George going to do?" I heard it in my mother's voice, digitized and pockmarked with bad reception. "Everyone's wondering what's George going to do." This is the story of how one man lost everything, then still managed to find some more things to lose. Job gone. Boyfriend gone. Gone like ribbons of sand across the shower floor, gone like the sands of time itself. And now a dragon, a snake.

"You're saying he just up and left in the middle of the night?" Mum said. I hadn't called and told her this in tears. We were only talking because of a letter she had received from a debt collection agency trying to contact me. "You guys didn't have a fight or something? You don't have to tell me." Everyone wants to know. No one wants to know.

I remember rolling my eyes. "We're always having fights," I said. "I guess we fought on our trip to Sitges one night, but that was a while ago." We hadn't actually. That was the one night when we should have had a fight, but we didn't. Why does a person leave?

"You don't have to tell me." That was how she did it—situate the lever just right, pry enough to lift, but *stop*, look away, don't tell me what's underneath. Spiders or snakes or dragons, you don't have to tell me. You look under there alone.

Now I was alone, clambering up the slope of the crater in darkness, a wretched bouquet of decisions behind and before me. I was too afraid to put them into words.

I remember the helplessness of that night in Sitges, of washing and only finding more sand, more layers of sun cream, my body a sandcastle lapped up by the tide, crumbling down the drain, and wishing I could do that too, break down and slip away. Or just drown.

Fuck stripper on beach. It was as if it had been scheduled on our itinerary. Tick. My boyfriend's reaction was not the end of our relationship, but the beginning of the downward spiral that ended with me coming face-to-face with the dragon, the devil himself. He (my boyfriend, not the dragon, but then again, who knows) made no show of things, even giggling along with all the other boys back at the beach house, watching a video of me and the stripper fucking in plain view. "Wait, pause it," I remember saying, so I could admire myself. I couldn't tell where the stripper ended and I began, an oatmeal of pixels and grime. I forced the guy who had filmed it to delete it, then forced him to delete it from his Recently Deleted folder, seeing it in a lineup of bad selfies, bad food pics, bad sunsets. We all felt the proverbial thump on the shoulders of it being gone, and the shame of having almost said out loud, "Can you send it to me first?"

What were we living for?

I wished my boyfriend had been angry or cold or even fascinated, anything. Instead he acted completely normal—not even acting like *nothing* had happened, but accepting what had happened as casual fact, an occurrence, like weather changing. He was in bed on his phone, scrolling through regular things. Mindlessness. We talked about tomorrow's flight home, remember to check in, where should we eat, what was the weather back in London; so afraid of sin that we had excluded ourselves from any narrative form and become these magnetized bobblehead ah-hyuck-hyucks. I almost said, "So that was a crazy night," to get some kind of closure at least, but I knew that doing so would only claw back all the airy words we had used to blow ourselves so far away from each other. And part of me was afraid of what he would say in response: not anger, not sadness, but something worse. "Yeah, that was pretty crazy, George. G'night."

What is George going to do you don't have to tell me. All in the same fucking breath.

I craved reality, I craved punishment. I wanted to believe

in the universe's counterbalances and that the vicious gluttony of having sex with a stranger on a beach had a calculable heft to it that eventually would swing back into me; something deeply human inside me had cried out for this, and look, finally, it took seven hundred years of time travel and a five-hundred-and-fifty-fucking-whatever-year-old dragon but I finally had it. I had wished for a world of consequence and raw humanity and I was given one: beat, imprisoned, living in shit and met with life's limits in a land where morality was a tangible, foreseeable element that interlaced all things. When I moved, Simon moved. When I moved, a dragon appeared. This wasn't God-fearing obsessive compulsion, this was gravity and evolution. Love, commitment, consecration—these are mechanisms with more command over the world than anything else, and when I had reached a point where I had so exempted myself from their reach for so long, they had pulled me rapturously through time itself. I deserved everything that was happening to me and more.

I looked back at the crater and saw the dragon's whole frame emerged from the earth now and I threw up. A ceramicist's gray splattered the ground. It felt incredible actually—a euphoric mixture of endorphins and adrenaline slid up and down my spine and I felt mania, crying until I was laughing, laughing until I was crying, here on the border between hell and home.

Did I want to go home?

And which one was that?

In the distance, the dragon stretched its magnificent wings, a silent, blackened moth. It stretched out its body, shook out its hind legs, laid its neck out long, and yawned—but it held its mouth open, it didn't close it. I held back and watched, waiting for fire or something, but there was nothing. He held his mouth open while resting it on the ground. Then I saw something. A figure ran across the crater's open plain, running toward the dragon. I squinted—it was a person, a man. He was dressed all in white and he wore a helmet, a round, circular helmet, not like a helmet from here because it wasn't metal, it was glass—and there was a light. An electric light. I gasped at the sight. The figure was unnaturally lit up with brilliant white against the dark blue dusk. For the first time in a year, I was seeing an artificial light. Inside the man's glass helmet, a ring of light illuminated his way forward as he ran toward the dragon, which was still holding its mouth wide open. When the man finally reached the dragon, he went—*what?*—yes, he went inside.

The man ran inside the dragon's mouth.

The dragon closed its mouth.

And then the dragon took flight. The largest bird on planet Earth flapped its wings. It hardly needed to run for takeoff, only needing to catch the slightest breeze with its sturdy sails. As soon as it was fully airborne, it reached a speed I couldn't make sense of, like it was both sprinting in place and zooming forward. Its body both stretched out and magnified itself. There was a blur and a contraction as it shot across the sky, and then it was gone. It disappeared like a fine loose thread pulled free.

"What is George going to do?" asked Mum, third-person, saving all parties from direct confrontation. I hung up.

Twilight bloomed around me in the forest, all manner of green things had turned blue, spreading coolness and leafy sighs. Oak trees towered over me—I had never seen oak trees this tall in modern England. Perfectly vertical lines of thick timber went straight up to the moon, where they exploded in a symphony of branches, squiggling in the sky, going every which way. Wood creaked and leaves fluttered and shook. And down this corridor of trees, appearing in flashes and spurts at first, was a torch. Light approaching. My man. What had I done?

I cursed. I wiped my tears and cleaned my face but this triggered a new wave of upset, a horrific self-pity and shame, and I had to wipe that away as well. I walked toward the light, steady but completely unsure. I walked toward Simon, but just seeing him made me cry again, made me run to him. I crashed into him, we embraced. In a perfect world we would have both reached the same apologetic conclusion, but I'm afraid mine was . . . I'm afraid . . . I'm just afraid.

"I'm sorry," I said. All I could do was say it over and over again, speak over the fear of the idea that roamed on the very edge of my mind. I wanted both of us to fall through the earth, no explanations, just meld and melt away. "I'm sorry, I'm sorry, I'm sorry." My heart snapped like a magnet to all the different ways it could betray Simon at the same time as I nuzzled my face into his chest.

But Simon was in tears as well. "No, I'm sorry," he said, and the pain of it twisted inside me. "You're right, we have to get out of here. Let's leave. Let's go to Scarborough or back to London or York. Let's run away and start over."

As much as my heart soared with how much of him was back in my arms after our days of distance, it dropped just as easily with what horror my mind had wrapped its slithery folds around. "No, no, no," I cooed. "You were right all along. I think we need to stay. We need to defend ourselves. We're meant to be here. This is our home." I tried to assure him. I don't know if what I was saying was a lie. I'd like to think I didn't know what I wanted yet, that I just needed a minute to think. I wanted to hide behind that minute for days. But we had run out of time.

"No—seriously, George—I don't think this is our fight anymore." Simon's face was white and sharp in the dark. "We need to get out of here because they're all here now. The army is here. They've arrived."

Human plague had swept over our smallholding. The land was barely recognizable. Prince Edward's abandoned tent had expanded into a sweeping festival of men, nearly as big as the king's battalion at Thirsk. A sea of men and horses and battle equipment and filth littered the land. Their occupation had come as instantaneous as if they had arisen right up from the ground.

"They arrived a while ago," said Simon. "While you were gone."

The men had come from the most exhausted front lines of the north. Like Prince Edward's harem of men, this new regiment seemed relieved at their dispatchment out here, a respite from the real war going on elsewhere. The men were joyous. This was a party. One of our sheep had already been slaughtered and was roasting over a fire, there was music, buckets of mead, the ground muddy from the overflowing canal, ruined by too many men bathing, pissing, wrestling, no order, ultraviolence, unintelligible speech—this was a horde not an army.

Prince Edward had made good on his promise. We could not pass through the encampment without pinballing into a man, a bonfire, a stack of metal armor, a tanklike pony, a pile of swords like toothpicks, a pile of arrows like hairs on a head, and even what appeared to be a catapult, complete with a gang of men crowding around it, hands on hips, chins stroked, deep in drunken discussion about wind direction and ammo and one of the men breaking away, spotting Simon and I, marching toward us.

A sentient mountain of fleshy bulbs introduced himself as Commander Smear.

"Spear?" I clarified.

"*Smear*, boy, Commander Smear," he bellowed. Four teeth in total lined a bread-flecked tongue too big for its own mouth. He clasped my shoulder with a giant, calloused hand. "Smear like what I do to my enemies. We're here to slay the dragon. Your squire said you've been out plotting its movements, examining its dung."

I almost corrected the commander and said Simon wasn't my squire but then I looked behind me and saw him—saw him carrying the cloak I had taken off, carrying my cough medicine, carrying a flask of water for me—and for a moment I didn't know what he was. Campfires and clowns reflected in his darkened eyes, and I did not see myself in them.

Commander Smear pulled me into our stone hut, which he and his men had completely taken over. We couldn't get through the front door and Commander Smear had to yell and barge his way through. He introduced me to other soldiers under his command—their ranks nonsensical, their names more variations of grunts. Our bed had been turned over to its side and pushed against the wall. On the ground was a crude map of the surrounding woodland and nearest towns. Scarborough and the sea to the east, Wykeham to the south, an expanse of forest to the west and north, with a crude drawing of a dragon in the middle of it.

Commander Smear garbled through his plan of attack, something about a staggered ambush, a surprise from all sides, the advantage of that western ridge where they could set up the catapult. The other men stuffed in the hut shared grins and even smug chuckles among themselves. This was all merry amusement, I realized, war as hobby. The battle-scarred commander was playing toy soldiers and the toy soldiers were just gig workers, half dressed, clutching flagons of beer. What looked like dirt and mud across their ragged tunics and leather armor was actually dried blood. They had seen the worst of humanity already. Hunting a reclusive lizard would be a holiday.

"You're all going to die," I said. I held a piece of charcoal in my hand. The commander had wanted me to indicate the size and location of the impact crater. Suddenly I had become possessed by a time traveler's hubris. "I'm sorry, but I can't take you there. I don't want to be responsible for sending you all to your deaths."

Some of the soldiers smirked and shared looks with each other, unbelieving. I felt Simon's questioning eyes on me. I had said we needed to stay and defend our home, but not like this, not with soldiers. I didn't know how to convey the dragon's clarity— the business meeting I had just had with him—how he wasn't a wild beast beyond imagination, but something worse. He was a coherent, coordinated thinker and speaker, and we were a dot on his schedule.

"The dragon doesn't give a toss what you want," said Commander Smear. "This is about what His Majesty wants and he wants that monster's head on a pike."

One of the soldiers called out, "Is the dragon freshwater or saltwater?" He broke into laughter with the goons who had dared him to ask.

"The dragon's bigger than this whole smallholding," I said. "It's real and none of you will stand a chance. Simon—you saw it, tell them. It'll kill everyone here with a swipe of its tail."

"Yes, it's huge," said Simon. "It took out a whole chunk of the forest, we can't let it do that again. There's a huge field of ash, we'll take you all there tomorrow."

"We can't," I said directly to Simon, my eyes pleading with him. I said to everyone else, "The dragon won't attack if we just leave it alone."

"And let the devil instate his globe of fire?" said the commander. Another soldier snorted with laughter. An elbow was thrown.

"I'm saying just wait," I said. "The dragon killed two soldiers already, but only because they were foolish enough to try and attack it. He isn't blowing fire because he wants to." Eyebrows were raised at my degree of personal insight. "He does it because it's part of his feeding process. They're his . . . expulsions. He has to hack them up and we have to stay out of the way."

"Like a cat," someone said.

"How do you know it's a *he*?"

Everyone was laughing except the commander and Simon. Simon looked at me like he didn't know who I was. I might as well have been wearing a suit and tie and giving a presentation— something I had never done in my old life, just as meager and helpless then as I was now, unrallied by cloying men, my own mind nefarious and tucked away, horny with nostalgic grief. "Simon," I said feebly, with nothing more to say, just his name like a plea to trust me, be the squire.

A torch was raised. Commander Smear stood in the center of the hut with a flame held high. "Here's the deal, Oh Benevolent

George. You'll take us to the dragon tomorrow, or we'll burn down your house." Flames crisped a stray piece of straw that dangled from the roof above us. "If you don't take us to that fiery furnace of Satan's pet, then we'll just have to build one here. Choose the place you want to die."

15

We marched in the morning.

March, march, march.

It felt embarrassing, corny, even. Because is there anything more brainless than this? Is there anything more embarrassing than picking up a shiny stick and thinking you can use it to hack the world into whatever shape you think it ought to be in?

Of course the soldiers formed a line. Of course Commander Smear gave a rousing, inaudible speech. Of course the horde cheered and stomped their feet, ejaculating blanks into the empty air, mouths still full of mutton right off the bone. The dragon could arrive any second, the dragon could arrive any hour, day, week; who cares when we can just play pretend and get the same result: a surge of adrenaline, animal yips, muscles flexing under fat.

I led the horde from our smallholding through the forest, everyone galloping and whooping at first, but slowing down as the reality of the narrow trails set in. All the horses and equipment struggled to condense. Plants and offshoot trees were flattened and the catapult got stuck multiple times. It took all day for everyone to make it through the forest and their awe at the crater's grandeur was tempered by the reality of needing to set up camp again, light the fires, feed the masses. War and conquest were an exhausting logistics game. At sundown, I left the crater and went looking for firewood and spent the whole time sitting on a log alone. I thought of nothing. I tried to empty my mind, be the peasant I was always meant to be.

Something licked my hand. I was back in the forest. Echoes of laughter and shouts from the soldiers weaseled their way through the trees. I heard the whiz bang of a firework—I didn't know fireworks had been invented already. Flashes of green and red lit up the sky, lost in the black teeth of towering trees. Then something licked my hand again.

I looked to my side and flinched.

It was a wolf. Its blue eyes locked with mine, cautious as it licked a faint crust of dried blood and ash from my hand. Its fur was mangy and gray, its ears tawny and alert. The wolf finished with my left hand and I presented it with my right, but it shrank and ran away when it saw Simon coming toward us, stepping through the thicket. The wolf disappeared like a ghost, like a dragon, and only the slobber on my hand convinced me it had been real.

"What are you doing out here?" Brambles cracked as Simon pushed through them. "They've slaughtered another sheep. They took all our animals out here. They'll be eaten by morning. You didn't want them to burn down our house, but you're fine with that? You don't want to fight the dragon, but you still led them here. Now you're hiding?"

"I'm looking for firewood." I stood up. Simon grabbed me.

"What's happened, George, what's going on?" He put his arm around my waist, he put his head close to mine and closed his eyes as if to listen to what was going on inside. I pulled away.

"What do you mean 'what's going on'? Your angel didn't tell you about this part? It told you all about me but neglected to mention the dragon and the thousand soldiers?" The sourness of my own words stung me and I stopped myself. "Sorry. I just think—" My head pounded with all the things I couldn't say, or couldn't decide—I couldn't do this but I wanted—I didn't want but I needed . . . "I think we just need to let the dragon do its thing. If we try and fight it, it's going to kill everyone here. More people will come, and more people will die, and it's just going to keep happening over and over." We needed to go but we needed to stay. *I* needed to stay. I closed my eyes and felt the purposelessness of the past, the dragon's denigration of it and how the myth of the future was just a pale imitation of the present. The date had tasted so derogatory on my tongue—he had called them entropy. The entropic zone. We were random chaos, viruses colliding. Simon reached for me, hands pulled for me again, pushed through the purposelessness I knew he also had to feel lapping at his ankles.

"Do you love me?"

I didn't ask it. I was stunned to hear it because it didn't come from my mouth. It sounded modern enough like I should have said it, but I didn't.

"Do you love me?" Simon asked again. "George. I need to know."

Tears pulsed down my cheeks. I felt an immense pain in my throat, a stifled cough I clung to, tasting ash and barrenness. I nodded my head, knocking more tears from my eyes like a child.

I said, "Yes." Meager and weak.

"Yes," I said again, into Simon's chest, closing my eyes, muffling my cries, "Yes" in this foreign tongue, "Yes," but I didn't know what love meant anymore.

The ring of encampments circled the lava field. We sat and ate dinner and watched soldiers run drills across the crater's darkened plain, horses riding back and forth in different alignments. Echoes swirled around the massive space like an open drain, their torches like fading embers. The catapult was set up and tested. Someone slipped and fell through a lava tube. Another sheep was roasted, two lambs were left to go—they stared at me like strangers with their oblong pupils. It was indeed another moonless night, but only because we had blocked the sky with our campfires, this traveling tailgate.

I wondered who everyone was. No one wore a uniform, carried a wallet, no ID. All of these men and they could only proclaim their selves to each other, scooped up into groups. I thought: it's a miracle nobody just lies. Or maybe everyone did and I was finally getting the idea. You can just say what you want, you can just say who you are, and be it.

A child soldier ate bread and stew across a campfire from Simon and me. The startling fact was that there were six-year-olds running around places like this—because who else will carve rocks for the catapult, light signal fires, scavenge the bodies of the dead? The boy watched me through the flames, fixated while he chewed. I could hear nervous words whirling in his mind. Simon noticed it too and smiled. Finally the boy lifted his bowl to slurp the last of his meal, then asked, loud and in a rush, "What does the dragon look like is it as tall as a tree or even bigger?"

I chuckled. "It's very big," I said. "Bigger than a house."

"Bigger than a castle?"

"Probably. I'd say it's bigger than the Tower of London."

"I've never been to London what's London like?"

"It's nice," I said. "It's very noisy. There's lots of people."

"I'm from York."

"I like York." All I could do was answer his fruitive little questions while a dirge of sadness moaned in my heart. The boy was barefoot and dirty. His cheeks were chapped and glazed. He carefully poked the last of the beans in his stew with a rusty dagger.

Simon had a better manner about him with children and took charge. He said, "The dragon's big but he's not very scary. He's got big, flappy wings and skinny legs like a chicken."

"I'm not scared," said the boy.

"That's good," said Simon. "Make sure you stay up here on the ridge when he appears, don't run down with the soldiers. The ground will be too hot, you'll burn your feet. Stay up here and keep any fire from spreading to the forest. You can make sure our house stays safe."

"Is that your brother?" The boy pointed at me.

"No." Simon smiled. "He's my boyfriend."

My spirit sailed as high as the banners of war strung above

our camp, and my spine, caught unaware, shuddered and winced and tried to pull it back down. I smiled but I'm sure I grimaced. I didn't want to think what I was thinking. I didn't want to decide what I feared I had already decided. I didn't know how to be honest with myself and say definitively what I wanted so I thought of only the things that I knew I didn't want, namely, child soldiers, babies abandoned in forests, heads on pikes, brutality, and ruthlessness—never mind the fact that these are timeless injustices available at any time period—but it was easier for my mind to play dress-up in this blatant outrage, a child soldier just a convenient excuse. I forced myself to think plainly like this and avoid the real question—no, actually skip over the real question entirely and jump straight to a masking follow-up question instead: Maybe Simon would be able to come with me?

A dog somewhere barked. A bone was thrown for it. Somewhere else, a soldier got out a lute and started strumming. Then silently and suddenly, a cruise missile shot across the sky.

It happened in an instant. A fiery line, followed by an explosion. A flash of white. Silently.

Sound was delayed. For two seconds there was the vision before us of the earth erupting, accompanied only by the sweet crackles of campfire and music, the final slurps of soup. Shadows lengthened. Faces twitched. Then when the sound hit: a roar unlike any other.

It was like a chunk of the sun itself. Don't stare into an open flame. I closed my eyes and I could still see it through my eyelids. Wings unfolding. A neck extending. Talons, horns, and a thorny tail. A mouth opening with a smile from hell. It was like the dragon had simply come home, kicked off his shoes, taken off his coat, slammed the door, and let out a scream.

The soldiers tripped over themselves and onto their horses, gathered their arms. Everyone scrambled for swords and arrows like you would rummage through a cutlery drawer for a sudden uninvited dinner guest. The most inspiring speech Commander Smear could muster now was "Divine," his face alight with pure white. "This is divine."

I didn't grab Simon. Surprising myself, I grabbed the little boy who had been eating with us. But of course he broke free from my grasp, held up his rusty dagger, and charged along with everyone else. I watched him disappear into a tornado of fire, his skeleton visible through his skin.

I think a lot of the humanity I saw in the world of 1300 and 1301 was my own projection. How I chose to see things was largely dictated by my needs of survival. I had to believe there was a reason for my initial capture and beating in Greenwich—a brutal misunderstanding, sure, but at least a form of understanding had occurred in independent minds. I told myself over and over again that surely my perceptions were biased and I just didn't understand where everyone else was coming from. I've done that my whole life actually—expected more from people, convinced of a greater substance operating within them that I just didn't understand and someday, with the right amount of empathy, would. But I realized then, as I watched hundreds of men throw themselves headfirst into a rushing flood of lava, that there wasn't a single thought in their minds. Like time itself, their standard mode of operation was to press forward unceasingly.

The horses swelled and burst like powder kegs. The men first lost their legs and arms like twiggy little spiders, then their stubborn torsos, their screaming teethy heads, their battle cries transforming into frothy childlike hoots. With Prince Edward, we had caught the dragon at the tail end of its cycle, but now the dragon was white-hot, electric even, his eyes white like meteors, his fire and lava a pole, a sword, a constant funnel of destruction, turning and swirling all over the place like the hands on a mixed-up clock. The future and the past collided. I jumped out of the way of a flaming Toyota, a rapid splash of melted computers, a radiator, an oil barrel, a garden trellis.

Soldiers fired arrows, but these evaporated in midair. The catapult fired a boulder but it crumbled apart like tossed sand. Still it was the first thing that had managed to touch the dragon and he paused. He licked clean his teeth like a dog and looked along the ridge, taking in all the archers and their fruitless arrows and a second wave of infantry getting ready. When the dragon noticed me among the lineup, I swear he winked.

"We've got to get back," I said to Simon. I pulled him by the arm, hauling us away. "Get down!" We jumped off the ridge of the crater into the forest just as a mouthful of new molten lava flew through the air. Trees caught fire, the crater began its expansion. We lay flat on the ground as the earth shifted and sunk like a porous blanket. What had been stable was now slope. Uprooted trees, rocks, animals, soldiers all tumbled down around us, falling into the dragon and his swirling vortex drilling deeper into the earth. Some soldiers took advantage of the slope and came sprinting down it, their gallantry undeterred. A new infantry charged out from the forest, another hundred men ready and willing. They sprinted and tumbled, others simply leapt and soared. Another hundred men, then another hundred men. An endless supply of brawn. The men in the battalion, the men in the nightclub, the men at the office—all they could do was press forward. All this death, all this destruction—the pointlessness of it was just as the dragon had explained. It felt the same as it had then. It felt the same as it did now. This was the past.

For the first time in a year I thought about Pringles. I thought about a Big Mac, a bacon and egg McMuffin. I thought about Snickers chocolate bars, Maoam Pinballs, Jaffa Cakes, a double-shot espresso and a flat white and a croissant and pizza and Greggs and Pret and Diet Coke, sertraline, Adderall, paracetamol, finasteride, and cigarettes, and clotted cream on scones, muffins, pickles, pornography, and couches— I hadn't sat on a couch in a year, I hadn't been comfortable in a year and I wanted to check my email, I wanted to charge my phone, I wanted to watch TV, take multivitamins, take photos, take drugs, think about going to the gym, text people I hated, forget birthdays, drive a car when I knew I could walk instead. I wanted to smell petrol and polluted rivers. I wanted palm oil and corn syrup. I wanted an army of British bankers and Californian private equity vampires, not these unshaved, unwashed barbarians.

"I have to go," I said.

Simon didn't hear me. He was coaxing a lamb into his arms to save it from tumbling into the dragon's void. It was bleating and dangling from a ledge. Simon reached and flexed. Debris continued to fall. I pulled myself up, then reached and grabbed Simon and the lamb and together we scooted carefully away, finally reaching a point where the ground evened out. The dragon already sounded farther away from us, his destruction echoing up from the deepening well as the avalanche of men continued. Different factions huddled and shouted orders, made plans and arrangements, which proved futile once they started charging and the ground slipped out from under them. Instinctively—

I don't know what instinct—I stood up and went to follow them, taking a step toward the dragon. Simon grabbed my arm and yanked me back to the ground with him. He clutched me to his chest along with the lamb and I couldn't speak, only strain. Something was fanning its wings inside me. "Just stay, George," Simon said. I think he even said "Shhh." There were dents and divots where our clunky armor pressed against each other. The lamb's tight little curls reflected in them.

"I have to go," I said once more.

"Go where?" said Simon. "We have to get back to the smallholding. We've got to get out of here. There's nothing we can do."

Violently, I broke free from his embrace and stood up. Embarrassed with myself, I turned my back to him, ran a hand through my hair, shifted my weight, and checked the sword holstered at my side. Then something dawned on me, a new idea. Confidently, I turned back around to face Simon with the lamb, both looking up at me bewildered. I motioned in the direction of the crater. It took every muscle in my throat, every falsity in my mind to sound brave, to sound noble, to not sound like the convenient excuse I knew I had tricked my heart into thinking it wasn't. "That kid," I said. "I have to save that little boy. I have to go."

16

The earth was sinking in on itself, lava and rage swirling into a pit of pits. The smoke was so thick it felt like swimming, like I was sloshing across a new firmament built from ash. Stalactites of comets of trash hurtled in every direction. I witnessed men crumble and splatter. I witnessed a pile of them enveloped and blackened. That little boy? There was no chance in hell and this was hell.

My lungs felt like bags of compacted ash. What little air my chest could take wheezed through a pinhole in my throat so I moved slowly and I tried not to weep as it dawned on me what I was doing. I told myself that I was going to be able to come back. The dragon had sounded so assured and official, his voice like a name tag, like an email signature. I'd be able to go back and speak with the dragon's manager about everything that had gone awry and even claim compensation for myself and my partner—not my boyfriend, my partner, my perfectly nonspecific ungendered partner, my co-filing dependent—when could

I go back and get him? How might we apply for a time traveling green card? Maybe our love story would get written up in some wretched newspaper column.

If those are all the things I told myself, then why was I weeping?

The dragon was up on his haunches, working away. Muscle contractions started at the bottom of his abdomen and tremored upward, his neck shuddering and heaving. He didn't really spit fire so much as he gagged on it. Elsewhere, fiery human arms reached for me, mouthlessly. The last of the soldiers had been eviscerated. Instinctively I touched the hilt of my sword, afraid the dragon would mistake me for one of them, but he didn't. He smelled me. He saw me and smiled. It was like I had stepped into his office for a scheduled appointment. He swam through the earth toward me. He shook droplets of magma from his leathery hide.

"The man of the many hours. I've told them all about you," said the dragon.

"Who?" I asked.

"The people I work for. My handlers. They're as amazed as I was, but willing to do a favor for you. You'll go right back to twenty twenty-sixxxxx. The pathway is all set up. You're lucky it's still in the entropic zone so there's no harm done, nothing matters."

"Well . . . I think some things matter," I said. "What do you do now, you just eat me?"

"Yes." The dragon hissed long and serpentine. Sparks flew from his teeth. His breath didn't smell of charcoal or venom, but like chemicals, like paint thinner, bug spray, and bleach. I took a deep whiff of it and felt, for a second, pleasure.

"So a dragon is just going to appear in London in 2026 and spit me out?" I asked.

The dragon laughed his abominable laugh. The bellows echoed off the rocks and I realized we weren't inside a cavern like last time. We were deep inside the earth but like a massive open well. There was open sky above us and through breaks in the smoke when the wind picked up, I could even see stars. It was strangely quiet.

"Well, it won't be London, for one thing," said the dragon. "You'll still be here, just seven hundred and twenty-five years in what you would consider the future. You'll need to pay your own fare back to London, if that's where you want to go. My people said they would not be compensating you for that. And I will not be there. You go alone." His mouth was held in a vicious smile. "When I swallow you, enzymes from my stomach react with your hormones, triggering the same conditions you experienced when you first time traveled here. This happens slowly, so you may experience some mild discomfort, but by the time you reach my intestines, your body will have combusted fully back to your time period."

I raised an eyebrow. I didn't know how I had imagined this working, but it wasn't like this. "I saw a man the other night," I said. "He was wearing some kind of equipment and he went inside your mouth before you flew away."

The dragon seemed surprised by this. "Oh, him. He was a flight passenger. That's something different."

"But I can't do that? I have to be digested?"

"There's no digestion taking place, George—I don't think

I've fully digested anything in at least three hundred years. My stomach enzymes interact with your human stress hormones, causing the combustion. It's a process that occurs solely within your body, like an allergic reaction."

Suddenly I felt dizzy and weak. I took off some of the heavy armor I was wearing and sat down on a rock just in chain mail. I leaned forward and rested my head on the hilt of my sword. "Sorry," I said. "I need to think this over for a minute."

"I don't have minutes, George. Now that I've finished my expulsions, the process begins. I can't pause it." He hocked a loogie of magma.

"It just doesn't sound very safe. I thought you'd like, carry me in your mouth or something and we'd fly into the future together. That's what I saw you do with that guy. That seemed easy enough."

The dragon laughed again. I worried about Simon up on the ledge and what he might hear. I needed to do this now if I was going to do it.

"I fly at half the speed of light," said the dragon. "The inorganic material that makes up my diet are the only things able to withstand the pressure of that kind of time travel. The stomach enzymes are a nice alternative to what you would otherwise need specialist equipment for. The man you saw was wearing an airlocked pressure suit with a liquid cooling system and a thermo-polycarbonate glass helmet."

"Well why can't I have that?"

"It's not available." The dragon smiled. He moved his massive head closer toward me. He rested it in his hands as if he were a bored teenager on a bed, but I could tell he was choosing his next words carefully. "What you need to understand, George, is that there are a lot of moving components to maintain this . . . ecosystem. We're going out of our way to do you this favor. I'm honored you want to fly with me, but I promise the digestion option is just as painless."

"You just killed hundreds of people—that's what gives me pause. How can you act like this is business as usual?"

"George . . ." The dragon rubbed his eyes and sighed. Long streams of smoke poured out his nose. "I know you've already made up your mind." He said no more and laid himself even farther across the ground, flattening his chin to the earth. Slowly, he opened his mouth. His jaw unhinged like a snake's to reveal a vast inner cathedral. His tongue unfurled like a set of stairs. He closed his eyes, and down the barrel of his throat, a hallway of muscles relaxed and expanded and I stood at the gateway. Surprising myself, I reached out and touched one of the dragon's teeth. The totem pole of white enamel was surprisingly cool after all the magma purging. Again I smelled that inorganic stench. The mouth smelled like new carpet, a new car, new shoes, permanent marker. It was intoxicating in all the best ways and it felt—easier than it had been to feel in the past year—like home.

"George?" said a new voice.

Behind me. Skidding on rocks. A halting of breath. Then a great fall and a landing, a horrible crash.

"Simon!" I let go of the tooth, I turned around. Simon had fallen from a ledge and landed hard on the ground, barely avoiding a stream of lava. He winced and cried, bending forward over a leg that was broken at an angle unnatural enough to cause it to suddenly bleed. Blood flooded the ground.

And then something happened. Simon looked up at me broken and terrified. "It said your name! The dragon said your name!" he screamed. And this horror created what I can only describe as a rip or a kind of smear, like the world around Simon had boiled itself to an evaporated state and formed this millisecond injection of pure undiluted stress that I think would have killed him if it hadn't done what it did instead.

Simon vanished.

He didn't get up and run away. He wasn't incinerated by the dragon or swallowed by it, he simply vanished into thin air. I saw him there, lying crumbled on the ground with tears of a thousand types of pain, and then I didn't. His body, his blood, his presence, everything about him, completely disappeared. The ground was clean.

The most unyielding silence filled the bottom of the well. Everyone had died. Everyone was gone. Only myself and the dragon, this whale of the sky, remained, and even his breath was silent, his nostrils like the exhaust pipes of an idling car. I broke into screams.

"What did you just do?" I demanded. "What did you do?!"

"I didn't do anything!" The dragon was humanlike in his reaction, eyes wide, mouth askew. He even skurried backward like a fool caught in a bind, shaking his head, insistent denial. "Who was that? How did he do that?"

"He just disappeared!" I felt sick. The unreality of what I had just seen didn't register in the right place in my brain, fueling nothing but words of sharp exclamation. "Where did he go? His leg was broken, he was bleeding, he needs help, where the hell did you send him?"

"I didn't send him anywhere. That right there was spon-taneous combustion. Remarkable. Who was he?" The dragon seemed genuinely surprised. "I smelled a dash of a pheromone, something lovely and nostalgic. There was a delicious amount of fear in there too." The dragon crawled over to where Simon had laid seconds ago and sniffed. "Completely gone, not a trace, but what a delicious smell that was. Pure combustion. In all my five hundred and fifty-five years I've never seen it with my own eyes before."

"He's my boyfriend," I said, no doubt about it now. "Now send me to wherever he went. Eat me, eat me now."

The dragon turned his head and smiled at me, narrowing his eyes. The corners of his mouth practically touched the corners of his eyes. "Your *boyfriend*?" he said. "What a fun surprise. You've had a busy year out here, haven't you?"

"Send me to him."

The dragon shook his grinning head. "That's not how it works, George. My handlers have set up a pathway for you and that's where you'll go—to your beloved twenty twenty-six. What happened just now was purely independent combustion, unattached to my pathways. Now hold on"— the dragon leaned back on his tail, crossed his arms, thinking gleefully—"if he was your *boyfriend*, then why—"

"Just send me to him."

"You wanted to leave him."

"I thought I would be able to come back." Tears pulsed from my eyes and instantly evaporated in the heat. "Or he could come with me."

"You never said that." He pointed a claw at me and leered,

whip-quick. "That's an excuse. You're just like all the other boys—flitty little termites running from one shiny thing to the next. You've had your fill and now you want back. What do you want back to, George? Go home and watch *tee-vee*? Is that what you want? I probably have a tee-vee still in my gut if you want one, let's see—" He drove a fist into his soft and deflated belly. He stuck a finger in his mouth and started retching.

"Stop!" I said. "Please just bring him back. Go find him."

"You don't want him back!" The dragon spoke in a vicious bark, reminding me of the animal he was. "He can go find me for all I care."

"Then make me spontaneously combust! Breathe fire over me, slash me with your claws, you're right, I'm a fool. Come and attack me!"

"HAHAHA." The dragon's laughter boomed out of the well like a volcano. His wings extended and he flew upward. He landed on the ground with a seismic pulse on all fours, facing me head-on. "Only you can make yourself spontaneously combust." He snapped his teeth. "Go on, try it, George. Get more weepy, get more pathetic. Your boyfriend was able to do it. Obviously he cared enough. You're just not heartbroken."

"I am!" I sputtered and coughed. Thick whirls of smoke and sparks engulfed me.

"You're not! You're not heartbroken—I'd even go so far as to say you're relieved. You didn't love him, you're not devoted to him, certainly not as much as he must be to you. I bet you don't even want to go back to where you came from. You don't want to stay here, you don't want to go there, you just want to sit at the bottom of this hole with me and all my filth. That's what you want. You want to be me. You want to be a facilitator for filth. You're a shitty little bird, aren't you?"

I wailed and shook. My head pounded with blood and rage. Some warbly muscle sprained itself in the back of my neck, a pain in my stomach, but still I remained there with the dragon.

"Such empty passion," he said. He stuck out his forked tongue and wiggled it in my face. "You're not a bird. You're just a pig. That's why you want to go back to twenty twenty-six, to be back with your pig people. You couldn't be anything for your boyfriend here, so you want your old gobble-life back there. They'll feed you well, there's plenty of shit to shovel. There's a new Sainsbury's on the high street. You ever been to Scarborough? Trust me it looks about the same now as it does then, just more piss, meat, and mud. They'll sing a song about a fair there. There'll be a chippy and a vape shop and a Premier Inn and an Aldi and treacly little people complaining about the NatWest closing down and I know all that because I hear that from the people, I lie underground and listen to them bitch and moan, that's all you've got to look forward to, George. Money and food and petrol—those stupid little words you say in your stupid little language. 'Oi, did you see they changed the hours of the M&S and the car park went up a pound? Did you see they've gone and called a strike just in time for half-term?' Have you missed those conversations, George? Have you missed those drip people? The junkies, nags, and tramps? The bankers, voyeurs, and holiday home whores? The gilet alcoholics and gallstoned queerdos? The greenbelt low-culture gadflies? The diabetic pod-people constipating the highways, counting chemtrails and credit card debt and missing me, flying above them—they don't even know it—

the flames that await them—you want to go back there? That's how bad you want it?"

I nodded my head, surprising myself. Suddenly clear-eyed. Like raising my hand in class. The pulse of rage had passed and a sense of finality trickled through my brain, skinny-dipped in my cerebellum. I could have almost laughed at how easy it suddenly felt. I wore chain mail, leather, cloth, sword, boots, helmet, but I couldn't feel lighter, lifted by grief high above my station, richer than any pain or hatred could do. "Yes," I said. "Yes, that's exactly where I want to go. I want to go back. And I want to go now."

The dragon guffawed like the worst kind of man, shrugged his shoulders like the devil he was. "I can't tell your head from your tail, diva. But fine. Dust to dust, entropy to entropy. Let's get it over with." He lay back down again, pressed his chin to the ground, and opened his mouth one last time. It's true, he was a facilitator, nothing more. I walked up his tongue and shuffled between his teeth into the cavern of his mouth with its wretched smell of freshly pressed plastic, jet fuel, and printer ink. I stepped across taste buds and ducked under a uvula. "Easy, easy," the dragon said. A hundred fleshy polyps echoed his voice. I stepped carefully down into the hallway of his throat, already feeling sensations of a future that didn't exist, a past that was no longer mine. Memories pitter-pattered across my skin like acid rain, memories of dogs, hay fever, ranting boyfriends, rising rents, smeared bugs on white walls, but mostly just tastes and sounds, of sweat, rubbing, smoke, and sand—as I clutched the hilt of my sword. As I unsheathed it.

In one solid motion, I knelt and staked the sword through throat and into ground.

The dragon reacted instantly. He whipped his head up, but with my sword stuck through him and the ground, he caused a hole to rip right through his neck. Suddenly I was back outside of him, still kneeling but on a rug made of his throat. I looked up just in time to jump away from his claws as they came swiping at me. With his other arm, the dragon clutched his neck and screamed but a vicious damage had already been done, his scream corrupted into a gargle. Blood mixed with bile, mixed with leftover embers and debris, and while he struggled to keep these things from bubbling up, dribbling out, I grabbed my sword again and ran and leapt and stabbed into the top of his chest, ripping the tear even further, pulling it down his belly, spilling lava and all the things I never wanted to see again. The flames and embers of liquid modernity rained down over me, melting and mixing with my armor, burning my clothes, my skin, I screamed along with the dragon, along with my heart that had been broken—it was shattered! Simon! oh Simon!—my tears as proof, wiped away by fire and guts—stomach enzymes, what kind of madness? I licked at the rain, mouth open like a crazed dragon myself, lapping up his pseudoscience. "Simon!" I cried. "Bring me Simon!" as I drove sword through crocodile skin and dinosaur bone and python eye and godless, empty skull. Soot—that is all there was. Soot that coated all sound and all alive as the lizard rattled and melted and finally died.

17

2026. I can say the year without shame. When I was in the grips of my self-immolation back then, I took comfort in the clear timeline: fights with boyfriend, dishonesty at work, debauchery in mind and on beach, all these stones skipping easily, predictably to my sinking. It was simple cause and effect and while the effects were of a great magnitude (unemployment, unlovability), I never looked back on them with bewilderment. I was never really surprised. I was never shocked.

There was only one moment when that calm turned slightly on its heel and the grief of reality slipped in. It was early in my dog walking endeavor, before the overstuffed wolf pack, back when I only took one or two dogs at a time. I was at Greenwich Park watching the sunset over the skyline. It was early summer. Frisbees and green clouds of parakeets swam through the air. I was sitting in the grass with a black Lab and a terrier sufficiently exhausted on either side of me, my body telling me this was the most satisfying day of work I'd ever had despite my mind feeling otherwise. Suddenly the Lab's tail began to wag and he perked up. He stood, whimpered, and nervously skipped over to another dog walking across the field. I did the usual smile and nod to the owner and we let the dogs sniff each other and play for a few minutes. Something in them had clicked in that unspoken way of animals and they were instantly giddy together, no hesitancy or fear, only quick yips of excitement, a whine and a wiggle of the hips, a game of chase performed like a well-rehearsed ballet, like they knew each other from long ago. And I remember a distinct, painful longing opened up in my heart as I watched them, an ache that swelled throughout my whole body, that almost made me cry aloud: I wish I could have that.

The thought was as simple as that, and it caused me so much pain.

1301. In the end, it was only me who remained, no other living thing—and I doubted that even of myself. I stayed with the dragon long after the shores of lava had hardened and my clothes had burned away and blisters had risen in welts across my skin. I smelled burning hair and burning men but found nothing organic, only phones and tablets, plastic bottles, forever chemicals, car parts, and metal beams, chains, buckets, nails—all this undigested dragon kibble etched into bricks of charcoal—not a hand in sight to grab, not a face, no one crying "George!" and no one to whom I could cry "Simon!" This, now, was real silence, punctuated only by weeping and a hacking cough, my calls to no one eking out of me as whispers and strains, the throat in my mouth a cave inside a cave.

Fire lapped up the dragon's skin and chewed through muscle

right down to white bone. His coiled head remained mostly whole, coated in ash. His mouth was left open, as if it were permanently aghast at me peering inside—in fact I walked back inside it, standing and sitting and curling up and waiting with a feeble hope Simon would crawl out from some hidden bowel, walk magically through the forest of teeth. Under the dragon's tongue there'd be a portal I could step through into whatever world Simon had disappeared into and I'd come out the other end and see him there in jeans and a T-shirt, nice trainers, phone charged, ironic and mawkish about how easily he had embraced the twenty-first century, or twenty-second, thirty-seventh, eighty-fifth, who knows, and it would look good on him, better than it had ever looked on me, and he'd smile, pick me up, clean me up—we'd shower together like we used to share a tub together but there'd be limitless water, limitless soap and towels and perfumes and red cheeks—and I wouldn't even have to say I'm sorry—because I'm sorry. I'm so sorry, Simon, I really am. I don't know what came over me back there. I had thought to say that in the moment—words of denial had crossed my mind almost as if in parody. "It's not what it looks like!" as if he had caught me and the dragon in an unseemly tryst. I was an embarrassment and a cliché right up to the moment of van- ishment, right to the very end. I looked out from the jaws of the dragon, saw the gray, decimated world, and cried. Tremors drove through me and all I could do was collapse and weep, unable to breathe.

I stayed in the mouth of the dragon for a long time. It was comforting in a strange way to be in hell, to be at the very bottom and know that there was nothing farther below me. Ashes coated my body and all my surroundings, creating a new silence I had never experienced before. The silence from when I first time traveled had been surreal and almost a body-horror, but this new silence was exactly what it was: it was silent. I heard nothing. I felt nothing. There was no ringing sensation in my ears, no alien croaks from deep within my body. There was only absence, complete void. The empty, secluded glade of a zero.

Then One.

"Sir?"

A child's hand touched my shoulder. A child's, I guessed, only because it felt small and weak. In all other ways it was older than would be considered humane, dead almost and brittle, coated in cuts, blisters, and ash, dirty fingernails, actually, missing fingernails.

"Sir George?"

I rolled over and my dry eyes stung, blinked, coated themselves in acid tears, blinked again, saw a form, saw a visage of gray, the form of a child—*the* child, the kid from dinner. My god. The kid, my excuse. I yelped like a lunatic. I grabbed the kid and clutched him to me.

"You killed the dragon," he said.

Words failed. I could only cry. I stood up and stepped away, coughed and spit, tried to compose myself but that only made my vision clearer, so I could better see the shell-shocked kid and how one of his ears was blown off, foot pointing the wrong way, his new tremor and dried blood, the rocks embedded under skin.

As clear as when I had first arrived in this world, I called for God. I watched the six-year-old pick at his wounds, pick at mine, wince with every movement and I waited for God to step in and say something. Here, God, look—here's another casualty of this thing that's slipped through the netting of time and threatened to ruin it all, nullify this whole grand experiment in earthing, do you mind? Do you care? Don't you want to step in and say something? If I leave this kid here, will you mind? If I take him with me only for him to run off and die in some other battle, will you be fine?

I sat with the child in the mouth of the dragon while we sutured our bleeding, wrapped sprains and breaks in what cloth was still salvageable. No angel appeared. No voice from heaven. No eyeball of God, blinking once for yes, twice for no. Again just that silence.

I sighed—no, I smiled, actually. It was the physical reaction to the buoying of my cheeks against a sudden lightness, nay, a sudden emptiness, but it was a smile nonetheless and this was enough of a hydraulic to keep me upright, to stand and move and climb. We left the dragon and clambered over rocks, scampered up cliffs. Half the well had landslided itself into more of a modest slope, so this wasn't pure mountaineering, but it was arduous. I carried the child on my back—the child whose name I never bothered to learn, who I'm sure is dead by now from sepsis or tetanus or maybe he never even had a name, just a cattle-prodded serf, purpose-built for rote tasks dressed up in the temptation of bravery. I was going to put him on a horse and send him off to the king with news of the dragon's demise, which reminded me—"Fuck!" I said it like forgetting my keys, the last gasp of my own modernity. We were still in the crater, but out of the well. A bright gray sky was above us. "Stay here," I said to the kid. He stared straight ahead, only bones and gristle. I ran back down into the crater. I tripped and fell three times but what did it matter at this point. I grabbed my sword and went to the dragon's head one last time. With the sword as a saw, I extracted the smallest tooth from its mouth, rubbery gums still succulent, great big nerve endings floppy and alien. It took even longer to climb out of the well with the tooth strapped to my back, but I made it. I found a horse. I loaded it with the child and the tooth—its knick-knock legs buckled slightly. Then I said goodbye.

I did not accompany them to Scarborough. The mammoth tusk of a tooth would speak louder than anything I'd be able to say. I didn't even bother going back to the smallholding. I left Yorkshire. In a way it was like I left England completely, left the entire United Kingdom, which wasn't a kingdom yet and had far from any semblance of unity. A year ago, time had removed me from itself, and so now, this time, I took the clear, decisive action to remove it from myself. I went away and embraced my end.

THIRD EPISTLE, concerning the insistence of peace despite borders

Written by the hand of EDWARD by the grace of God King of England, Lord of Ireland, Duke of Aquitaine, Conqueror of Wales, Hammer of Scots, Uniter of kingdoms, grandfather, father

Smoke drained out of the valleys and moors and was never seen again in such a lacquer, the countryside reverting to its familiar controlled burns, its celebratory bonfires, its cozy hearths, each of these appearing on the horizon like gentle trails of seafoam across sand. News of this change in weather pattern reached us while lodging at Peebles, our pocket of peace, where the sky was already a beaming Scottish blue, yet still I turned my head southward, waiting for something, watching and listening, greeted by only the sweetest noise—the punctuation of children laughing. Grandchildren.

A sword stuck me clear through the back. The wooden nub of it slipped around my side and I mimed a gallant death, collapsed and beaten with tickles by soft little hands. Gilbert and Mary and Elizabeth piled on top of me and for once, without the cushioning of armor, I felt the exposure of my age in my joints, in my shoulders as the children clung to me and by admission of defeat my daughter Joan had to call them off. I yielded to their terms of surrender, granting each child candied oranges and a rose bestowed by Queen Margaret, and these were my goings-on when a battered mare flanked by soldiers approached from across the garden. A starved child rode the mare. The mare towed an enormous white effigy, sharpened like a spear, dragging across the grass.

Queen Margaret called the tooth an elephant tusk. She showed me her ivory comb. "Feel the texture," she said. "It's the same." She sent a servant all the way to her palace at Marlborough to retrieve an ivory platter for further comparison but by the time he was on his return we had moved on to Berwick and the servant wrote to me saying he was stopped at the border and that was what sent me into a rage, Margaret's first of mine to witness. "Stopped at the border." Be it tusk or tooth I broke it in half. A crystalline pulp at the core crumbled across the ground. I dug Margaret's comb out from her hair and snapped that in half as well. How am I meant to unlight a fire like that? How can I not raise my voice and bark and scream at this encroachment, this casual treason in my own home?

THERE IS NO BORDER. I could barely scrawl the words myself. I screamed them into the ear of my scribe, stabbed the pen right through the bloody parchment while everyone— Margaret, the Prince of Wales, Thomas, Mary, the kids, the urchins, the usurpers—looked on, dead-eyed and too young. I don't know how to be unseething and unscreaming when they look at me like that, when I see their ingratitude for the land they live in, their assumption that everything there is simply there, because it's there. Thousands of countrymen have not died with spears through their heads and swords through their bellies for your parcels to be "stopped at the border." A border does not exist. A border is a consignment of the devil, and how dare you freely give it to him? A border should only be an ocean, nothing smaller, like that which lies between us and France, and yet even that I can step over. I step north, I step south, people pop underfoot like berries and bleed red, their skins like that of thin tadpoles. There is absolutely no border. How dare he say he's stuck at the border like some misbegotten cow. If the servant dares show his face with that plate, both will be split in half.

I digress.

I take strange comfort in the thought of George and the ███████. I don't believe what Margaret said about the tooth being feigned. It wasn't ivory. She is young and unbelieving in many things, as young as everyone is in this world—a world that feels too fragile, constantly newly born. She is pregnant again. How can humanity refresh itself at such a maniacal pace? As old as I am I feel myself alone in this battle against a slate that is continuously wiped clean, "borders" repainted like black iron mullions, when in reality they are movable, I have moved them, I have shattered them; still I bang against these windows, still I walk to all these places. I've outlived every horse I've ever owned. I've spent every last coin in the treasury. And so the comfort of George, as I was saying, is the unspent youth I saw in his eyes. They were not deadened. They were fey. I remain haunted not by their depth but by their wide absorption.

With the ███████ slain, George's role is fulfilled, but if a troublesome time befalls this disunited kingdom, I can think of no greater guidance than his to seek. If he really was from a world still to come, then there is comfort in knowing that there will be children of our children, there will be a continuing branch despite what I only see as a constant culling. And what I say here about George, I suppose, I mean to say to you. You who will one day be in possession of these records by the sheer happenstance of our sacred calling. You who will one day be me and for that I've spent your life in so much loathing of you, from fear, from agony, and yes, from love. You, my son. My heart.

18

I was hauling a bundle of dried flax on my back when a town crier announced the death of King Edward in September, in 1307. The king had died two months earlier, in July, six years after the last reported dragon attack, when the love of my life had disappeared into thin air.

I dropped the bundle of flax and stretched my back while the crier went through all his pageantry. This was in a market town on the outskirts of Cambridge. This was during one of the musty last days of summer when I'd mistake weariness for wariness, rub melancholic muscles in my arms and shoulders, and feel the length of all the different paths my life could have once taken.

The king's body was going to be marched down the main road here on its way to Waltham Abbey, where it would lie in state for a time before burial in London. A conflicting series of shrugs passed through the crowd of villagers gathered around the crier—some relieved that all the needless drama with Scotland might finally end, others wary of his son's more dangerous predilections. Hah, I thought, how's that for time travel?—we're back to year one. Year one of King Edward the Second's reign. Long live the new faggot king, his child bride Queen Isabella, and his soothsayer-lover Piers Gaveston. I toyed with the idea of writing to them or doing something to climb into those circles of privilege before the opportunity completely dried up. I still had my summons letter from Edward I and a letter of thanksgiving for all that business with the dragon, a royal seal. I could hire a scribe. I could go view the body as it lay in state, rub shoulders with a knight or earl and remind them of who I was, what I did. I kept these ideas as the toys they were. I had more timely matters now.

I took the flax to a weaver, who helped me soak and break out the fibers. I whipped these through a series of combs, then refined and spun them into yarn, which I decided I would sell to the weaver in bulk instead of trying to weave them into linen myself. I baked the leftover flax seeds into a bread, I planted the rest. Another month passed. The weather turned sour. I moved to a different village. It was autumn, then winter.

What I'll say about time is that even the coronation of a new king could not punctuate its droning hum down corridors of bare trees, across the crystallizing surface of ash-flecked lye frozen over every morning, steam rising off my back as I washed, every day more hunched and sore and—I'll use this tempting, modern word—happy.

Is that how I used to use that word? *Happy?* To describe the vigor of a blister popped, infected and gnarly? To explain the sensation that washes over me when I reach a new city's walls, see the bloodstained stones and naked prisoners on parade, kept in stocks, shitting like dogs—the sense of disgust I feel from all the barbarity and how it comes from a place of twisted kinship, as if to say, *I was once like you and you will one day be like me*, not with vitriol but filled with a pain I know so well that it inverts into the tastiest, richest dish? Then yes, happiness. There's no greater reminder of what it's like to be alive than to have nothing and to be whipped, hung, drawn, and quartered. God, how good would it feel to be stretched like that. After living in this world for so many years it's hard not to feast on this, our one shared reality and all its violent unfairness. I envy them, almost, as I watch life pulled from them like thread from a spool—that rush of aliveness, one last hurrah. I had always wanted to die happy, and now I was happy.

Which is all to say how unprepared I was for the shock of naked sadness that came over me, years after the new king's coronation, when I was given an unexpected letter. A messenger of no affiliation approached me one night at an inn and pressed the note into my hand. It was addressed to me, from no one, and inside the folded paper read only one single word: *Scarborough*.

The word rattled a jar in the back of my mind.

I caught the messenger at the bar. He hadn't darted off into the night. He was sipping an ale.

"Who sent you?" I demanded.

"Friend, all I know is the name on the envelope," he said. "Ah—but I'm glad you caught me—I nearly forgot." He reached into his satchel and riffled through envelopes and scrolls. "I was supposed to give you this too."

He handed me a clear bottle. It was empty and slightly tarnished. There was no label and it was strangely light, too light to be glass, and it was bendy, made from a material almost like wax, but more solid. I was transfixed.

"Strange, isn't it?" said the messenger. "I have to admit, I spent some time admiring it myself. It's like a kind of rubber, but translucent, super light and unbreakable. Bouncy glass, I call it."

"No, there's a name for it," I said. "I know this." A sudden tremor came over me, a hidden revulsion. The bottle felt so familiar. My fingers wrapped around it like it was second nature and squeezed slightly. The material bent inward, snapped back. There was a word—but a fit of tears came over me. I excused myself and went back to my table, ignoring sideways glances and raised eyebrows. I sat with the crumbled bottle before me, watching the warbled reflections of a dozen candles flickering in its surface, in this material I could no longer remember the word for. A word that time forgot.

In my early days of grief, I spent most of my time in hysterics like this, traveling aimlessly. I would wander in a kind of dawdle you couldn't even call traveling. I wouldn't *travel* to York, I would simply keep walking until I ran into a wall and it would be York's splendid walls. I'd collapse and cry and this was acceptable because most people have at least one or two things to collapse and cry over. But York would prove too close to the pain, too filled with memories like the worst kind of drunkenness and I'd flee because I craved Simon. Not a place, not a thing. I craved Simon. I would say it out loud. In pubs, in streets, in fields, sometimes in the arms of men who weren't him. I'd whisper it into voids, I'd press my lips into nooks and crannies and say I crave Simon. "I crave you," praying he might hear—no—praying *to* him, God just an eavesdropper, the moon my only intercessor. I'd whisper my recitations and run a lock of Simon's hair across my lips. We had exchanged these once, cut and tied with thread, and I had laughed him off at the time.

"What am I supposed to do with it? Wear it?" I had put the lock of hair on top of my head and wiggled it around, pretending it was a tiny ponytail.

"I don't know, it's just something lovers are supposed to do," Simon had said. Then he asked for a lock of mine, and I let him take it. I felt his hands comb through my hair, gently gather a small collection—less than he had given of his. He cut with sacred precision.

"We're lovers," I said.

"We're lovers," he said.

I would repeat this aloud to myself in the silent rooms of inns and churches, treasuring the dark coil of his curl more than my sword, my coin purse, my knife and holster, wishing I had more of him, a fingernail or a tooth, his whole body, his eyes. What was he seeing now? Was he off in an even more ancient past or some fantastical future, some mundane future? What was his commute like? What was his status on WhatsApp? The last photo he had posted to Instagram? What was his favorite sandwich, drink, holiday destination, film? Did he still like cabbage and venison? Thyme, chamomile, and sage? Did he still hum little songs I had never bothered to ask the names of? These were all the thoughts and old words that flooded my mind now, in the fifth year of the reign of King Edward II, as I held the letter in my hand with its single word: *Scarborough*. I rubbed the surface of the strange not-glass bottle and remembered the smoothness of Simon's skin, the marbled bend where his hip met his rib when he lay on his side and I'd trace it with my tongue, my hand, our breath our only clothes.

I let out a cry that made patrons drop their flasks, that sent horses running from their posts, a wail like a roar like the dragon I was.

It took a month of aimlessness and ale before I made it to Scarborough. I wandered a long time and often not in the right direction, as if hoping I could trick myself and end up there on accident, not wanting to stir up hope inside me, or fear, or guilt, or anything. Still, nothing could prepare me for the memories of the region—recognizing particular trees along the roads, how the wind bent around the castle on the cliffs and blew down to the rocky walls of the town below, the briny air and constant wet.

I got a job at the Peasholm ferry trading hall, unloading cargo, sorting and cleaning fish—I say job but what was that? I showed up and money was there, not a lot and not enough, but there and easy, as common and precarious as beads of water on a cobweb. I kept a room at the White Boar Inn and each night expected a knock at the door but nothing came. What was I expecting? I'd pick fish scales from my fingernails in silence and try not to look out the window at the faraway hills and imagine our old smallholding out there. In the eerie quiet, as waves slumbered in the harbor below, I said Simon's name out loud and waited. I analyzed the handwriting of *Scarborough* and wondered if it was his. I allowed myself these delusions only because I had survived so many years of elemental living—seeing magic only in dried herbs, bloodletting, and idol worship, free from dragons, angels, time travelers, love. I could allow myself this desperate, unanswered whisper.

"Simon."

The whole town hung in this stasis. Scarborough Castle was in the middle of a siege, which didn't mean anything bombastic, just more silence surrounding the complex and frustrated fishermen unable to trade up their catches. Occasionally there'd be a sharp yelp in the middle of the night from the bluffs and I'd wonder: Was I supposed to have done something? Was a whole world of sequence and history happening without me? I felt excluded, but for once, I felt peace—again, pain as happiness, the brutality of the world and its loneliness my succor.

"George?"

It was the next morning. I was sitting on Merchants Row eating bread and cheese on a lunch break when the town vicar saw me and stopped in his tracks.

"I can't believe it," he said.

I stood and we shook hands even though I was filthy and stank of fish guts. The vicar was cheery and round as ever, dressed in his same old robes. He patted my arms and looked me up and down.

"How long has it been?" he said. "It must have been years—I don't know how I recognized you but the name just came to me. You've got to come to church tomorrow—or even tonight, for evensong. Do come."

I was amazed he remembered who I was. Simon and I had met the vicar at church that one time all those years ago, then seen him a few more times only in passing. If we had ever held conversation, Simon would have done most of the talking. I'm sure our names were on a registry somewhere, but Scarborough was an increasingly transient place, no other townspeople had recognized me. I must have been looking at the vicar question-ably because there was an anxiety in his voice as he filled the silence between us.

"Are you here alone?" he asked. "Is your lord here as well? I'm afraid I've forgotten the name of the man for whom you were a squire, if I remember correctly."

I blinked and stammered. I almost corrected the vicar but stopped myself, unsure what to say. "Simon," I said. "His name was Simon. And yes, I was his squire. He was my lord, you're right. He was. Everything to me. He's not here. He's gone."

The vicar's discomfort remained right at the surface of his expression. "Well," he said. His eyes darted left then right. A seagull cawed in the sky. "You need to come to evensong. I insist. There's another Lord you should always remain in service of." He winked. He blessed me. He left.

I went to evensong that night and sat in the back of the church. The vicar and clergy sang their incantations and while their voices found little melody, it was nice to sit in the pew, on a cushion, and watch the angels in the stained glass windows shape-shift and shudder in the glowing candlelight. Their halos were perfect circles. Their robes were bright red and blue. I felt the vicar watching me from the choir as he and his clergy droned on in half Latin, half mumbles, the gist of which was a plea for forgiveness for us sinners and fools. When they finished, like a bubble popped we were forgiven, it was that easy. The parishion-ers relaxed their shoulders and I wished, in a moment of child-like wonder, that I had done this more often, that I had run here after every mistake I had ever made no matter how small so that I could have grown accustomed to the sensation of its erasure. If

I had ever been forgiven of anything, I had never learned how to accept it. I couldn't feel it. I didn't believe it.

After the service there was soup, bread, and ale, and I stayed near the back of the nave, keeping to myself. The vicar still shot glances my way through the crowd. I thought over what he had said earlier about Simon, calling me his squire—hadn't he recognized our relationship all those years ago? He had blessed us, called it a romance. Simon and I had held hands in these pews. Simon had kissed me in the churchyard. Had that all been just a brotherly, servitial love to the vicar? Was something lost in translation all those years ago? Suddenly I felt unwelcome and uneasy.

"Sodomite."

I heard a man say the word. I homed my attention in on a group of men and women. Someone said it again. It was the first time I had heard the word said in a wholly derogatory way. They were discussing the king.

"He can't bugger Gaveston anymore so he's buggering the whole town."

"I'd bugger a sword up his ass but I'm afraid he'd enjoy it."

I had no reaction. I didn't feel insulted by what they were saying, it was clear they were venting more about the state of the nation than anything else. The land, titles, and castles King Edward II had given his lover over his little time in power had already caught up to him. He was nearly bankrupt, and the knife-edge victories his father had left for him were only just that. Still the malice from the congregants felt oddly modern. It tickled something inside me that had gone dormant long ago.

"Couldn't keep his dick clean so the country's gone to shit. He'll burn in hell."

I listened to all this, fascinated. There was even a gay couple among the group, but they also relished this new weapon, this shade of homophobia that was hatching. I felt a trickle, almost, of shame. I found it all puzzling and maybe not unwarranted, but certainly ungodly. I went and thanked a member of the clergy for the meal and quietly left the church. But in the darkened street as I walked back to the inn, the vicar caught up with me.

"Wait, George! Why did you leave so soon?"

"What are you doing?" I whipped around and instinctively touched the handle of the knife I kept in my tunic. "What do you want from me?"

"Please, just come back," said the vicar. He was breathless, having run to catch up to me. "I swear I don't mean you any harm, but I just need you to come back to the church." We were alone on a darkened lane at the top of a hill. All of humble Scarborough was dashed out below us, houses faintly lit if at all. The castle hung over everything like a ceiling of black stone.

"Are you the one who wrote me?" I asked.

"Yes," said the vicar, but he stood there flummoxed and unsure. He shifted uncomfortably and wiped sweat from his brow.

"There's been another dragon," he said finally.

My breath caught on itself. I felt the prickle of a chronic cough. Suddenly I was aware of every candle flickering in every window along the street, like I could smell each thin line of smoke.

"How?" I asked.

"It comes at night," he said. "It's terrorizing the countryside, eating all the sheep, it's burning women and children alive."

"That's impossible."

"Please, George." The vicar grabbed my arm. There was genuine desperation in his eyes regardless of the unbelievable claim—not unbelievable, but veiled by something else, his expression ultimately unplaceable. "The attacks are happening more frequently. All of Scarborough is at risk and now with the siege and all the pressure we've been under . . . I just need you to come with me. Please, George, please if it's the only thing you do. There's someone who wants to meet you."

Dragons don't eat people. They don't eat sheep. They eat rubbish and spit up what their fiery bellies can't digest. They fly through time as they please and sleep underground and live for centuries without end. And there's only one—there's only one dragon and I killed him.

I knew the vicar was lying. The more I questioned him as I followed him back to the church, the more extravagant and false his claims became. The dragon flew in from the sea, it snatched children with its talons and carried them away into the night, it had bewitched the water supply. It was insulting to listen to but still I followed him back to the now empty church, up the nave and past the choir, through a door into his private quarters. His hands shook as he hurried me inside and told me to wait just a moment. He left me alone. Somehow, through all the unease and strangeness, it dawned on me what was happening. I smirked, even when the vicar slammed the door behind him, even when a figure stepped out from a darkened corner of the room and raised a bow and arrow. I held up my hands in submission but couldn't pretend to be surprised by who was there.

"Hi," was all I said.

King Edward II stood alone and trembling, barely able to keep the arrow held aloft. Silent, desperate tears streamed down his face. I wasn't going to flinch and he wasn't going to shoot me, we both knew this. He put down the bow and cursed.

"You don't need to make up stories about dragons to get my attention," I said.

The young king shook his head. He wiped his eyes and rubbed his face. Edward had aged handsomely over the years. His hair was longer and coiffed. His clothes were stately but pared down, presumably in order to be here incognito. "I'm not making anything up," he said. "There's been another dragon sighting."

Impossible. I bit the inside of my cheek and said no. It was strange to be on this side of disbelief for once. "I killed the dragon," I said, definitively.

"I know you did," said the king. "I remember the tooth you sent my father and there's been no sightings since. But I sent my men on a search for it—for the bones, I mean—and while they were out there, they saw it. They saw it from a distance. It flew right over their heads."

"Well, your men are lying to you."

"That strange bottle I had the vicar send with my letter— that's from its debris."

"That could have been left from years ago. There was only one dragon and I killed him. He was five hundred and fifty-five years old and he spent his life traveling back and forth through time; we would have known if there were more than one." Suddenly, two thoughts dawned on me. The first was the nature of the dragon itself—it's possible Edward's men had really seen the dragon, but a younger version of it as it flipped through time. If that were true, there was still nothing I could do about it—the dragon's death was right back there in 1301 and any portion of its life before or after was beyond stopping now. The second thought I realized was more imminent: the king wanted to use it.

"I need you to take me there," Edward said.

"Have your men take you."

"They're not"—his voice broke apart—"they're not my men anymore. They left." He looked away in teary shame. His arms twitched slightly with the thought of maybe raising the bow again and threatening me with force but turned into a self-defeated shrug. His solitude and loneliness settled like a fine dust across the floor. Elsewhere in adjoining quarters of the church, dishes were stacked, basins of water were cleaned out, dogs were given scraps. A fly danced in candlelight. A threadbare kingdom stood on the brink. A heart was at the point of breaking.

It took us all night to reach the crater. I was surprised by how much I could remember of the terrain, even in the dark. We walked there, just the two of us, off main roads and cutting through forest trails, and I was amazed at how the land, as its own living breathing creature, seemed to have eroded and pulsated at will, each year washing away old trails and hewing new ones. The woods and marshes, rocky bluffs—they enveloped me like Simon's arms and I nearly forgot that I was alone with a king of England, alone with the pure weight of history's fate in my hands. If I were to direct the king off the wrong peak, if I were to push, provoke, or even just say something, an idea, what chain of events was I toying with? What history book was I rewriting?

But no, that wasn't right. Long ago, the dragon had sworn up and down that the past was immovable. Anything I did now would only contribute to history books already written. My life was a neutral zero, unfolding in a history already unfolded. Yet still, I felt the presence of something way beyond me, reaching.

We arrived at the crater just as the sun was beginning to rise. The lava field was covered in greenery now. Heather and reeds of red and yellow were dusted with a springtime down of emerald needles. Waterfalls of moss poured from the charred husks of felled trees, and lazy hawks in the sky relished the open landscape, dipping with ease for breakfast mice and rabbits and I thought to myself if only Simon could see what our world had become, how beautiful it still was. He was right, the volcanic rock was good for the soil, I'd have to tell him that—I didn't correct myself. I forgot where I was for a moment. I almost didn't care for the king's desperate fossil dig, for the caution needed as we scaled down the gentle slope of the crater, to the lip of a narrow ravine, the well of the disaster.

"It's down there," I said. I looked around the bowl of greenery. There was no indication of another dragon having appeared here. I pointed this out to Edward but he only shrugged and moved past me, beginning the final descent down the hole. I recognized the single-minded expression on his face and knew I could only follow. I knew the hopelessness that awaited him. I filled my lungs with green and blue and descended.

The ravine opened like an hourglass hewn into the earth the deeper we went. I took a few desperate leaps across the rocks and cut my knee. The aerated lava rock crumbled too easily, both cushioning and cutting, and that old familiar acrid scent filled the air. My cough was unperturbed—sticking to its usual rhythm of one cough every twenty minutes or so like a running tally of how much time had passed since the fateful day I was last here.

At the bottom, a cavern opened up, forming a long, tubular space. There was stagnant water, moss, and fungi. Tiny birds startled and flashed into the open air above us. And there, entombed in matte black sand and solid curving rock, were the craggy remains of a dragon. Bones. Scales. Claws. A flesh of dust more delicate than cobwebs. Its body was a broken globe of jutting ribs, deteriorating into the whims of nature. Edward rallied himself and made one final leap onto the sandy ground. He stumbled over to the dragon and ran his hands across its bones, the segments of broken neck, the pieces of what could have once been its legs and claws. The skull was half submerged in sand. I brushed some of it away, wiping sand and dust from divots in the eye sockets, feeling the cold coarse rock that had once been white-hot. There were massive teeth, a jaw, a pointy snout. This had all once been of so much consequence. And now?

This was all so solidly in the past and the past was dead space. The future was a myth. But what about the present? What about all the people existing in their own immediate realities at any one point in time? What if we were all present, wherever we were?

"Do you remember Simon?" I asked aloud.

Edward was inside what had been the dragon's abdomen, under a cage of bones. He was digging in the blackened sand.

"You called him my squire, but he was my boyfriend. He disappeared the day I killed the dragon." I touched a hole in the dragon's skull that I must have created all those years ago.

"I spent so much time back then being afraid of what I wanted, being stubborn. Simon's devotion came so easy for him, which scared me because I thought it meant he was neglecting some other part of himself and I was expected to do the same, but that wasn't the case. There were no expectations. I didn't understand that his devotion to me was a baseline, not a branching path. He had given me his whole heart but I had been so balled up in myself, so scared of newness, that I ran back to all the old ways I knew how to love, when they weren't really ways at all." A calming breeze flowed through the ravine and disturbed nothing. No sand shifted, no plants moved, not even a delicate fern, but my mind was further drenched in memory. Our old smallholding was only a few miles away. I remembered the calculus of the fields and their harvests, the digging of the canal, the felling of timber, and how I had once thought myself so clever with my modern know-how, my imagined unfair advantage, my laundered intellect. I had based my survival out here on the subjugation of the world to me, but the truth was that vitality, goodness, and peace all hinged on the subjugation of myself to it—to long hours spent in fields under the sun, boiling snow in winter, gutting fish, tracking stars. All this had been embodied by Simon, how he treated me, how he loved me. We had survived because we were together. "I think I really was his squire all along," I said aloud. "I was meant to have learned something from him, but it happened too late."

Edward was paying no attention to me. He was furiously digging, only finding darker and darker veins of sand. He was a curious, scavenging animal. When he gave up digging, he went to one of the hanging ribs and tried snapping it in half. He hung on it like the limb of a tree and pulled, straining to break it. There were tears of frustration in his eyes. His cheeks were flushed and hollow.

"How did you do it?" he cried. "How do you use these?" He gathered a handful of shattered bone and held them toward me. I backed away. "Go on," he said. "Do it. There has to be a way. You have to try."

"Try what?" I said. "Time travel? This is why you had me bring you out here?"

"Well, there's no living dragon but we can use the dead one. We can do something with the bones—the marrow—something, anything—I've read about it. You have to try." The king was on the very brink. A desperate madness wired through him.

"There's nothing you can do," I said. I moved farther away. "It's a dead animal. It's bones and dust. And even if it were alive . . . I never time traveled with the dragon. You need specialist equipment if you want to do that. That's not how I got here." I looked for a clear pathway out of the cave. The mysterious letter, the bottle—it had all been for this nonsense. It was a mistake to have come back here and indulge this. I started climbing back up the ravine.

"They're going to kill Piers," said Edward, his voice breaking. He called out with wretched despair. His skin, still smooth with its perfect royal sheen, was stained by blotchy red anguish.

I exhaled long and steady, of course recognizing that anguish. "I'm sorry," was all I could say. I wished I knew more about history to say something of comfort. All I knew now was from gossip and hearsay. I felt the strange honor of being in his presence and the holy shame of having nothing of value to offer him. I felt like a peasant.

I turned away from the king and climbed out of the ravine.

The snapping of bone and cries of despair continued behind me as sunlight and birdsong greeted me back on the surface of the crater. A sea of wildflowers undulated and glittered. I felt oddly at peace. For a moment, my worst fears had walked back into my life, but there was no sign of another dragon. There was only a memory buried deep underground and I could walk away from it.

Back on the surface, I looked along the treeline, in the direction of the smallholding, contemplating a decision to leave or stay, the mathematics of grief and hope. Then there was a flash of light. Farther up the slope where there were fewer wildflowers and the grass was shorter and blunter, sharpened sunlight reflected strangely off something in the ground. A glare shone right in my eyes. I held up my hand and walked over to it, curious. I thought it would be another bottle. A piece of leftover debris. A piece of—

PLASTIC.

The word finally dropped from a ledge in my mind. That was the word for it—but this wasn't another plastic bottle. This was larger and more curved. I knelt down and carefully dug around the shimmering object, moving small rocks to reveal not a bottle, but a large glass bowl or a sphere. It wasn't fully glass and it wasn't fully plastic. The rim or the opening was lined with rubber and inside were metal wires and plastic components strung in different formations. The glass was a perfect sphere slightly larger than my head and it was in perfect condition, it wasn't broken or covered in debris. It was as if it had been hidden here intentionally, not buried and forgotten. A tightness caught in my throat. A memory, a vision awakened in my mind.

Then something hit me hard in the back. I turned around. Edward had climbed out of the ravine and thrown a chunk of bone at me.

"Help me!" he cried and ran toward me. I dropped the glass sphere right before he tackled me to the ground. He punched me in the ribs but he wasn't made for this. His fists crumbled before they could cause any real pain. He broke into clumsy tears and wallows. "You time traveled! You know what's going to happen to us! You know what I need to do!"

"I don't!" I said. All I could think to do was hold him as he wept. "And even if I did, you can't time travel and fix things like this. You'd just make things worse or get trapped in some paradox and I'm sure the dragon knew that from the start. It's only fit for rubbish, nothing good comes of it."

Edward got off me and we sat side by side. He cried big heaves of sorrow and I saw myself in him, the loneliness and incessant want.

"It'll be OK," I said and patted his back. "I wish I knew something, anything, that could help you, but I guess I never paid enough attention to history at school." I had never heard of Piers Gaveston in my former life. Granted, I had never heard of Edward II either, or at least nothing memorable enough to keep him sorted from all the others. I'm sure one day his face would be on a kitchen magnet at a gift shop along with all the other kings and queens. I knew some met grisly ends and I hoped he wasn't one of them. "I think you'll make it out of this," was the best I could think to say.

"Piers won't," said the king. "And I was the idiot who kept calling him back. I kept wanting him. Needing him. You know how that feels? It's unabating."

"It's love," I said.

"I remember hating my father for keeping us apart, sending Piers away at every opportunity. But now the worst of all this is I realize he was only doing it to protect me. To protect both me and Piers. He knew what these people would do to us. They get more fearful every day."

"I think it's more about what they see as unfairness, rather than you and Piers being together." I chose my words carefully. "This world constantly surprises me with its openness. I think they taught us the opposite of that in schools where I came from so we wouldn't get any ideas."

Edward looked me in the eyes. "How did you do it?" he asked. "How did you time travel? If you didn't do it with the dragon, how did you get here?"

"It was accidental," I said. I recounted that night at the park, walking the dogs, fighting over the phone with inner— interned—what was the word?—*internet* providers, that's it. "It was a moment of pure undiluted stress—that's the best I can describe it. Being pulled in multiple impossible directions at once." I thought about how Simon must have felt the day of the dragon's final attack, falling into the well, wanting to protect me, but then seeing my ultimate betrayal. The same compounding fractals of terror I had once felt were what had caused him to vanish, sending him God knows where. God knows when. Out the other side, he would have felt shock, then anger, then I hope, some level of forgiveness and understanding. I felt immense sorrow.

"But why here?" asked Edward. "Why this time?"

"I don't know," I said. "Just destiny, I think."

"Destiny to sit in the dirt and do nothing? To spend your life slaving away on smallholdings, being no use?"

I laughed. "Honestly, I think so. I think the only thing that can pull someone through time like that is another person—I think it's love. And I think Simon was the great love of my life, just like Piers is yours, we just happened to be centuries apart. And there's no grand plan there. Sometimes it's just two people pulled together, sitting in the dirt. I don't know."

Edward and I looked at each other and for a moment, he took on a wholly modern visage. We could have been two salary-men sharing a table on our lunch break, inching together toward devious self-fulfillment, lust, the opposite of prophecy and hope. I saw in him what I had once been—a whole other life played out so poorly, ending in annihilation.

"I think there are things happening around us that are just beyond our understanding," I said. "And I think more often than not there's nothing we can do about it." I thought about the angel Simon said he saw. I thought about all his silent prayers. Maybe he had been tapped into goodness to the exact same degree I had been tapped into despair and it had snapped us together like magnets. An angel had appeared to him. An angel.

Edward wiped his face. The thrum of grasshoppers began again after being startled by our scuffle. A bumblebee squiggled through the air. Wind moved the grass, the wildflowers, the brambles. You could never have guessed what had once occurred here.

"Is that another one of your bottles?" asked Edward, nodding over to the strange glass sphere that had rolled away from us.

"No," I said. I went over and picked it up. The glass had remained sturdy and clear. "It's a helmet."

"What foolish soldier wears a helmet made of glass?" said Edward.

"It's not for a soldier," I said. I turned the helmet in my hands, inspecting the strange technology attached to it. The spark of an idea whizzed around in my mind, afraid to grow into anything more substantial. My breathing remained steady. "I think I'm going to stay here a while longer," I said, looking around the crater.

"Well," Edward scoffed. "I'm certainly not." He stood up and brushed dirt from his clothes.

"You're not worried about the dragon your men said they saw?"

"They told me what I wanted to hear. They defected right after I paid them. Plus if you're staying here, I think we'll be OK." The king sighed, then extended a hand to me. "Thank you, George," he said. I shook his hand and he pulled me into an embrace. "And I apologize for what I said earlier. Your destiny was more than to just sit in the dirt, I'm sorry. My father spoke very highly of you before he died—he thought you should be made a saint. You slayed the dragon and saved us all. I think I just needed to come out here and see the bones for myself. Something I needed . . . to better understand—I don't know. Him. My dad. He knew how to do all of this much better than me."

"I think you're doing all right," I said. "And I wish you luck, Your Majesty." I truly did.

We let this temporary peace settle over us and went our separate ways. The king would go to Scarborough to play out the long path of destiny that awaited him. I remained on the edge of the wildflower meadow, clutching the glass helmet, my reflection curving around it. The king turned back around as he walked away. "Hey, I'm letting you keep that helmet as payment for dragging you out here."

"Oh, how generous of you," I said with a gleeful, old-timey sarcasm. I put my head through the hole at the bottom of the sphere and tried it on. There was no visual distortion, the glass was perfectly clear.

Edward gave a thumbs-up. "Ready for war. It looks good on you. You look like an angel."

"A what?" My heart skipped a beat involuntarily.

Edward yelled back, "An angel. Or a saint. It looks like a halo around your head." He drew a circle in the air. "There you go—Saint George."

He turned around and kept walking, leaving the crater and disappearing into the thicket of brambles and trees. But I stayed where I was, on the periphery of something much grander than myself.

I took off the helmet and inspected it again. At the top of the helmet, inside, there were tiny electric lights. It's true, if you saw someone wearing this out here all lit up, it would seem otherworldly, an angel would be your only reference. And judging by the way I had found it—not exactly buried underground so much as intentionally hidden and with care—I wondered if whoever had worn it was still here. An angel falling through time.

19

It took me hours to find the old smallholding. The forest surrounding the crater had grown denser and wilder. Our old paths had been wiped away, and more than once did I get helplessly lost, guided only by the ground's meager incline and the sound of running water—the canal that had eroded back into the creek it was always meant to be. Then the faint yet sudden smell of smoke.

There. I spotted it through the trees. A thin line of it led down to an old thatched roof held up by stone walls—what had once been our home. A fire was on. Someone was inside.

The hut was not a dilapidated ruin. It hadn't been forgotten about—or it had, but it was recently being cared for. The surrounding meadows were overgrown and ruined with weeds and brambles, flooded with swampy ponds dotted with chattering birds, but the house itself was alight with new activity. Foliage had been pulled away and cut back from the rocky walls. Small repairs had been done to the roof.

I knew instinctively, against all logic and reason, who was here. It's a strange thing how love can pull you through something, even if it's through complacency and peace into a state of what I could only call at that moment fear as I approached the house. It was worry I felt as the door opened. Worry of the impossible and all that it entailed.

There was Simon.

He stood in the open doorway. He was older, just as handsome as he had always been, and looked at me through the confident stalemate of our love. He saw the glass helmet I carried and sighed. I approached him with caution. Air between us was like a skin twitching and contracting. We were old lovers confronting our snubbed-out wicks. I couldn't even say his name, only "You."

But he could say mine. "George." He ushered me inside the house, but the expected warmth of the place was stale and drafty, an echo of heat. We kissed like strangers, clumsily, and only as a means to try and puncture the doubt and fear still between us. We couldn't converse, only quip: "Sorry." "It's OK." "I'm so sorry." "It's OK, George." "I'm so, so sorry." Emotions spurred and faltered. Then a debasement of the miracle: "*How?*"

"Shhh." Simon pressed his fingers to my lips. He closed the door behind me and shook his head, his curls following their same old helixes, now flecked with gray. He took the glass helmet from me and set it on a table. "It doesn't matter."

"That night," I said with trembling urgency. "The dragon. When you saw me. I wasn't thinking straight. I was only wanting to know more. I wasn't going to leave. Or maybe I was, but not without you. I just wanted us out of there. I wanted us safe." I had spent years rehearsing these words but they still tumbled out of me like excuses. "I was a coward."

"I know," said Simon. He tried to smile but his face could only warble and grimace. "I've had a long time to think about it. I was angry—but not toward you. I was angry at my reaction. Angry at how it had zapped me away from you. It was weakness and fear, pulled in a thousand directions at once." I noticed his accent, how it had changed. There was a rigidity where there hadn't been one before and I could tell he was actively sanding it down to fit back into our older, shared dialect, frustrated with its limits.

"Where did you go?" I asked like a peasant to a god.

"The future," he said. "At first." He invited me to sit down, but both of us remained standing. His blue eyes had gone stony and gray. He looked at me, but only through me, searching for words. "It was . . . deranged. There were so many people, but none of them could help me get back to you. I could only rely on myself. Everything was so closed and paved over. The ground— right here, even—it's so smooth but hard at the same time, like it's all one giant tile. The whole world is tiled over. The whole earth is baked. And clean, really clean, like my hands"—he flexed his fingers—"are constantly dry—*were* constantly dry. They fixed my leg. I was lucky this place was paved over because I got help right away. And I got all that other stuff you get there. Identification, accounts, logins, cards." He looked at me with another forlorn smile. It couldn't hold back the shimmer of pain in his eyes. "And I wanted to get back here. Immediately, George, I swear, I did everything I could. I promise you, George. I did everything."

"I know, Simon, I know." Saying his name made my voice break. I reached to put my hand on his shoulder but both of us flinched, unaccustomed. Simon stepped back.

"But, George, you don't know." He turned away from me to

face the smoldering hearth. Light cut through the smoky haze—sunlight. I noticed there was a window. We had never had a window before. On the wall opposite the door was a four-panel glass window that blended seamlessly into the old stonework. I wondered how long Simon had been here waiting for me, fixing up the place. The roof had also been fixed and smoke from the hearth lingered heavier in the air, filtering slowly but not enough through a new chimney. I cleared my throat, then asked, "What do you mean you went to the future 'at first'?"

Simon's shoulders rose as he inhaled but they did not lower when he exhaled. "I could only rely on myself," he said again. His back was still to me. Trees moved breezily in the new window—a window that would have needed to be formed from molten glass, a fiery furnace, carefully cut.

"It took a long time to find you once I discovered how," Simon continued. "Time travel isn't precise. You'll be in an open meadow one second and the next it'll be a car park, or a drainage pipe, or a stadium, or something you can't even imagine, or an ocean. The world changes a lot. It sweats and dries out, floods and freezes. I got lost." He went silent. A gust of wind droned outside. The window rattled lightly. I watched a spasm crinkle across Simon's shoulders. "I'm devoted to you," he whispered, and that was all. Forgiveness pierced my heart with its gold needle.

I opened my mouth to speak but made no sound, battling waves of nausea. I could only cough and watch Simon watch birds dart across the window, fleeing into the wind that had picked up. I waited for him to turn around, but feared what mad pleading I would see in his face, what confessions it harbored.

But how? I didn't ask it aloud. The smell of the place was suddenly overwhelming and I couldn't breathe. Smoke from the roaring hearth. The memory of our skin on each other, our winter and spring. My throat wheezed. I really couldn't breathe. It was the hearth but when I looked over at it, there was hardly any fire. The hearth was nearly out. The last embers had faded and only coal remained.

I went to open the door and air out the remaining smoke—

"Don't open the door," said Simon, and finally he turned around, but his face was stoic and calm. He looked at me no longer with the endearment of shame, but with eyes that had seen the whole arc of human history and decided this moment, our union, would be its apex. "Please," he said. "If you don't want to know, don't open the door."

But I already knew. Opening the door would not let out the smoke. It would only let more smoke in. I saw it pouring steadily through the gap under the door, flooding the hut. The sweet heat and memory. The grandeur of being exactly where you're meant to be, no matter the cost. No matter the cost. It had to be no matter the cost.

I pushed open the door and the air was no clearer. Time was as fettered and constant as it always was, our present moving along with all its orchestration and terror. And there it was, perched there on a tree branch, smaller, younger, but still enormous with its same sly grin and leathery scales, its knowing yellow eyes and all the hundreds of years they were yet to see.

ACKNOWLEDGMENTS

Special thanks to writers and researchers John Boswell, Walt Odets, Nicholas Orme, Ian Mortimer, Barbara Tuchman, Simon Roper, Charlotte Tomkins, Paul B. Newman, Marc Morris, Michael Prestwich, and many other time travelers. Thank you to everyone at William Morrow, InkWell Management, and The Blair Partnership—especially Peter Kispert, Naomi Eisenbeiss, and Hattie Grünewald.

ABOUT THE AUTHOR

RYAN COLLETT is a writer, animator, and knitter. He grew up in Oregon and now lives in London, where his first novel, *The Disassembly of Doreen Durand*, was published in 2021. He also runs a popular YouTube channel dedicated to knitting.